STAR BRYAN

STAR BRYAN

a novel by

Jerry Rabushka

QUEER MOJO
A Rebel Satori Imprint
Bar Harbor, Maine

Published in the United States of America by
REBEL SATORI PRESS
P.O. Box 363
Hulls Cove, ME 04644
www.rebelsatori.com

Book design by Sven Davisson

Library of Congress Cataloging-in-Publication Data

Rabushka, Jerrold.
  Star Bryan / by Jerry Rabushka.
    p. cm.
  ISBN 978-1-60864-057-7 (pbk. : alk. paper)
  1. Gay men--Fiction. 2. Gay couples--Fiction. 3. Interpersonal
relations--Fiction. 4. Race relations--United States--Fiction. I. Title.
  PS3618.A3265S63 2012
  813'.6--dc23
                    2012029891

CHAPTER I

All the time they were together, Brad acted like it didn't matter. He sent off *didn't matter* vibes; he slid over those vibes with the virtuosity of a smooth jazz musician. So who was he to say that now, when they were apart, that it mattered? For Star it was different. It mattered to him then, and it didn't matter to him now. That was more the way it was supposed to be, since he had moved on, left Brad, and started his own life.

It was to be expected. Not *for* anyone, not *because* of anyone, but simply from walking down a road paved with a red carpet of neglect. Star's six-five dark muscular frame withered away like a rotten walnut overlooked by a well fed squirrel. He was nothing when he left, a black shadow in the doorway, khakis, polo shirt, hand on the door quietly pulling it shut.

"You look white today," was all Brad could think to say.

Star had come back to this house for five years, hoping one day Brad would notice him, hoping one day Brad would change back into the man he moved in with. Now it took one click of the door and it was over. It was that easy. Easy after five years, never easy before.

People didn't give Star much credit. "You got yourself a white boy for status, not love." Disapproving friends dropped like flies descending upon a Zambian refugee camp. Star didn't care – one look in his man's eyes and it didn't matter that he had swum away from everyone and everything to this wealthy west St. Louis County refuge.

Maybe they were right, maybe they weren't. Brad sparkled, his smile could make Star forget his worries, his lovemaking could make him forget everything else. That ended about three years ago. Brad still sparkled, but Star watched from a distance, and making love, from Star's vantage point in the cheap seats, turned into having sex with the available manpower.

Star, 30, tall, handsome, trimmed goatee and nearly shaved head; five hoops in his left ear, three in his right, one through his eyebrow. He used to work out; he'd stopped awhile back. Brad didn't care how toned his body

1

was, so neither did he.

Brad always looked good. Same age, about five-ten, blue eyes, brown goatee, short hair. Brad stayed in decent shape, played a lot of squash and racquetball, and that smile, on the increasingly rare occasions when it was meant for Star, made it all worth waiting for.

Brad took the heat too. His friends didn't enjoy having this big black man hovering around them, an import that they knew Brad was using to fulfill a fantasy and not for love. His family was scandalized; they accused Brad of living with the man solely to upset his mother. Well no, but it was a good side effect.

Star's love was good. Too good. Brad didn't have to work for it, and soon he stopped the effort. Unconditional acceptance led him to test exactly what heights *unconditional* could reach. As a result, Star was no longer the man he initially loved. He was a beggar. A refugee. A victim of abuse. Brad created it; Star knew at this particular click of the door he was going to reclaim himself. Brad wanted to rewrite the last three years but couldn't find a pen, so he made up stories to his friends and came home alone. Suddenly it mattered.

Star got himself a condo back in the city of St. Louis. He wasn't hurting for money. He had a decent law practice, money put away, yet he felt he was starting over as an alien, slowly coming to earth and realizing that this oversized mass he carried around with him was the body he had recently acquired and would be forced to inhabit for the rest of his life. Now he had to find a heart and soul to put into it. Those, he might have to snatch from somewhere else. Someone unsuspecting, some panhandler who had no use for them anymore. Who would know the difference? For a quarter he could get started, but of course those were men who hated themselves too; a beggar with the audacity to call someone else cheap wasn't a good place to regain ones spirit. Star had been a beggar himself, but he couldn't live any longer off Brad's occasional pennies.

"We need each other," Brad said.

"I know that. You know that. But, it doesn't matter."

"It matters now."

"No, it doesn't. You've made me stop caring about myself, so caring about you, and particularly caring about *us*, is impossible. I'm a lawyer,

2

and I know such things."

Guys who date across the lines of race often find themselves marooned on that uncharted south sea island called ostracism; or labeled – suddenly it was a fetish, a fantasy, no one could believe it was love if your man was picked off a color chart.

Star went to the bar, alone. People were eyeing him like he was a boss searching for a new set of boobs in the secretarial pool. They didn't notice his eyes turned inward, barely aware of their drunken semi-human shapes. He was afraid to meet someone, to fall for him, to have this happen again. He knew he wasn't fodder for much. He wanted to be around people, but people who would ignore him. Brad was dating someone within hours of the breakup to prove to himself it didn't matter. Star could see him at the other end of the bar, kissing someone, eyes brokering Star's direction hoping to pick up a hint of jealousy. *Finally, he's paying attention to me.*

To Star, to whom it really didn't matter, a cover up wasn't necessary. All that *did* matter was preservation. Piece by piece, he got new furniture. He got African art at T.J. Maxx... *Never ever the same place twice?* They've had this shit for months! *No, I don't have the soul of a white boy, and I don't have a heart born and bred in Wildwood. I'm not that suburban. Come see, come listen to my tale of woe. I just want something of myself back, but I can't remember who I was. Brad has it all. He's got my sparkle and I have my broken heart. But... it doesn't matter.*

Star had big hands, and when he worked out, biceps that molded themselves sharply against a blue sky. His hand over a basketball was a work of art; when he was growing up someone sculpted it. Someone who then kissed him and said, "I can make you feel as beautiful as that work of art." Star didn't think the sculpture was that good. It was a hand and a basketball, without much motion.

"You should see me shoot it," he said.

"I will," said the man.

It was at his sculptor's pressing that Star's hair went down to a quarter inch; the goatee came out, dark around an oval long dark face, and he was suddenly a new man – a man to reckon with, foreboding, powerful, all because of a head shave and a goatee. But it worked. This transformation from geek to stud brought his artist friend to a new rapture, and the reaction on campus and in the press groomed Star into thinking he could have sex with anyone and everyone. For a short while, he did.

They'd show him on TV, on the bench with his muscles boasting better definition than Webster's, the round knobs on his shoulders, solid curve of his biceps, his arm rising gracefully in the air, shooting the ball with a deadly arc of accuracy like a missile riding its way on the night sky from Baghdad to Tel Aviv. Every new piercing found its way into the local sports section. For awhile there was a cult of Star Bryan, 20 years old, and he had lost himself.

The artist grew tired of it; too many egos clashing and too much neglect. Star knew he was not the man his excesses portrayed, but his actions spoke louder than his apologies. He was a young buck for sure, but who wanted quiet love and acceptance. The shaved head, the arc of the foul shot, the move by move documentation was not him, and he watched again like that alien in a space ship, waiting to land, wondering what mind was taking over his body.

No one could satisfy him as well as his artist friend, but he felt compelled to explore. More than one face would smile at the thought that they were his chosen one, even if only for a moment. For Star the pursuit of that smile became all important, and addictive.

It mattered to the sculptor; it didn't matter to Star until it no longer mattered to the sculptor. "I cannot hear you above the roar of the crowd, and you obviously love yourself more than me," he said. "Right now, what you want is more important. Right now, anyway, and later, it will be too late."

One morning Star found the sculpture shattered, like the heart of its maker. It brought everything back to earth, put it all in perspective... and like the back door of a truck slamming on a load of imported Chinese prostitutes who realize this really is the end... it really was the end. It hurt, and no one else could touch him or make it better.

He was good. Not NBA good, but at least his parents were affluent and far sighted enough to insist he get an education, so that he did, and a law degree from that same Saint Louis University that made him famous for the hoops. The family supposition was that he would use his earrings and education to help the black community through its scrapes and scuffles, but instead he popped one through the eyebrow, married a white boy, and hid out in the county doing white boy stuff. He became an anomaly rather than a man.

Learning from his mistakes with the sculptor, Star gave Brad his life and his soul, but now all that was tied up somewhere in a laundry bag in a garage on the wrong end of the county. Star searched for it again in the aisles of T.J. Maxx. West African, East African, South African, all that tribal regionalism could get ugly if warring spirits found themselves staring at each other across his rehabbed three story Soulard neighborhood town home. Just south of downtown, Soulard was known for its jazz, its bars, a couple gay hangouts, old dwellings, and lots and lots of rehab.

It was weird, being a gay guy buying gay books and a black guy buying black art. It always seemed that he was trying too hard to assert his identity through acquisition, rather than just being who he was.

"Star Bryan!! Bro!" Hendrick Pardee, from the ball team. *Been almost ten years. Damn!* "That's some cheapass African shit!"

"Hendrick!"

Smiling, genuine, happy. "You is looking good!"

"Ya think?"

"I always thought so. Just never thought I was good enough for you."

Star's sexuality was the most well kept secret in the college. Well kept by everyone, that was... but Hendrick? He'd grown up a bit. Looked scrappy. Looked tough, but only on the outside, Star could see a sweet sunshine in the man's eyes.

"What you buyin' all that shit for?"

He looked into the eyes of some wooden female statue with a bizarrely distorted face. "I want to feel black." It was a joke, sort of, but not really. He more wanted to feel human.

"You is beautiful black!" said Hendrick.

"What you been up to?"

5

"Jail, mostly."

"Ouch."

"Coke. But clean for a couple years. Ouch is right. But you can't surprise me with nothin'. Cept buying knockoff shit from the Maxx."

"I've been in a prison of my own for five years," said Star. "The love police came and arrested me."

"I always thought about you."

"Oh you did not."

"Yes I did."

"No you didn't."

"Well I used to. And now I think I want you to take that shit back."

"Let's see how it looks, first."

The art never much gave him any sense of identity, but it gave other folks a sense of *his* identity. Or it scared them off. *He's black first, man second*, said the guys who were gay first and men second. White folks in Rhodesia listened to Ella Fitzgerald and they never made the connection. It's all an imported world, and so is this. It can't be your culture if you don't know what any of it means.

Hendrick was shorter than Star, maybe six-two, grew himself a bit more hair, left the scrap on his face, and worked as a cook at a Bob Evans in Kirkwood just up the street from the T.J. But he hadn't lost himself after all that. He was upbeat, taking his new chance on life. His eyes bright, his teeth flashed, one was gold, nothing pierced, but a gang tattoo someone needled on him in prison marked his shoulder, a dark green eagle in dire need of extinction.

T.J. Maxx was selling all kinds of African art, but yet the Kirkwood police didn't like the idea of two big black guys in the parking lot eyeing each other and discussing their culture. One cop recognized them both. Saint Louis University, back about ten years ago?

"Yowsah!" Hendrick wasn't too scared, by now his blood was so pure a minister could use it to baptize children. No prison, no probation, no parole, just cooking up pancakes at Bob's. Someone turned him on to the white horse at college, and by now he didn't miss it. Well, he did, but he knew better.

"You just be careful," said the cop.

"Why?" Star asked.

"Because, it's Kirkwood. It's dangerous."

"For a black boy?"

"For a boy, period. And for a gay boy picking up scrap in the parking lot, yep. This what you left Brad for?"

Memory came shooting back. Squash? Croquet? Some event everyone attended but no one enjoyed, just to say they'd been. Some policeman's ball. Some policeman's balls. Who knew? "Yes, it is." Turned to Hendrick. Starved for attention. Very, very starved. "Come on, Scrapdawg. Let's git."

Hendrick got so turned on with that nickname he didn't think he could control himself on the way home. Star knew where all that art was going. He'd seen it languishing in the aisles for weeks while he spent hours at home wondering if purchasing it would admit to the clerk that he had an unfulfilled need for racial confirmation, or if the clerk even cared. *Hey, you're the one who gets the magnum condoms!* Do they really remember?

The last clerk was some distracted white chick who didn't even look at him. She said have a good day like she didn't know what one was. She bagged the stuff as if she knew she lived in a materialistic America where the merchandise wasn't even relevant to the owner and its acquisition just a time filler. Racial identity crisis? Probably never crossed her mind.

Some thick female head on a very long neck went on a glass shelf, a couple masks hung on the wall, a fertility icon on a coffee table in a corner. Star bludgeoned everything into place, because he'd already visualized it there for so long while contemplating the agony of those two minutes and fifteen seconds at the checkout counter. He remembered vaguely that he was used to people paying attention to everything he did, until Brad whisked him from the public eye under an ever dwindling pretense of true love.

This was a shock to him that it came back, that he thought it would matter when the only thing that mattered before was something that didn't really matter at all. Brad, a lifetime away, but still influencing everything he did, and still hurting. He still wished hard enough that Brad loved him, and now the chance of ever seeing him smile again, or to feel his lips, his fingers, and his love, just the chance even, was gone, The real thing had been gone a long time. Star, by leaving, was just admitting the truth after wasting three years of his life making excuses.

Something hit as the last artifact was consigned to ethnic eternity on a glass shelf. Just about filling the door frame, Star looked to Hendrick pacing the floor like a hungry Roman tiger let loose at The Last Supper. He was being deferential, or maybe scared, since he was a bit smaller. Could be the prison thing. Could be he was used to being took. Could be he was a crouching tiger, hidden dragon who was stalking his prey.

"Scrapdawg!" Star looked at the man smiling across the room; bowed head, raised eyes. *Some Enchanted Evening*. The room wasn't crowded, but it could well have been, and Star wouldn't have noticed.

"Woof." Maybe Brad wasn't the only one who knew how to sparkle. Star was just getting used to someone being attracted to him and wanting him. It's hard to comprehend after so long without. After being consigned himself to ethnic oblivion and being a work of art, to finally...

He pinned Hendrick up against the door, spread his arms out over the wall, kissed him with three frustrated years of loss, grace, and desperation. Dawg's arms curled in and pulled him closer. *Maybe he was really thinking of me all this time*. Finally they broke free, Star looked deep into this scruffy face, just a couple inches away. Hmm. Taking all that shit back? *That* would be a rejection of identity, not to mention totally implausible. Too many refund slips and too many unanswered questions. "I ain't ready for this," he said.

Hendrick smiled, ran a hand over Star's goatee, over his face, over the ammo factory hanging from his ears. "Bro? Like I give a fuck." Another kiss, so elegant, he wouldn't have expected it.

Star could feel a heart beat, amazed, someone was this excited to be with him! Not just a man, but *him*. A new feeling, one he sort of remembered, but with the b-ball career down the tubes, and the word "attorney" not being much of an aphrodisiac, it had to be him. "I wanna be your dawg," Hendrick said. "You started it."

CHAPTER 2

There's a reason kiss rhymes with bliss, though most think it's for purely poetic motives, Star hadn't ever experienced anything as deep as all this. "Someone who really wants you isn't afraid of any of you," Hendrick postulated. "And he isn't afraid to show you."

That was bullshit, but Star was ready to hear it – on the other hand, he was ready to be alone, reconstruct himself alone, put his life back together alone. He wasn't sure if having someone at his side would work. Neither was Brad, who had acquired Star's new address for purely political reasons, and found that living alone really sucked. Once again, a door was closing on him, but he had done it himself, like shutting a French door on a patio to let people smoke dope in peace outside and ignoring the consequences— that one day it will be locked and they'll be trapped between the police on one side and that bolted door on the other.

Brad found himself squarely on that patio when he thought he could retreat to the comfort of his own room, now missing the smell, touch, and sweat of a man that he'd never realized had any of those three in such pleasant abundance. The cleaning lady doused out the last of it during a laundry run, and Brad was beside himself.

Brad watched too much TV, especially these days, and so decided to drop over without calling, a prerogative of folks on TV shows that no one would ever dare in real life. Folks who try it find themselves very unwelcome, very quickly.

Hendrick was over, they were playing CDs, in fact it was a South African band called Mango Groove, whose heyday was the '80s and whose music sounded like the '60s, but Star was tired of rap, Motown, and Destiny's Child. Hendrick didn't care, he had his boy and so the rest of the world was irrelevant. Star had nothing. He was reinventing, and Hendrick, he knew, was just going to be there come hell or high water. It didn't matter. Sadly, it didn't, and wouldn't... hopefully Star could accept this good fortune before Hendrick left for someone more self assured.

But he kissed like nobody's business, and cooked up a good set of eggs. He got Star working out again, and he loved sleeping close to him. And he didn't snore, which made all such things possible.

Is that what you want? the voice echoed within him, and came out of Brad's mouth as well in one of these unexpected visits that should have been reserved for an episode of *Empty Nest.* "What can he give you that I can't?"

"Come here Scrapdawg." Hendrick popped over and they kissed in full view. It was a performance, but not without sufficient rehearsal to fully offend its audience with its perfection. "That, sir." There certainly was a refinement about it, and a passion, and it made Brad feel whorish about his own sexuality, and incompetent.

"You got yourself a bitch," said Brad. "I can do it just as well."

"That's cuz you're a better bitch. You made me nothing, and worked at it more intricately than anyone I have ever known."

Brad, undaunted, hopped up and clamped his lips over Star Bryan's mouth. Damn! Familiar, longed for, home home home!!! Why now?

"Bro! You ain't kickin this dawg off his porch!" Hendrick yapped, slung Brad away, and sent him careening into a wall where a giant wooden African mask dislodged and fell over his face. It must have hurt, but it looked pretty damn funny to the other two.

"I'll have you for assault!" said Brad.

"Have me? Don't think so," said Hendrick. "You didn't want him when you had him Now do not fuck with me. I've done time, and I'll do more for *him.*"

Star took the mask and hung it back up. "That's some heavy magic. Namibia." Brad looked at him quizzically. "I don't know where *I* come from," Star said, in a bizarre self revelation. "But one of these has to be close to home. I lost everything being with you."

"Heck, you've probably been here 350 years," Brad offered. "Longer than I have. You just as soon come from South Carolina as Namibia. Three hundred fifty years ago, there was no Namibia."

"Hey, can we can the history lesson here? You git!" Hendrick was drooling and huffing. Brad was taking away his time with his man, and worse than that, taking away his man. However brief, he could see Star light up at Brad's touch. Love and like having so little to do with each other, he was scared. Guys in prison had been damaged for less, just sometimes Hendrick had to remind himself he was again living in polite society.

"We'll talk. But not now," Star said as Brad went out the door. He'd been cut just a bit. Star wanted to lay him down and douse him with peroxide, but there was too much pressure from without.

He sat on the couch, the new couch from Humble Abode, confused, and feeling alone. Hendrick came up to him and took his hand, touched his face with the other, ran a finger over his lips so Star could run his tongue over his finger. Hendrick really was a dawg, and this lick would calm him down. Star was confused – why would a lion invite him back into a den except to lock him up again? Still the face next to him was scared, lonely, and foreboding.

"I love you." Hendrick laid it on the line. "And I would go back for you. If he comes for you, he won't have you."

Sealed with a kiss, he just about felt Hendrick clasping a chain around the back of his neck, hanging an albatross in front. A heavy, smelly, dead white bird. His heart hung heavy, and his life was suddenly out of control after he'd worked so hard to hang every detail in place. These two idiots were fighting over him suddenly. Suddenly everything mattered, and again, over something that didn't matter at all.

Actually, it *was* about 350 years. No one knew for sure, but his family lived as free blacks for a long time before that combination was generally considered *en vogue*. His father's family owned a few slaves of its own, a fact hidden imperiously until it popped up on a radio talk show hosted by someone who'd done damaging research under the pretense of historical accuracy but really trying to undermine Mr. Lancer Bryan's hopes of remaining a city alderman.

"Yes, it was wrong," retorted his father, "but it happened a long time ago. I can hardly be held responsible for it." Of course some angry white folks suggested the same thing, that they were tired of being so accountable for something that'd been over since 1863, and there was no way of explaining the difference. In any event, no one was sold up river, and they'd stayed reasonably affluent, though ostracized by just about everyone, for almost two centuries.

Star met Hendrick on the basketball court at SLU. They'd shot a lot together, and played well together, but he never realized that Hendrick wanted the playing and the shooting off the court as well. Never, really. He was too busy being sculpted, being rich, and being made love to by folks who wanted a big name in their notebook. A name that would flash on TV and they'd say "I've had him." Star was educated, Hendrick was ghetto trash with talent, but they were friends.

Neither of them made the NBA; Star turned to law, Hendrick to cocaine. He got caught dealing, went to jail, got out, paid his debt, he was over it. He never forgot Star, and wondered in prison of the difference it would have made in his life if he had confessed his love... no, at the time, just a face in the crowd, just a nobody in the shadow, right now he wanted that shadow, and since he had the shadow and he wasn't about to let it go or ever come out from under it.

It was being engulfed in someone, *the sparkle is not me, it's you!*

And if it's me, Star thought, *then if Brad lost his, what did I do wrong?*

Don't mention Brad. Brad's history.

No, he's not. He's meeting me for lunch. It was five years. We need to talk.

I love you.

Dawg, I know. I love you too.

Don't meet him.

I have to. It won't matter.

It will to me.

Trust me.

Even his fingers looked scrappy, his arms kind of beat up, still lanky like a basketball player—the big hands, the muscle definition, lately a mustache growing in like zoysia grass taking over a suburban lawn. Star could look down a few inches to his face, and already be used to so much, a man so close to his eyes. It was new, and exciting. This was probably what being loved felt like. But Brad was comfort, and Star, a horse running back

12

into a burning barn, waiting and hoping he could be set on fire again.

Apparently one can't purchase a new identity or a new soul. T.J. Maxx, never being the same place twice, made stability difficult.

Hendrick really was frightened – he knew he'd found Star way too soon after a breakup to have much chance of making it work, but every day they were together seemed to push it a bit closer, to make Star a bit more accepting that despite the bad timing, it could be the real thing.

Star and Brad met at Bob Evans in Kirkwood, a concession to prove to his Dawg that he could trust them together. They would do it under his eye, and in a family restaurant where two guys wouldn't be making out. If they were, Star would be picked up for DWB – Driving While Black – and given a ticket because someone didn't like his pierced eyebrow.

"Your boy cooks up a good dinner," said Brad, who in trying to ghettoize Hendrick, thought he could win Star back to the wild side one more time.

"My boy cooks up a lot of good stuff," Star replied. He didn't even react to Brad's plays on racial insensitivity, because he already knew the game. Belittle him for returning to whatever roots he had and for daring to like one of his own. He wasn't sure it would be worth returning to Brad's apartheid government in the hope that he might receive new freedoms arbitrarily granted by someone who had breached his trust and taken too much control.

On the other hand, and the other hand was big, he remembered now that he didn't leave Brad because he fell out of love with him. And he still hadn't, despite Hendrick's constant evangelizing. Here, being polite, conversational, and attentive, was the man he loved, however irritating the conversation was. He wanted to hold his hand across the table, or bend forward and kiss him. At five-ten, it was quite a bend.

"I'm sorry," Brad said.

"For what?"

"Everything."

"You can't buy that all back with a meatloaf," Star told him.

"He's a cook!" Brad said. "That's all he is."

"And what are you? Things would have to be a lot different. I'm not sure they can be. And I'm not sure I want to come back."

13

"I think you do. I don't think you're over me."

There's absolutely nothing snootier one man can say to another. Even the waitress knew it, and so tossed off her long standing rule about keeping out of her customer's business, particularly since Hendrick had her keeping an eye on the proceedings. Her eyes glanced from one to the next, from Brad's arrogance to Star's biceps newly cutting out of a muscle shirt. Right about now, he was too damn sexy, and no one could look without being ashamed at what they felt.

"I think he's over you." It was worth it. Star would make up for Brad's tip, she was sure.

"I miss you. I miss everything about you, and I guess I didn't realize until it was too late how much I loved you."

It's amazing what goes through someone's mind at times like this – Star felt silly for acquiring all that art, and realized he'd have to take it all back if Brad was to come back into his life. It was like it was okay to be black, but not to be an African-American. Anything he'd discovered about himself, or had gained, would be immediately returned to TJ Maxx. But then again, everything he'd done was just a façade to show the world that Brad didn't matter. I would only work as long as Brad didn't say "I love you." It didn't matter if he meant it or not.

"I saw you kissing that thing," Brad said. Hendrick had been demoted.

"He's better at it than you."

"That's all he can give you."

"That's enough," Star said, and realized that it was. "That's all I wanted from you, and I never got that. You can't make up for it with fancy appliances."

"I'll do what it takes. I can't be without you anymore. I just didn't realize it."

"You had a date eight hours after I left. I bet you had a few before I left, too."

"You think about it."

"I have." He'd never really stopped; he was always hoping for this proof that Brad really did love him, but now it wasn't so easy. Going back into the burning barn, those same comforts of home could scorch him to death. Star felt, strangely enough, like Scarlett O'Hara looking back at a flaming

14

Atlanta. Brad licked a bit of coffee out of his mustache, and the flames burned hotter. The good news: if Atlanta was destroyed totally, there would be nothing to return to. Or, rebuild it from scratch, and make it better.

Star stuck a long leg out from under the table and tripped the busboy as he walked by. "You play ball?"

"Sorta."

"You know who I am?"

"Nope." The guy was about 16, too young to know Star in his heyday.

"About time you found out. You get me five guys and a hoop, and I'll turn you into something."

"Why?"

Star got up, rising to his full height slowly, and it was compelling. "In my day, I couldn't miss."

He looked important, and the kid was impressed. So was Brad, seeing him that tall, arms strong again, and mid-20s confident... Star himself had no idea why he just did what he did, but it might help his father's political ambitions, his mother's self esteem, and it just seemed like the right thing to do.

Hendrick was miserable in the kitchen, waiting on reports from the waitress, who wasn't sure what was really going on. He was happy enough to see Star looking in over the counter into the cooking area, shouting, "See you later, Dawg," and striding out the door. The name stuck, and now every time someone called him that, he could think of Star. It was good.

Brad was livid, and wasn't about to be put in his place quite so easily. The parking lot was a better place to vent.

"What the fuck are you doing with that loser?"

"This isn't either/or," said Star. "If he goes, it's not like I'm running back to your fucked up ass."

"He can't even cook a meatloaf."

"You said you liked it in there, now don't start changing your mind."

"You're wasting your life."

"You saw to that! What do you want from me?"

"To see things realistically."

"I have," Star said.

"Honestly?"

15

"Honestly, I love you. But you're very very bad for me. It took me three years to learn that. Scrapdawg don't have your money, and he don't even have your looks, but he ain't a loser. Don't think by getting him away from me that it'll get me running back to you. Once you get me back, it will be the same old thing – which was nothing, and lots of it."

"You still love me. You'll be back soon enough."

What a prick! Star had to vocalize it. "What a prick!" Right now, being white would come in handy, because he could punch Brad's lights out and get away with it a little easier.

"Please!"

Whoa!

"Let me touch you once again, and see what you feel."

In Brad's car, his hand running up Star's fingers, gripping him with a longing that his recent condescension was doing his best to hide, then a small kiss in the encroaching darkness, a slip of the tongue, licking him back into the world he left with so much reluctance, the waitress looking out the window at that precise moment, hearts beating faster and more miserably than ever.

CHAPTER 3

"You sat in the car with him for an hour!" Hendrick was understandably unhappy.

"I thought we were done talking, but we weren't."

"Penny says you were way past done talking."

"I don't know where I am in my life."

Hendrick picked up that distorted woman with the long neck. "This bitch ain't gonna help you."

"You know all this! I've been honest with you."

"I watched you during college doing everything and everyone, and I stayed on the sidelines, afraid. I'm not going to sit it out again."

"I'm not the same guy I was in college."

"Neither am I," said Hendrick. "I spent five years in jail and you spent five years in Wildwood. So I don't want to hear about getting your life together, or misery, or any of that shit. I got mine together, and I didn't ask for sympathy, patience, or for someone to watch me being indecisive while I jerked his ass around. I cleaned myself off of coke, but you ain't got the white shit out of *your* life! And you're willing to pay whatever price to snort up more of it."

Everyone was throwing race at him, and it was getting annoying. Actually, it really hurt. No matter who his friends were, someone was insinuating it made him less than a man.

"John Taylor-"

"Is a geek. He don't know a fork from a knife," Hendrick sneered.

"Is getting his friends together and we're gonna teach them to play basketball."

"What the fuck are we gonna do that for?"

"Because we can. And so his ass doesn't have to do the same five years yours did." Star changed gears quick, and then back again. His mind was all over the court. "You want to stay with me, you deal with me. Or get out.

And if you want to stay with me, your ass is gonna be there teaching John Taylor to play basketball."

"Well then you tell me what you was doin' in that car with Brad for an hour while I was stuck inside making Roast Beef Roasters."

Star grabbed the back of Dawg's head and kissed him breathless, chewed on his lips, and sucked his tongue so far into his mouth that it still hurt the next day. He was about to say *That's what I was doing,* but Hendrick lost interest.

"Fuck!" said Hendrick.

"Yeah? That's next."

Star wore shorts and a muscle shirt, Hendrick just a pair of shorts, his scrappy smooth body sporting scars and tattoos from his years in prison along with a set of muscles no one wanted to mess with. He wasn't in the mood to take any shit from a bunch of 16 year olds, and doffing his shirt was a silent way of saying he had taken all the shit in a lifetime that he was going to take.

It was Saturday afternoon, 94 degrees, the only hoop John Taylor could find with a moment's notice was the one slung up over his parents' garage.

His father remembered Star Bryan and Hendrick Pardee; he was old enough for one, and he lived and died SLU basketball for two. Not that he went to SLU, or to college to begin with, but it was a team, close by, and affordable, and back in those days just about anyone who read the paper heard of Star Bryan. No one believed that he never went professional.

Here he was, one leg up on a chair, one on the ground, dribbling the ball in the Taylor driveway, not far from Hendrick's own efficiency in Maplewood – but in the city in south Dogtown. A working class neighborhood just south of Forest Park, where the world's fair was so long ago. Mr. Taylor looked out the window in admiration, across the street a white crotchety neighbor looked out in trepidation, seeing what he believed to be an illegal number of black boys congregated in one place.

"I'm Star Bryan, and this here's my buddy Scrapdawg," he began. He'd rehearsed this speech like he was s trial lawyer going before a jury. He wasn't a trial lawyer, but one day, maybe, so he might as well get ready. His earrings glistened in the sun, his body starting to sweat, he and

Hendrick both looked like oiled up porn stars. The younger kids just had the appearance of boys who were uncomfortably hot and would rather be thumbing a Game Boy.

Star had a million reasons for doing this, none of which he felt like he had to justify. Making mama proud was pretty high on the list; pissing off Brad even higher. That, and he was feeling important. Wow. Once again, a basketball god.

"We used to play ball for Saint Louis U," he continued. "Ten years ago, I was the best thing that happened to the place. And Scrap here, he was the second best." He put a hand on Scrap's shoulder, the hand was sweaty, the shoulder was sweaty, and Hendrick's shorts too thin to conceal how it made him feel. "If you don't got the talent, there's probably nothing I can do. If you do, I can probably help get you on the team, and maybe on the college team if you're willing to work at it. There's millions of y'all playing ball in the parking lot, and about 300 of y'all playing in the pros. I was damn good in my time, and I didn't make it. Scrapdawg here was damn good, and he's just done five years in prison for selling coke on the street corner. He's got his life fixed up, and there's nothin' you can throw at him now that he can't throw back a lot harder.

"Another thing..." he slid his other hand across Hendrick's other shoulder. "Three or four days a week I wake up to him in the morning. And three or four days a week I make love to him. He's my boy. So if any of you niggaz have a problem with us being fags, you can take your down low road back home to mama. If not, let's play ball."

Homophobic black folks annoyed him particularly, and sadly, he knew his acceptance, like it so often was with high school kids, lay largely in his athletic ability. If the ball went through the hoop, he could fuck whom he pleased, and if not he'd have to land a date with Destiny's Child – all of them – to get himself out of the fix he just created.

Three shots arched effortlessly out of his hands – one on "niggaz" one on "fags," and one on "mama," one by one curved in the same arc and swooped their way through the hoop. It was three strokes of luck, but Star knew there was a lot riding on it. Each drop of the ball buried Brad a little deeper, and he saw five sets of eyes light up, plus a sixth, as John Taylor's father still couldn't get over the fact that these two guys were teaching his kid to play ball in his own driveway.

Hendrick, hearing himself described as the man's lover in front of a crowd, suddenly felt legitimate. His fear was gone, at least most of the time. John Taylor, in deference to Star, shaved his head and tried to grow a goatee, and looked a lot less like a geek than he used to.

As week progressed, the daily newspaper *Post-Dispatch* came by and did a story about the coke addict done good and the former college star giving back to the community, just a little human interest story made all the more interesting by John Taylor's insistence that Star and Scrap fess up to being lovers.

John Taylor was tired of being a geek, and here he was looking up to a man that his father admired and who was gay; needless to say this choice of a role model was geeky in itself – people who your father like and who are gay are by necessity frowned upon, unless of course... unless... yeah unless.

"Boy, what did you do that for?" Only Star could get away with calling John "boy." "Everybody else out there doesn't get it. You keep your mouth shut, or someone's going to put this to an end."

Indeed, the *Post* got letters about two gay guys and a bunch of 16 year olds, but someone on the editorial board thankfully declined to print them. John Taylor was lonely, frightened, and tired of being a geek that got the crap beat out of him at the city schools. Star mentored him into a clean shot, showed him the geometry of sinking the ball from all angles, and finally John dribbled his prowess up to school, sunk five in a row, and found that people were willing to put up with a gay geek on their team if he could win them the game. It's a sad realization, when acceptance comes from athleticism, that one really *can't* be accepted for who one is. But he was accepted finally, and that was good enough.

Roof Howard's mother, on the other hand, was less than thrilled to see this in the paper, and stormed out of her car after her kid on yet another sweltering Saturday afternoon. She didn't seed some fag-ass slave owning lawyer trying to make whoopee with her kid in the Taylors' garage, and wanted to pull her son home.

"I'm doing this to make my mama proud," he said to her. "You wanna take away my mama's pride? Or are you just scared that I could turn your kid into something better than you can?"

"Roof's a lot of trouble, but at least I know where he is on a Saturday afternoon," his mother replied, a bit stifled after Star pulled out the mama card. "That's more than I used to say."

"Well for five years, we always knew where Scrapdawg was, and it was behind bars."

"And you think teaching someone to shoot a ball is going to keep him off drugs?"

"I don't know. But it's worth a try, ya think?" Silence. "I said, do you think, Mrs. Howard?"

"I don't know. As long as ball is all you're teaching him, I guess it is."

"You let your kid work with me, and I promise not to shove my cock up his ass. Deal?" He smiled, and she couldn't resist.

Nether could John Taylor, who said later, "You don't have to make that promise with me."

Mrs. Howard had a different proposition. "You oughta start a league," she said. "Because I'd love to see Roof kick the shit out of the boys from Vashon High."

John Taylor was one of the best things that happened to Star. He felt important, and it had nothing to do, on his end, with love, sex, or the acquisition of unauthentic art. The fact that John was gay was a nice by-product, the fact that John had originally no self esteem – endemic in most busboys anyway – made him a good fixer upper. The fact that he was 16 and wanted Star in bed would hopefully go away when he found a kid his own age.

Unfortunately, Hendrick heard the comment, and saw the friendship, and he wasn't happy. He particularly wasn't happy when John pierced his eyebrow, apparently with Mr. Taylor's blessing. *John's been a new kid since you tripped him in the aisle,* said Mr. Taylor, unaware of the politics going on backstage, just happy that his son was motivated and had buzzed off that awful '70s "do." The goatee was sparse, but it would come in over time. One time Star put his bare arm around John's shoulders to help him aim a shot. John shivered with passion and Star's life became messy again.

But... a league? Hardly! In St. Louis it meant a chance for someone to steal someone else's money and some other politician to grandstand that he didn't do it. Whichever race wasn't the thief had the upper hand on local radio talk shows for a few weeks; whichever race held the mayor's office would probably lose the next election. There was nothing more disgusting than St. Louis city politics. It was disgusting what it had done to his father, and Star wasn't sure it would do anyone any good to organize his good will.

"A league?" Hendrick was on a tirade again; Star was beginning to wonder if it was better being ignored than monitored. Even that tongue sucking trick wasn't going to settle him down all the time. "What you got going on with John Taylor?"

"He's a kid. I'm being his friend. I'm making a difference," Star said, almost sarcastically, but he was, and it felt good.

"He's in love with you."

"Most people seem to be," was the reply. "I can't help that."

"You're going to go for it, aren't you?"

"He's 16! I'd go to jail."

"I was having sex when I was 16," said Hendrick. "And he was 30. I loved it, so I kept my mouth shut."

"You were ghetto trash when you were 16."

"You better watch yourself there, nigga!"

Star bust out laughing, but Hendrick didn't particularly think it was funny. "You watch your*self*, boy!"

"See! You've been calling John Taylor *boy*! I'm your boy, and I don't want no one else bein' your boy, and no one else thinkin' they're your boy."

"He *is* a boy. He's 16 years old."

"You don't call him boy like that. You call him boy like you call me boy. You got a man in love with you, so don't you go working no one else."

"I am not working no one else!" Star mimicked. "And your grammar is be atrocious."

"I is ghetto trash, remember? So you must be into dinge."

Dinge? He'd heard it tossed about. Someone who likes messing with the homeless, the addicted, and the rarely-bathed-if-ever. Hardly. "I'm feeling like a good man for once. Why are you turning it against me? You've been with me every step on this. Everyone knows you're my boy. I cleared that up right quick."

"I work with him, don't forget. He asks me what it's like being with

22

you. Making love with you. And I don't ever want him to find out. You just stop being so buddy buddy with John Taylor, and stop calling him boy."

Prison mentality? Not sure. "You don't trust me, do you?"

"Why should I? You're still in love with Brad!"

"Then don't come over any more."

"You don't mean that."

"Yeah, I do." For a split second, he did.

"Star!"

"Hendrick!"

Ouch! That sounded foreign. "I wanna be your dawg."

"Then heel when I tell ya."

"Tell me to roll over."

"You gotta heel, first!" *Yeah, I gotta heal, first.*

CHAPTER 4

Star liked making love to Hendrick's glistening sweaty body after a Saturday afternoon outside. He wasn't even thinking of John Taylor. Everyone else was. John was interviewed locally because Star Bryan turned his life around; Mrs. Howard got quoted too, with a chance to say that Roof wasn't a bully any more. Way too much attention was being paid to everyone. Maybe it was because no one expected St. Louis black kids to amount to anything, so it was news when they tried.

It didn't matter now. What mattered now was the steam coming off Hendrick's chest and the sweat rolling down it; as Star would lay him out on the bed, kiss him all over, get his face full of his buddy's sweat, lick off what was left. Hendrick looked up to see this big man bending over him, broad shoulders, bulging biceps, shaved head, and drool strands pouring like a Roman fountain from his mouth, leaving slimy pools on his chest, his stomach, his face, paying him all this sweet attention, feeling the soft lips and the scruffy goatee, and for awhile it assuaged his fear, quelled his anger. This particular afternoon, Star was hoping if he gave enough, Hendrick might finally shut the hell up. That, and like Brad, it was finally becoming comfortable. He couldn't bear the thought of his boy being upset with him. Particularly for no good reason, particularly over John Taylor.

"Ain't no one ever took time to love me like you do," said Hendrick.

"Nope," said Star. "You remember that. No one ever will."

"I hope," said Hendrick, "that you're the last man I ever make love to."

Star made him squirm and writhe and moan and lose himself in an unusual and lengthy display of unselfish edgy servicing. Dawg was howling from deep in his throat, shot a perfect arc, a perfect score, and had to admit he'd never realized the human body was capable of such pleasure.

Then don't fuck with it, Star wanted to say. Instead, "That's yours, whenever you want it."

Hendrick was sweatier than when he started, and messier, and more tired than shit for a man who just laid there. Star let himself spurt out over his partner's face. "Deal with it, Dawg."

"Oh, I can."

Hendrick couldn't deal with much, and it occurred to Star that despite all this love, affection, and basketball, that he didn't really know much about the guy. They'd never talked prison, they'd never talked lawyering. Star was no more lawyer at heart than a convict, it was just what he did, at the time, to please his father. But he didn't hate it, and he didn't hate himself any more either.

Hendrick didn't much care for the prison life. He was a good boy; he went into rehab, did what he was supposed to do and got out in five years. His cell mate was a dark skinned Muslim gang leader named Rashad Ali, who tried to force both Islam and his cock down Hendrick's throat. The Islam never much took; the cock wasn't a bad trade for safety. Being Rashad's boy meant the others would leave him alone, and Rashad was kind of hot, if not, unfortunately, oversexed. Other than that, there was nothing to recommend the man, but Hendrick, while big enough to protect himself, didn't always have the stamina. If he let down once could never go back. At least this way, if there was a gang of folks unhappy with him they had to deal with a gang of folks who owed favors to Rashad. Everyone owed favors to Rashad – whether they thought they did or not.

Rashad was bigger than Hendrick, his eyes starched white peering intently out from a heavy brow, pretty damn hairy and pretty damn mean. Sex wasn't something one could describe as intimacy; it was more Rashad getting his rocks off and enjoying it all the more for the force of it. Hendrick was trained well, and he gave up his self worth to save his life. The first could always be regained if he still had the second.

If Hendrick said no the protection was withdrawn, and he had the scars on his back and arms to prove that saying no wasn't a good choice. He learned how to be someone's boy, how to please someone, basically how to be a slave. He didn't much care for it, but for Star's benefit, he had learned to suck a mean dick.

With Star, the commands were more fun to obey, the sex was intimate, and Hendrick felt protected. That, perhaps, was what he needed most of all,

25

when all was said and done. To lose Star would be to lose the protection, to lose the love. Hendrick, upon the completion of his narrative, realized that Star comprised his entire world, but rather than diversify, he planned to fight to keep the status quo.

Other lessons he learned in prison – changing of the guard came with violence, and tempers were acceptable. It was hard breaking that mentality, but if Star could whoop him into an orgasm that would practically knock him unconscious, it was step one in learning to cope. Step two, he hoped, would be doing that again.

Star himself sort of liked it, watching that scruffy face howl and whine and yelp, so he didn't mind. But the baggage! Just when he had his own suitcase to unpack.

The tattoo wasn't voluntary, either – Rashad initiated him into the gang by holding him down and decorating against his will. Once they got started, there was no sense in getting up and leaving half an eagle on his shoulder for perpetuity, so he let it go. Every prick of the needle solidified ownership for one, humiliation for another.

Basically, prison sucked. He didn't want to go back.

Star, on the other hand, had a charmed life. He'd just wasted his voluntarily, though many might say Hendrick's cocaine dealings were voluntary as well. After that, though, his life was not his own, and perhaps now, it still wasn't in many ways. Star just gave his freedom up, investing in Brad like some tycoon giving all his money to an unproven broker. It fell like the Dow after a bad year at Microsoft. Little attention, marginally interesting sex, and tolerable friends. They didn't seem to have a problem with the black thing; Star's family could move in white society with little effort, but he was big, and they were scared. Big, black, and strong, even more scared. They were taught that fear as they grew up, those who weren't disgusted that Brad would let Star manhandle him were jealous. Either way, it sucked.

As an attorney Star himself was pretty busy, but so many nights Brad would work late, so many weekends he would work overtime... rent a movie? Go out on the boat? *Why did you buy that thing if we're never going to use it? Just hold me! Why am I too physical just because I want to hold you? Why are you too tired to watch TV?*

Star stopped asking, stopped making the move, felt forbidden from expressing the need, occasionally Brad would ask him, but when he did, it was quick and impersonal. Star sank slowly into oblivion, coming home, waving hello, and working on wills, divorces, and other domestic unpleasantries. He didn't cheat – he wasn't sure he could say the same of Brad; but he was in love, and... well... maybe still was, deep in the heart of the Texas of his mind was a big open space with tumbleweeds blowing across it, trying to cross it, trying to put the distance between him and Brad. From Houston to Amarillo was a long way, and a totally different culture.

So now things changed, and faster than he could have thought for one moored on the scurvy of a loveless island for so long. Hendrick was a mess, but Hendrick felt good. And as a dawg, fiercely loyal and ready to attack if he perceived his master was threatened.

Nonetheless, life felt good. He was his own man, had his own place, and the basketball thing was putting him bizarrely in the public eye as a good man. That wasn't the point of it. In fact, it was more to make a difference in his own life than to keep a few kids off the street, but that had to be a guarded secret if anything was.

Really, it was just the same five or six kids hanging out on a Saturday afternoon for a couple hours, but it made a difference. Sometimes it got up to seven or eight kids, sometimes he and Hendrick got a free dinner from the Taylors. John was in heaven, Hendrick would stay and eat because he was jealous of John. He never saw that Star's attachment to John had nothing to do with their relationship, that if Star left John in the lurch, he wouldn't suddenly have all that extra attention available for himself. Hendrick didn't get it, and John started wanting it really bad. John's whole self image was tied up in being with Star, or being like Star.

Now Star remembered why when he was 20 he slept with everyone and anyone. Because he could.

At the time, his infidelities lost him a man who loved him; later on he learned that love in itself wasn't really what made the difference. Brad took it for granted; Hendrick took it for gospel. On the other hand, Hendrick assumed the worst at a time when Star was dead set on maintaining his independence. Hendrick got scared if Star smiled at someone in a parking lot, and the basketball thing was just getting weird, particularly in light of John Taylor's infatuation. Oh, and the league thing, which was following him around like a police helicopter tracking down a criminal in an open field in Kansas.

Brad worked as stockbroker, but he took time from his busy schedule to call Star at work a couple times a week, just to keep in touch. Star was used to it, but threatened Brad to bill him for the time if he didn't lay off. It was over.

"You don't get it."

"You're talking to me," Brad would say. He would get smug, as if he knew it was just a matter of time.

"There's no other man in St. Louis you can go out with." Star said it more as a statement of incredulity.

"Not that I want to. Sure there is. I'm doing it now."

"So, make it work. I'm happy."

"With that?"

"With or without it."

Thing was, Brad turned into a good legal sounding board. He couldn't bring issues of the job home to Hendrick. He wasn't interested and he didn't understand it. Brad got it, and suddenly became a good conversation partner for Star's professional side. "Why can't we just be friends and not worry about the rest? Star asked. "You're shit as a boyfriend."

"Not any more, just ask Devon."

"So you're practicing on Devon to get back to me? You weren't so bad for awhile. Then... Brad, I don't know what happened. I couldn't buy your attention." He still thought about it, and still wondered what was so wrong with him that he lost the attention and love of the man to whom he devoted his life. It still made him feel half broken, still made him do things Brad would never find out about, just as a means of compensation.

"We could be friends," Brad said. "Except for one small point."

"What's that?"

"I love you."

"Then I'll sue you for malpractice. Because you suck at it." Still, the

28

words floated over the phone and rang like a spring breeze lightly tapping a wind chime, beautiful to the owner but annoying to anyone else in hearing distance. He was finding he really didn't like Brad very much, but he'd give anything to get past all that and just be close to him again. Now, it looked like it could happen; he could have the lovemaking and the love at the same time. More than once? Who knew? His lawyer's mind, which he was applying all too rarely to his personal life, realized Brad would lead only to misery. So would Hendrick, and that was more immediate.

If John Taylor had only known, he'd have cut off that mop of hair and dumped the gangsta wardrobe a long time ago. He was no good at fitting in, and by trying, whatever geeky qualities he had – and there were plenty – stood out even worse. He had a few friends, and now with Star in the picture, folks with hoop dreams started liking him – so even if it was for purely selfish reasons, he was getting friends. Girls at Bob Evans were smiling at him, the staff started treating him with respect, and he carried his head up.

"You wear clothes that fit and people might notice you have a body," Star told him.

"Then what?"

"Then someone might want to use it one day." Star felt funny looking at John now, with his struggling goatee and pierced ears, like he wanted to be a clone of the older man. "You keep practicing, and let your sister eat those chips, and you'll see the difference. If you look good, people think you respect yourself. Besides that, you look really stupid shooting hoops dressed like ghetto trash."

"Well, you look good." Ghetto trash was in vogue in some circles, John often thought, and it *was* looking good. Maybe not, if Star didn't think so.

"Thanks."

"You think you'll always be with Scrapdawg?"

"If he has his way."

"Then you won't."

"You've been asking him about us, he says."

"I just wonder. I've never done it before. I never met anyone before that I-"

"That you what?" Star knew where this was going, but it seemed getting John to say it would help him communicate it better in the future.

"Loved."

"And now you have." Matter of fact, and quiet, he knew where *this* was going too, and just wait until John opened his big mouth to the papers.

"You."

"You know you can't go there."

"Why not?"

"Cause you're sixteen." If for no other reason, Star thought.

"I'll be seventeen next week."

"John..."

"Star! Nobody knows about me but the two of you. If my parents find out, I'll lose everything. I don't know what else to do."

"You know I will always be your friend."

"I know. But I want."

"I can find you someone."

"I don't want someone. You're all I need."

"Is this cause I fixed you up and turned you into a man?" Star tried joking, but he knew it wasn't the time for it.

"It's cause I love you."

Well, that was the entire community project backfiring, and the whole Saturday basketball league failing for the very reason it was supposed to survive – a kid having some respect for himself and his elders. "You can always talk to me," Star told him.

John took Star's hand. "I know I'm too young. You just think of me as a kid. But I won't tell anyone. I have no one I can tell."

"Then do something for me."

"Anything."

"Drop about five more pounds and get that lay-up thing together." Star rubbed John's nearly bald head. "Once folks respect you, if they find out it won't be nearly as bad if you're a geek. It's just how the world works. It's not fair. Being black and being gay, we have no margin for error. You have to be better than everyone else just to keep the playing field even. The rules aren't the same for everyone, and whining about it isn't going to change it. Maybe in twenty years. But you and me? We don't have that kinda time."

30

"How does it feel?"

"What?"

"You know!"

"Lay-up, John. You get that lay-up, and you'll find out."

Star was about to puke—he realized that the only way out was to leave John Taylor tied to the porch, which would destroy him. Staying around would destroy him as well. Maybe by staying around though, he could help him on some sort of path, get him a basketball scholarship, and out of town. Probably not.

Hendrick couldn't abide Star being alone with John, or being alone with Brad, or just being alone at all. Star was feeling so trapped he wanted to just get rid of everyone involved and start over, just like he planned originally. Alas, now he was loved by three, and it was horrible. On the other hand, when all was well with Hendrick, all was great. Time alone was wonderful. Hendrick had a good heart, beautiful deep eyes, and a smile that could light up all of Soulard. Star could look into those smiling eyes, and damn! that hard muscled body and scrappy face just felt better than anything he'd ever known. Hendrick wasn't controlling by nature, but he was scared, and his fear made him violent. In prison, he couldn't show fear, and quickly it turned to anger and violence as a cover up. The reality that everyone saw in Star the same things *he* did... frightened him.

When Star was confident, everyone wanted to be close and bask in his aura. Star was very, very confident these days. He was what Brad fell in love with initially. Seeing that again, Brad wanted it more than ever. Brad particularly was going to miss 4th of July with the Bryan family, a reunion event with great food plus intergenerational dynamics that were better fireworks than anything on the Arch grounds.

This year it was Hendrick's turn to meet the family.

CHAPTER 5

Roof Howard was uncoordinated and an asshole, the first of which was a natural born talent, the second of which he learned from his mother. Star had promised to try to change his behavior in exchange for keeping his pants zipped. The first task would be impossible, the second a no-brainer. In any event, the idea of Roof becoming good enough to kick the shit out of Vashon High was remarkably short sighted on his mother's part. Vashon High, the building itself collapsing like the Ottoman Empire in 1914, had nothing left but sports and pride, and with sports being their path to pride, they were clinging to it like Kurds in their quest for autonomy in a brutal Iraq. Roof would just be a Kurd in the way.

Nonetheless, it was Mrs. Howard who opened her big mouth about the league, where it filtered through to Alderman Lancer Bryan, and where it stood firmly when Star and Hendrick went to meet the folks.

"They're not going to like me," Hendrick predicted.

"Probably not."

"Did they like Brad?"

"They loved Brad."

"Then they won't like me."

"I loved Brad, and I like you."

"You don't love me?"

Shit! "I love you and I like you. So you're one up on Brad." Star was wearing a polo shirt and khaki shorts. He looked white. Even Hendrick commented that all that African art hadn't chanced his core identity.

"The family likes it," Star commented. "And I like it. It's comfortable and it looks good."

"You don't look like a ball player."

"I'm not. I'm a lawyer," Star apologized. "We're upper middle class affluent black folks. If you want to think that's white, go ahead. Frankly, I'm tired of all that racial bullshit. And when you grow up with a father in

St. Louis politics, racial bullshit is all you have. I really don't want to hear that I'm a traitor because I own some Ralph Lauren."

"They'll think I'm ghetto trash."

"You have a prison record," Star said, realizing his tirade was wasted.

"I'm not trash."

"I'm not throwin' you out." He reached his hand between Hendrick's legs for a grope. It was that tough but sweet look Hendrick had that turned him on, the ability to put a smile on his face so easily. "Boy," he said.

That worked. Hendrick smiled and submitted. "Don't get me started. I'll be hoppin' for the whole picnic."

"You mean horny?"

"Yep."

"Good. Cause when we get home I'm expecting some hot action, boy."

Rashad called him boy all the time. It was comforting, and it defined his place in the world towards the men who could protect him. In prison it was about as affectionate as it got. Just like Star, he was running back into a burning barn, turning around to salvage one last bit of Atlanta, that same Atlanta that oppressed him in the name of Islam and Rashad Ali. "I am your boy, Star. You know that."

"You're my dawg, too," he said unequivocally.

"I'll lick ya!"

"Yeah you will! But later – here we are."

The sun cast Star's shadow on the house in the West End; a large three-story affair on Maryland Avenue that the family got for a song when you could sing your way into a neighborhood where no one wanted to live. Now it was worth about eight times as much, and as with everything else the Bryan family attempted, luck was on its side. Each home, built around the late Nineteenth Century, had just a couple feet of space between the homes beside it, which made for a very impressive block. Star took Hendrick by the hand and led him through the narrow passage between two houses to the family party in the back yard. Seeing them enter holding hands would send a clear message, besides, Hendrick's hands felt damn good – rough hewn, and powerful.

He knew the routine: mom was going to complain about his piercings, dad was going to try to turn him to some sort of political expedient, too many kids, cousins, aunt, uncles, it's been a tradition in the family, and no one would miss it for the world.

Star had a younger sister, Arielle, 27, and an older brother O'Ryan, 35. Ariel was blessed with a figure and a bustline that would ensure she'd never be without a boyfriend. Though she'd married about three years back, her figure held up even with the onslaught of two children. O'Ryan Bryan, cursed with a bizarre rhyming name, had been married for about 10 years, with three kids of his own. About twelve other people were around the backyard drinking, smoking, or eating vegetables, depending on where they placed themselves in the health spectrum. Mrs. Bryan learned early on that ranch dip outside in July was a sure fire way of sickening everyone in attendance, and stood clear of such things.

The Bryan kids got on well for all appearances – they were raised as examples, kept clear of the meaner aspects of popular culture, and were given a lot of good things. There really wasn't anything to complain about, they were told, but if so, they couldn't blame their parents.

Star kissed his sister, hugged his brother, tossed his polo shirt on a lawn chair and settled in for a beer. "C'mere boy," he said offhandedly, and pulled one up for Hendrick to sit next to him.

"Boy?" an uncle asked ready to start a fight.

"It's a black thing," said Star. "You wouldn't understand it."

Hendrick looked beautiful in the July sun, sweat glistening as it poured down the dark skin of his face, glowing like an angel, letting Star hold his hand, and saying absolutely nothing because he didn't fit in. Of course, they all remembered Hendrick from the SLU years, and so inquired about his dealings since then. He wasn't sure what to say. Prison? Short order cook? Cocaine? None of it seemed good.

Star cut in. "He's been my partner in the basketball thing," he told his father.

"What's this about you starting a league?"

"It's not my idea," he said.

"You know, when the sun hits your ears, it shines right in my eye," said his mom.

Hendrick cracked a smile, and that same sun glanced off his gold tooth.

34

Star pulled out a black scarf and tied it over his head. Like a doorag, but he never bought them ready made. It looked ghetto, and it annoyed mom more. They loved each other dearly, and enjoyed the game. She'd let him win for now. "Roof Howard's mom wants a league, and that kid can't play for shit," Star said.

"I thought it was up to you to teach him."

"I did. Used to be he couldn't play worth a fuck. Now he can't play worth a shit. Soon, he won't be able to play worth a damn. So he's getting better. Those other guys, they're pretty good. But a league? Six, seven teams, with expansion possibilities? That's administration. That's not what I want. I just wanted to help some kids out, and, Dad, to be honest, stop putting myself at the center of the universe."

"Funny," Mom said back. "You do that, and you wind up there anyway."

"It's a good lesson," said Lancer. "And don't worry about administration. We could use something to replace the mess that the mayor left. I wouldn't mind having my name on top of it."

"I'm having fun with it now."

"You've got kids admiring you and you're a role model. Think what you could be if it went citywide. It'd be good for your law practice."

"And your career," Star accused.

"Of course. The more people it helps, the better off it is."

"Your father's right. Go for it. Hendrick, what do you think?" that was his mother.

"I think-"

"Down, dawggy."

"Now you let him talk," she said. "You brought him here, let him talk."

"I think it was all Star's idea, and he should make the decision."

"That's not what you think at all," said Mary Bryan. "I can see that in your eyes."

"A league would be fun," he said. "But I defer."

"Do you always defer?" Arielle was putting the top and bottom question in a whole different light, and at an inappropriate time.

"You can have the league if you want." Star was getting a bit excitable. "I don't have to be part of it."

"But you will," his father said, not threatening, just knowingly.

35

"But I will." Star filled out his patio chair deliciously, with his arms covering the chair's arms, his legs sprawled out over the lawn, the black scarf wet with sweat and adding a bit of danger to his good looks. Hendrick didn't want to lose the moment, so he got up to fix Star a plate of food. His own black t shirt was getting soaked so he peeled it off and threw it back at Star. It landed over his shoulder; Star left it as a badge of pride.

"That's a gang eagle," said O'Ryan's ten year old daughter.

"How do you know that?" O'Ryan asked.

"I just know. Are you in a gang?"

"I was," Hendrick didn't know what else to say. "I had to."

"Did you ever kill anybody?"

Mary was incensed. She cuffed the girl quiet, but looked silently at Hendrick for confirmation.

"No ma'am. I made some mistakes after college ball. But I'm okay now. Your son, he means the world to me."

"He's just been through a lot," said Mary. "Be good to him."

"It's an honor," he said. "Truly."

He and mom had a good talk and downed a few beers, Star started up a hot chat with his brother about something irrelevant – well, it seemed that any chat with O'Ryan was irrelevant, annoying, or usually, both. Hendrick watched from the sidelines at his man having this whole other life without him being included. Scary, but he tried to let it go. *It's family, for God's sake, it doesn't mean he doesn't love me.*

"Does he talk about me much?"

"He does," said Mary.

"You don't mind that him and me..."

"There was a time I minded. He sat a home and moped about Brad for three years, didn't work hard, and turned into a big black blob on a red velvet couch. Yes, I minded. This, I don't mind. So whatever you're doing for him, keep it up."

It was her ultimate sacrifice, because she thought Hendrick was trash. Gang tattoo, prison record, didn't shave, and Star called him boy and dawg all afternoon – but maybe Star knew what he was doing.

Doubtful. That stint with Brad showed her he was an idiot when it came to men, but he was too old to fix now.

O'Ryan Bryan made the booboo, simply because he forgot Hendrick's name. "Dawg! Come here for a sec!"

It might be okay at Bob Evans, but suddenly it wasn't okay here. "I ain't your dawg!"

"I just thought that's what they call ya!" A few beers and the heat, and people would start calling each other all sorts of things. Lancer Bryan stayed sober, well aware that a bad night on the 4th of July could be a field day for the opposition in the press.

"It's what *he* calls me," said Hendrick. "It ain't what anyone else calls me."

"You got a prison nickname?"

"Yeah, it was 'boy.' You got a problem with that? You couldn't of stood it for five years. You ain't man enough to stand what I stood for five years and come out like I came out."

"No, I just ain't stupid enough."

"You know what I taught you about saying ain't," shouted mom. "I don't care how old you are."

"I know." For a minute, O'Ryan was 6 years old again. "You ain't supposed to say ain't." Then to Star, he grew up fast, and stood up in his taller brother's face. "Don't bring him on my playground and have him talk to me like garbage. Not in front of my family, not in front my daughter, and not in front of me. You take your trash back to where it came from." O'Ryan wasn't in the mood to be insulted, and he was too rich. "I don't have to put up with his shit."

"You don't know the first thing about putting up with shit, nigga!" Hendrick blurted out.

It was meant to light a fire, and it did; O'Ryan socked Hendrick in the face and sprawled him out on the yard, stood over him and poured some leftover beer on him; it bounced off him like rain off a metal fence. "We don't let niggaz in our yard," he said. "And more than that, we don't let people *call* us niggaz in our yard. It doesn't matter if you're white or black. You ain't supposed to either way, right mama?"

This was ugly. The boy and the dawg thing was driving Star nuts, and he was afraid that Hendrick would have to go. It would be too bad, he really did love the man. He loved his brother too, but this he wasn't going to

37

take. He knelt down and licked some beer off Hendrick's chest. It was a defensive maneuver, because everyone had picked out Hendrick as trash the minute he came through the gate. Drinking out of his chest cavity sent a clear message to shut up. Star looked up, calm as he could manage. "I guess it isn't a good idea for you to call him dawg."

Everyone looked his way with sorrow, *If you were straight you wouldn't make such bad choices, how can a big strapping buck like you like men? How can you ruin the party? We love these parties! Are you going to do this at Christmas?*

Gay folks called each other fags, and black folks called each other niggaz, but apparently it wasn't as funny as they thought. And what it meant, to Star, at least, is that you are the stereotype that the straight white folks say you are, so stop giving them ammunition. O'Ryan Bryan, insulted as he was, looked at it from a largely white point of view, that anyone using the word needed to be decked out. It was something else his mother taught him, about the same time she told him he ain't supposed to say ain't.

The only way this party would be a success now was for Star to scoop up his man and leave. It was too bad, because up to now he was having a good time.

Scrapdawg wasn't in the mood for any hot lovin' when they got back. He cried uncontrollably in the car on the way home. He couldn't say why; couldn't admit how he was so out of control, he couldn't risk running Star off by saying so.

He'd fucked up. Then he threw up. Then he laid down. Star walked him to the bed, laid next to him and held him close; his arm around Hendrick's chest, leg swung over Hendrick's, lips resting quietly on his back between his shoulders, eyes closed, a light taste and smell of the man calming him down. He didn't want to fall asleep, he just wanted to feel his man, quietly next to him, content. They were both relaxed, Hendrick was safe, Star was quiet. Sex could wait, in the wake of love.

CHAPTER 6

It wasn't the black scarf itself, said his mother, but the ease with which he put it on that was frightening. He'd already got in trouble with it once, telling Scrapdawg it was a present from John Taylor. Now his deft fingers were getting him a bad rap for that coordination which gained Star his fame ten years earlier.

"You looked like a gang member," said Mary Bryan.

Mary particularly enjoyed the day after a party, since she could call everyone up and rag on their behavior. It was expected, and in a sick sort of way everyone had learned to enjoy this. In this instance, she commented that the sole talk for the last five hours of the party was Star kneeling over Hendrick and drinking beer out of his chest. From a corner of the yard, Arielle snapped a picture of it and had already posted it on the Internet.

"What would you have done, mom?"

"Just about anything but that."

"That's all you talked about the rest of the night?"

"That's all. And that you called Hendrick *boy*."

"It makes him hard, that's why I do it." He knew he'd have to come out slinging with the Hendrick thing, or he'd be playing dee-fense the rest of his life.

"I really don't need to know that."

"Yes you do. It's not a race thing, it's a sex thing. And a good one."

"He's a piece of-"

"Ass?"

"Trash!"

"He loves me. And he's a good boy," Star said.

"Boy, dawg, what's gotten into you? In front of the whole family. You bring *that* here!"

"*That* helped get us into the NCAA!"

"*That* was 10 years ago."

39

"Your son punched him," Star reminded her. "I was standing up for him."

"He called my boy a nigga."

"You just called him a boy."

"He *is* my boy!" Mary apparently thought she could delegate the use of *boy* as she saw fit.

"And Hendrick is mine."

"It's not the same."

"It better not be."

"If anyone called you a nigga, I'd expect the same from you."

"Well mom, what am I?"

"You know what you are," she affirmed.

"No," Star admitted. "You kept us out of the black community and the white folks just thought we were some sort of curious addendum. I have no idea what I am."

"I was hoping you might worry more about *who* you are than *what* you are. That's how I raised you. Everyone else is worried about what color they are rather than what's inside. Your family, for the 400 or however many years they've been on the American continent, has not had that problem. I dare say they're the only one. And it's your father's mission to impart that wisdom to the St. Louis electorate."

"I don't want O'Ryan thinking he can get away with-"

"Defending himself? I do. Your dawg needs to show some respect. Or he's not a true dawg."

Star was blown away. His mother was street-smarter than he thought. "Wow. You're right."

"What did you expect?" They both laughed.

"Mom." Star got serious. "I'm afraid of him."

"Do you really love him? Do you love him like you loved Brad?"

"I don't know."

"I hope not," said Mary. "You loved Brad too much for your own good. You did forget who you were. We can all see the difference now. You're a smart man, but you can't pick a partner for shit."

"Mom..."

"Hendrick is not our kind of person. He's not what we want you to have. But if you love him, I'll stand by you with it. If you don't, then–"

"I do!" Star felt like a little kid, not big enough to fill out his 230 pounds. "But I can't convince him of that."

"Well you'd better, or you're going to be the next one laid out on the ground."

Star spent a whole night keeping Hendrick quiet, and just looking at him. Looking deep in his eyes, through them, to his heart, his soul, just trying to find him. A kiss here and there, a candle burning behind them, Luther Vandross for atmosphere.

"I like this," Hendrick said.

Star kissed him gently. "I do too." Trying to decide if he could spend the rest of his life looking at this, and what he had to give up, keep, or change to make it happen. No answer. He remembered the change, so quick, when O'Ryan called him dawg. Trying to find, now, where that was, and how to stop it. No clue. It wasn't here now. Just the same scrappy man he ran into in the parking lot. Something so luminous about those eyes, the smile, and when Star ran a dark hand down his face, he lit up more, more than Brad ever had, more than any man he'd ever seen.

Hendrick couldn't hide anything, and seeing him so luminous transported Star to a higher realm. After the horror of prison, most men couldn't pull themselves together like Hendrick did. But it wasn't enough, if he couldn't conquer the violent streak that it bestowed upon him.

"If I'm going to forget Brad, you're going to have to forget Rashad," said Star.

Star's condo was tall and compact, perhaps like Star himself. The first floor had a living room, dining room, kitchen, and small bathroom-of-convenience, plus a little bay window at the back. Upstairs were two bedrooms and yet another two bathrooms, and the third floor a finished open space where his hooked up computer and could display the picture of him licking up beer off Hendrick's chest like a dog lapping out of a bowl, so innocently posted under the "Bryan Family Party" page on Arielle's family website. They all had a mean sense of humor; it probably wouldn't have worked without the strength the family acquired through being outcasts for several centuries.

The higher up it got, the less African the décor. Most of his statues and hangings were on the first floor. The bedrooms had a few, he never got around to decorating the third floor so it was just an off white with a beige carpet with a surprising amount of sun coming through the windows and the skylight. Hardly anyone ever went up there, but Brad finally got the complete tour.

Brad and Star had revised things, more or less, and had become friends—friends who realized that there was unexplored potential and that it was all Brad's fault that it wasn't more than it was now.

But it was good. Brad could tap into the part of Star's intellect that he couldn't unveil with most folks. They could talk about seeing other people without anyone getting hurt. Brad was seeing someone he didn't particularly like, but he was used to seeing someone, so he kept at it diligently.

"He doesn't do for me what you did."

"I didn't do much for you either," Star reminded him, "so this must be quite a letdown."

"Yeah." Brad was introspective, and for the first time in ages, the arrogance left his eyes. "It is quite a letdown. Star, I'm sorry. I'm sorry about it all."

"Let's not go back to that now. If you don't like him, dump him. Find someone else. Or stay alone. It worked for me."

"You're not alone."

"Yeah, in a way, I am. I'm seeing someone, but I'm single. It's how I feel. I don't see anyone else, and we're in love–" that always felt dubious – "but I'm independent."

"You're fucking gorgeous!"

"Ya think!"

"I always thought."

"You should think out loud more often."

"I'm afraid to lose things by telling the truth."

"If that's the case, then it's something you don't have. And never did." He went into lawyer mode, imitating a TV announcer. "Mrs. Smith, are you accusing Mr. Smith with libel when he calls you a bitch, or are you just upset with him for pointing it out? Isn't it true that it's not so much an insult as a definition?"

"I see your point."

Brad made scrupulously sure his next flame was a white guy in order not to be permanently categorized as "into black" by the gay community. There are a couple kinds of white guys when it comes to this: white guys that only date black guys, or white guys that date either but at this particular moment *happen* to be dating a black guy. The second group of white guys is usually more defensive about its position and more confusing to their friends. Theoretically it means he likes the man on the inside, but nobody buys that. It's all chalked up to lust for the exotic, wanting someone *because* he's black, rather than in spite of it. It's almost like a gay married man saying he's bisexual when everyone knows better.

While white guys dating black guys were considered fetishists, a black guy ran the risk of being thought of as a wannabe by some of his own. All this from a gay society whose members wanted to be accepted for who they were. Still, Brad's new love was a lot smaller than Star, and seemed at this moment so much less a man. One more time, at least, he wanted to remember what he was missing.

So did Star, come to think; he could justify the ensuing kiss by remembering he didn't leave because he wanted to, but because he was pushed out the door by Brad's inaction. He clamped his mouth over Brad's and had at it. Brad remembered the delicious strength Star brought with him, Star remembering every last detail of his lips, though it had really been years since they kissed with such aplomb.

Brad was a bit flushed, and Star might have been, but he was pretty dark and no one would know the difference.

"Wow," said Brad,

"Wow," said Star.

"What do you think?"

"I just said. Wow. Other than that, we shouldn't go back there."

"I wish we could."

"No."

"I've changed, Star. I'll dump him, if you give me a chance to prove it."

"I've changed too."

"I know. I like this better. You were always a mope around the house."

43

"Yeah," Star laughed, not bothering to cite the obvious. "You're a handsome boy, but... just friends." The doorbell rang a few times, on the third floor it was harder to hear. The builder fell short on that point, and Star hadn't bothered getting it fixed. He glided down the steps, surprised to find Hendrick waiting for him, impatient. It was a breach of protocol, coming by unannounced. Although it seemed as if he was over all the time, it was always pre-arranged. He'd just gotten off work, and smelled like Bob Evans. A slight tick in Star's eye gave away something was wrong.

"What you doing here?"

"I was driving home and I just wound up here." Hendrick came in to see Brad coming quietly and suspiciously down the steps. It's not hard to tell when two people have kissed illegally, and prison taught Hendrick to read the worst into everything. Suddenly Star was forced into being a Clinton to an Arafat and a Sharon, and without a Lewinsky to provide any quick relief. He wasn't sure who was who, but he could see Hendrick ready to attack.

"I didn't tell you because I didn't think you'd take it very well. We're just friends now. We talk about lawyer and stock stuff. You'd be bored."

Hendrick's eyes went to from Star up the steps, and back, as if reading in a book that he assumed was *going* to be written, if it hadn't been already. "I don't think I would," he menaced.

"I knew it would upset, you, so I didn't tell you. I guess I was wrong."

"Yeah. You was."

"Brad knows you're my boy."

"He thinks he's so much better than me. Look at him."

"No, I don't think I'm so much better than you," said Brad, without a hint of sincerity. "But you are luckier than me, to have who you have."

"You do still love him, don't you?"

"It doesn't matter. He's yours now."

"Both of you have that look," Hendrick analyzed. "A look that *friends* don't have. Something was going on upstairs. See, I don't read a lot of books," he said, "but I can read men. In prison, it's what keeps you alive. You is writing chapters I don't like reading. And I don't think people should have their exes around the house if they know it's going to upset the current. It's just a sacrifice you're going to have to make," he said to Star, both as a threat and as a declaration.

44

Star didn't have a lot of friends, not that he could just shoot the shit with like this, and he knew if he gave in now, things would be horrible in times to come. Might as well break Hendrick in now. "You have to learn to trust me. If you can't trust me, or already don't trust me, then you can't have me."

Hendrick was operating under the fallacious belief that by getting rid of the competition, his man would stop cheating, rather than the truth, which is that a cheating man will always find someone to cheat with, or the more important truth, that Star, however much he might want to, wasn't cheating at all.

Star put his hands on Hendrick's shoulders, trying to calm him down, but it just stoked the flame a little hotter. He pushed Star away roughly. "Don't you play games with me, boy. I play to win."

"Hendrick, calm down!"

"Oh, so now I'm Hendrick. Not your boy, not your dawg. Just Hendrick Pardee." He said his own name like it was obscene. "Well fuck you!" He pushed Star into the wall, where his head cracked into the plaster, then he bounded up the stairs and caught Brad unaware, picking him up by his chest and his belt. "And fuck you too!" He heaved Brad down about ten stairs, watching him pound against the banister and the wall, then crumpling onto the floor. "Now get the fuck out of our house!"

That was impossible, since Brad couldn't move, but he let out an embarrassing howl, like a lonely wolf calling to a blue moon. Star, dazed slightly, ran to Brad, knelt over him, and looked up at Hendrick in his white cook's uniform, stained, dirty, smelly, and more recently, violent. "What you do that for, boy?" Star was shaking his head, thinking ahead of all the bad that could come of this.

Hendrick saw Star running to his enemy's aid and not his own. He flew down the steps, kicking Brad into unconsciousness with a heavy work boot, to the stomach, the head, the legs, the back, Star all over him unable to control him, and in enough pain himself that he wasn't at the top of his form. "I want him out of here. And out of your life." Finally he let up, panting, sweating, palpitating like a sputtering engine in a 19th Century steel factory. He flung himself up on the staircase. "You said he was gone! Now he's gone."

45

Brad, kicked up against the door, bleeding. Star over him, holding him, afraid to move him. Hendrick coming slowly back to reality, letting Star's eyes and sad gaze guide him down the steps back to the real world, and like Agave, the woman of Greek mythology who ripped off her son's head in a Bacchic frenzy, slowly the clouds left his mind like the clouds left hers, to where she could slowly see the world realistically. It wasn't a lion's head in her hand as she thought but her own son, and so Scrap saw the destruction he'd caused while temporarily out of his mind.

He started shaking, grabbed the banister and started to cry again. Star moved to hold him, tried to surround him, keep the outside world away. Even Star's big arms couldn't shield the man from his own ruined heart or from Bacchus' terrible revenge, but Hendrick held onto him as if it could make the difference, tight, close, clutching, almost suffocating, and afraid to let go. It's what he lived for, Star holding him. It's the only thing that made him feel safe, and now he could practically feel it being ripped away. "I don't want to go back," Hendrick cried. "I don't want to go back."

"It's okay, boy. Maybe you won't."

He looked into Star's eyes, desperate, filled with tears. "I can't. Please. Don't make me go back."

Brad was bleeding profusely, and probably had some bone or other broken, so Star went to pick up a phone and call 911. Hendrick, like Scarlet drooping after a deserting Rhett, fell up over the stairs in despair. He was just trying to save himself; now it was all ruined. "I love you. I only did it cause I love you."

Two police cars and an ambulance pulled up within minutes, blue and red lights grazing the sky and the row of town homes, voices over a walkie talkie, Brad being carried out on a stretcher, Hendrick being led out to a police car, taken away, cuffed, and feeling that final push of the head into the back of the police car. It was assault, plain and simple. Star had a choice of going to the hospital or the police station. The test of his loyalty was ridiculous. He should have thrown Hendrick to the wolves, but finally, finally he understood.

With understanding, there's hope. Also a really good news story, given that Lancer Bryan was a city alderman, and that Star Bryan and Hendrick Pardee were openly gay lovers giving to the community through a hoop over John Taylor's garage.

Star felt his own eyes tearing up on the way over; he'd finally seen inside his man's heart, looking up the steps his whole psyche opened up like a rain cloud releasing a torrent, so much love, so much hurt, so much confusion; being inspirational was not without its drawbacks. Hendrick's eyes were a mirror, and Star could see back into his own soul, and realized that life was still torture.

CHAPTER 7

"Let me finish!" It was mom. "All I'm saying is if you wouldn't walk around in black scarves and eight earrings and an eyebrow piercing that you wouldn't attract those kinds of people. That's all I'm saying. That's all."

It wasn't all, and they both knew it. Ever since Mrs. Howard opened her big fat mouth and said the word "league" everything Star did seemed to be of much greater importance than it ever had been before. It affected him, and worse than that, affected his father.

"Your father wants you to know-"

"Then have him tell me himself."

"He's busy."

"Well then I guess I won't find out, will I?"

"Your father thinks the boy should do time. It's the only way out of this."

"I love the boy."

"You do not. You love him because we don't think he's right for you."

"I loved Brad too."

"And you should go back to him."

"Mom! Ouch!"

"You know this is going to have racial overtones, and your father is in a ward that can't afford to upset the balance."

"Oh, so that's what my father wants me to know."

"It's wrong, but it's how things work. A gay lover's quarrel isn't interesting. Black on black isn't remotely interesting. Black gay guy kicks the shit out of white gay guy in jealous rage over black alderman's son – that's news! Whatever happens in your house reflects on the entire community."

"It shouldn't."

Mom was getting louder. "It does. So stop living in Oprah's world of what should be and get your horny lawyer ass back to reality. I don't want to live with your father if he loses the next election because you're banging a piece of street trash."

"Mom!"

"Star! I'm still your mother. Sometimes, I have to tell you the things you don't want to hear."

Star picked up a newspaper next to the phone and opened to the Metro Area News. "Shit, mom!"

She could hear the rustling through the phone. "Shit is right. That's only the beginning. If you're going to hang out with trash, I expect that's what you'll become."

Hendrick's Bacchic atrocity reverberated through the family, once again, like a scud missile had landed in the back yard. A family meeting was called, held outside with beer and weenies. O'Ryan acted like big brother and tried to lecture Star into cutting the ties and creating a distance; Arielle wanted the gossip angle for the family web page. The family hated her family web page – the immediate family that was. The rest found it indispensable.

"Right about now, a little support would be nice," Star said.

"You we'll support," said O'Ryan. "It's him. And we can't support you supporting him. We don't like what it's done to you."

"It sounds like you don't like what it's done to our father," Star corrected. O'Ryan looked more like dad than Star, but a little taller than Lancer. "I can't imagine my own welfare interests you in the slightest. And pouring beer all over him, brother, that wasn't so mature."

"Neither was licking it up off him," said Arielle.

"Yeah, with the shit you drink it tasted better. And if you touch him again..."

"Hold it!" Lancer tried to restore order. "We need to focus on damage control."

Star wasn't happy with this intervention. "I need to focus on saving a man's life. Dad, you've built your career out of helping poor underprivileged black folks. At least you've built a career out of *saying* as much. I've *done* it. I've done it in John Taylor's driveway. And Scrapdawg, he's got some sorta mental thing goin' on. I could see it. Because unlike you, O'Ryan, I is

49

one smart nigga. And if you ever touch my boy again, I will fucking wreck your life." Up in his face, with devastating intention. O'Ryan was right to be scared.

"Star, what has gotten into you?" Mary was not pleased.

"I'm working on it, Mama, and I'll let you know when I find out. But there's sort of a new guy inside of me. And I like him."

"We're not sure we do," said Arielle. She didn't care one way or the other, she was just more interested in keeping it going. It sounded more like she was imitating her mother.

"What about it don't you like?" Star said. Then to Lancer. "Dad, if you really try to make a difference, sometimes you get your ass whooped. And *you* are too damned afraid of getting your ass whooped to really make a difference."

"If I get my ass whooped, I have no chance to make the difference," Lancer replied.

"Yes, you do. I just got whooped wanting to help one kid play ball." Star looked around at everyone. "This is not the family I remember!"

"You're not the son we remember," said Mary.

"Yeah," said Arielle. "You were mopey, miserable, and self obsessed. Brad this and Brad that. Brad Brad Brad all day long. All that whinin' over a white dude half your size. We liked that better, didn't we mama? Now we got a strong man with a mind of his own. A man like you raised him to be. He did what you wanted him to do, so shut up about it."

Arielle's quest for gossip had hidden her intelligence quite admirably. Every now and then it poked through. Star kissed her on the forehead. "Thank you."

Still, things were far from over, both on a personal and city wide level. The race baiting radio shows on WGNU 920 AM were having a field day, and Star was finally putting two and two together, that the grouchy white man across the street from John Taylor was the guy causing most of the shit over the airwaves.

It was a circular argument, that somehow Hendrick's emotional folly proved the superiority of whites over blacks – the entire white race vs. the entire black race was summed up in one poor emotionally crippled

Hendrick Pardee.

The black folks called in and raised hell, acting like if they could get this one man to change his mind, everything would be different. By demanding he retract his beliefs, they gave him all too much credibility, much more than they would have by simply tuning him out. It was easier, and more fun, to assume that all white folks were like him.

Then white folks called in to agree, saying yep this proves exactly that. If you can't trust one, you can't trust any of them. The entire radio show boasted an IQ of about 86.

The newspapers, of course, had to run it from the angle of the alderman's son's lover – how this affected the alderman himself was only briefly touched upon, but the fact that it would, and badly, was much more a creation of the media rather than an accurate observation. That, and did we want unstable homosexuals teaching our boys to play ball?

"Yes we do!" screamed Althea Howard at an impromptu community action meeting that people hold when they're feeling particularly oppressed. "And you have no reason to worry about having a dick shoved up your ass as long as your head's in there taking up all the space," she shrieked at some self-appointed religious leader.

It got her on the news, made the league a reality, and kept some other candidate from spitting in the face of Lancer Bryan all too publicly.

What everyone forgot at this juncture was that the whole league at this point consisted of five to ten guys outside John Taylor's garage. It wasn't a league. A league would take paperwork, administration, and – since it was St. Louis – bribery. Anything to get Roof out from under her substantial bra strap, Mrs. Howard took on the job.

There's the old joke about being a criminal lawyer. "Aren't they all?" Star for the most part wasn't. He did wills, divorces, the usual stuff, and usually he was out the door by five or six o'clock. A lot of folks who didn't trust a man with a briefcase and a stupid haircut gravitated to someone who looked like one of the people. They liked the earrings, the polo shirt, the goatee, and the fact that they had a guy who was six-five and 230 on their side made it worthwhile.

Star did get a charge out of helping people out, plus $120 an hour was a good bonus. Sometimes he'd lower it if folks couldn't pay it, usually he felt worth the $120. Coupled with Hendrick's salary, they had a combined hourly income of $128.50.

There was no way any court was going to simply slap Scrap and send him home. Brad was broken, hurt, and in the hospital. Just before falling into unconsciousness, he reminded himself that this was a great chance to put Hendrick away and have unlimited access to Star for several months, depending on what kind of assault sentence was handed down in court.

Star talked to Venda Bratton, a lawyer friend of his who had more expertise in the area than he did. Most of Hendrick's mental mess came from being in jail to begin with. Putting him back? Just make it worse. What if he was put into a psych ward? Forced into counseling? Anything to make him better, not compound the damage. It would make Star's life more tolerable, punish Hendrick for the crime, but fix him so he might not do it again. Catching that look in his eyes that night, Star realized that Hendrick wasn't really responsible for it. And yet – he was.

Brad had a cast on his leg, stitches on his face, and surgery on his elbow. The cracked ribs would just have to heal on their own. He couldn't watch sitcoms because it hurt to laugh. He watched reruns of *Two Guys and a Girl* or *The Weber Show* because they weren't funny. Star looked down on his sleeping friend, studying his stitches, looking at the hand on the uninjured arm peeking out of a hospital gown. It looked a bit beat up, but that was from playing squash all the time. Actually the roughness imparted more masculinity to Brad than he could rightfully claim. A few light hairs sprouted out on his fingers, some others crawled up his forearm, again reasonably muscular from all its time in the squash court. That was all about to change. This recovery process was going to take some time – so would Hendrick's, if he would be allowed any.

The word "love" started flashing in his head in neon, and it all seemed so stupid; seemed to be what brought him to this crossroads, a switching yard where there was a train coming at him from every angle.

He took Brad's hand in his own. Brad's eyes opened slowly and he smiled as best as he could. "Don't make me laugh," said Brad. "It hurts."

"They fixed you up," Star said.

"You're dumping him, I assume."

Star shook his head. "No."

"Look what he did to me."

"Well I can't dump him now. If I fuck you I break you."

Brad held back a chuckle. "Go head. Something has to feel good."

"Brad, I'm sorry. Scrap – he's a bit messed up. I didn't realize. And I was, and you were, and we all are. And he's afraid of you."

"Well," said Brad, carefully repositioning a leg – every movement was an ordeal, "I think he's bad news." Star took Brad's free arm and started massaging it with his oversized hand. "I like that," Brad said. "It's the only thing that doesn't hurt. The other one doesn't seem to work."

Star didn't say anything for awhile. Then, finally. "I know you're going to press charges. And I don't blame you. And you know I'm going to try to keep it light. This is very hard for me."

"Then stay out of it."

"Can't."

"I know. But it will give me a chance to win you back."

"Can't. You've become a good friend, Brad."

"What do I have to do to change that?"

"Fuck over Hendrick, and you'll change it big time."

"Hendrick fucked me over."

"I know. There's no winner. But Brad, you really damaged *me*. I'm not willing to give you that chance back again."

"I've changed."

"So have I. You do what you have to do. Don't try getting rid of Scrap just to get back with me. That's when justice turns into revenge."

"Justice *is* revenge. It just has the law behind it. Someone should pay for this."

"I guess so. You look like shit."

CHAPTER 8

Star trudged up to the third floor and turned his net connection to Arielle's family website. Everything was archived, so he could click on July 4 and see all sorts of events, duly documented by the eye of a secret reporter. There were newspaper articles from the latest family brouhaha, including the *Post-Dispatch's* objective report, which objectively mentioned race at a very conceivable opportunity, and a nasty editorial in the second rate *St. Louis Argus:* "Are The Bryans good For St. Louis?" The answer was no, given the open homosexuality that was corrupting black youth, and Lancer and Mary, who by operating outside the "in" crowd, at least the "in" crowed as defined by the *Argus*, were obviously its enemies. Throughout the years, it claimed, the Bryans had advanced themselves at the expense of – rather than through supporting – the black community, all the way back to their slave owning days in South Carolina in the 1800s. It was Virginia, Arielle corrected them, and it was better to be slaves to the Bryans than to white folks, she further editorialized. The *Argus* would probably have disagreed.

The gay oriented *Vital Voice* ran a different perspective, a story about two basketball players who'd found love off court, and how one was going to be unjustly persecuted because he was gay. Some reporter came out to the Taylor's garage once to put his take on the story. There wasn't much of a story, Star said. He was just showing these kids how to get the damn thing in the basket. He didn't see what the big deal was, or how it had come to *be* such a big deal.

The real story, that Hendrick went nuts and clobbered the shit out of Star's ex lover, was reported only in Arielle's own weekly roundup. She was aghast that everyone thought this had to have such negative ramifications for the blacks and the gays. This was a story about *three* people, and not 500,003. It was just a case of jealousy crossing a few lines – lines people didn't want love crossing to begin with.

She was unaware of a major back door deal; Lancer's influence carried to the city courts, and Hendrick didn't have a chance in hell of going to a psych ward.

It was more of a hearing than a trial; everyone knew who did what, it was more a matter of what kind of punishment had to be doled out. Venda Bratton, a young, slightly plump black graduate of law school, pleaded Hendrick's case in an orange dress, some gold jewelry, and with a good deal of empathy. Brad had a coat and tie lawyer, a balding blond guy with glasses and a gray suit, sexy without knowing it, and Brad was in no position to show him.

Getting Brad into court was thorny enough, since he got around with great difficulty, as he told the judge while reliving his beating and partial recovery for all concerned. "You've been through a great deal," said the judge.

"I have. I can't eat by myself, or dress myself, and I don't know if this arm will ever work right again. I don't know if I can play sports again, and I haven't been able to work."

Venda Bratton's argument that Hendrick would be an asset to the community if he could be cured of his mental disorder fell pretty much on deaf ears. Hendrick sat between her and Star, clutching Star's hand with a death grip. He didn't care what it looked like. He couldn't help himself.

"Here's a man who is so lonely and troubled that he loses control of himself when he feels threatened," she pointed out. On the other hand, look what he's done with the basketball thing. Sure, he should accept responsibility for what he did to Brad, but don't we have a responsibility as a society to make sure we give him the help he needs so he won't do that again?

Well, not terribly. "I can tell by looking at you," said the judge to Brad, "that you've been through plenty of pain on account of Hendrick Pardee. Mr. Pardee seems to think he should be let off because this is a crime of passion. Sir," he addressed Hendrick, "if a straight man beat the crap out of you, and he pleaded a gay panic defense, I would think you'd be rightly insulted if I just sent him home to mama. And so here, it's insulting to think that out of control jealousy should get you off the hook. To be fair, however, I will order a psychiatric evaluation, and you will get whatever help deemed necessary by your evaluators. I see you are contrite, but you still have a debt to pay. I hereby sentence you to six months in the city jail."

Six months was do-able – it could have been a couple years. Six months? Well... it was still six months. Star stood up and approached the judge. "Your honor, can I-?"

"Take it up with your father," he said quietly, almost ashamed, and turned away.

Hendrick hugged Star, their bodies pressed tightly against each other, Hendrick's fingers spread wide around the back of Star's head and pulling him into his shoulder, fear radiating out from him like bad cologne. It was an odd education for most in the courtroom.

"You're a tuff dawg," said Star. "Remember that."

"I love you."

"I love you too. Be strong. I'll wait for you."

Brad could see Star meant it, and his work was cut out for him – that was, once he could walk again.

Hendrick, led away, bit his lip. Not too hard, now. There was plenty of time to bleed later.

Star went to T.J. Maxx, oddly enough, but he remembered that's where they met, and he was comforted that it wouldn't be the same place it was from before. Maybe they got some new stuff.

They did, and he bought it. He went home and paced his floors like a leopard in a small cage who was secretly wishing he could pounce on some small children and tear them limb from limb. He flipped on the TV but couldn't concentrate, went on the net but couldn't concentrate; finally he turned off all his lights and lit a candle. He spent hours watching the flame flicker and the wax burn down. They had taken his boy from him. All of them. No one wanted him to have his boy, and they conspired to make it so. Slave-owner dad sold his boy to a new owner to teach his son a lesson. It could have come out differently. No, it couldn't. Hendrick did it. He deserved what he got. No he didn't. No one ever saw what Star saw. But if you can't punish the mind, at least you can punish the body. Punish the body that doesn't need punishing, and ignore the part that committed the crime.

The family was behind it, his friend was behind it, there was no easy answer, just by taking his boy they would all show him who was boss. Payback for having a law practice with a black scarf and eight earrings. He did realize, finally, that there was no confusion about loving the guy. Having just discovered that, to lose him was going to hurt.

"Take it up with your father."

Oh yeah. Ohhhhhhhhhhhhhhhh yeahhhhhhhhhhhhhhhh.

"Some of you may have read in the papers that Scrapdawg's been taken away for awhile. And if you're not reading the papers you should start." It was cooling off, and soon they'd have to find a new place to practice or call it quits. Star noticed a chink in the mini blinds across the street, where the neighbor was curious as to how things would go. "Remind me to have a talk with that man," he said.

"I can't say that Scrap didn't deserve what he got. He beat someone up pretty bad. But he's got some problems, and I hope he can get them worked out. If not, I'm gonna help him through it when he gets back out. But he needs to know we're all behind him, and that we all care, and I'll need y'all go to with me a time or two to see him."

"How are *you* gonna get on without him?" Roof Howard showed every sign of sincerity. For Star, that made the entire summer worthwhile.

"I don't know."

"Family's what my mama says gets us through everything," said Roof.

"Yeah, family. Now you're gonna make Scrap proud, and learn to play this game."

John Taylor had taken the summer to turn into a man. Not just a man, but a *man*! He'd gotten leaner, more muscular, he grew a few inches after everyone thought he'd stopped. He was up to about six-three. Those same features looked so much more incredibly handsome than they did when Star first tripped a detached busboy at Bob Evans. Girls were smiling at him when he cleaned up their mess, the staff treated him with more respect, and he'd dropped those five pounds Star ragged him about earlier. Then he put it back as muscle and dropped it again. Maybe all this, and being 17, could convince Star that things could happen between them, and that he'd never desert Star by going to jail.

They sat on the front porch of John's small house, just up the street from Manchester Avenue and the St. Louis Marketplace, a rather unsuccessful shopping center built on the site of the old Scullin Steel plant.

"That eyebrow thing hurt?"

"Not any more," Star said. "You wanna get one?"

"My dad won't let me."

"He's a smart man. Wait a year, and make your own decision. And don't do it because I did it."

"That's not why."

"Yes it is."

"Yeah. Will you come inside?"

"I don't know if I should."

"Why not?"

"You know."

"I know. But maybe you need to talk," John suggested.

Star was amazed. He wasn't sure what good would come of talking to a 17 year old with a crush on him, but he had yet to hear a voice of reason in this whole thing. Maybe a younger perspective would help. Anyway, it would be good for John. "Yeah, I do."

"Will you let me hold your hand?"

"Yeah I will."

"I just wanna say this," John proposed. "I wish you and I could be together."

"I know you do."

"Don't you wish it?"

"I'm sure it'd be nice."

"He's gone now, and you'll need someone to take care of you."

"I'll take care of myself. Lookin' as good as you do, you'll find someone soon enough."

"I did it all for you, though. I don't want anyone else."

"John, you said I was supposed to do the talking."

"I know." He moved to kiss Star before Star knew what was going on. "I've never kissed a guy before. I just wondered what it felt like."

"We better stay friends."

"Too late for me." John's heart rate increased noticeably.

"Can you handle this?"

"You're gonna tell me how much you love somebody else, when I wish it was me."

"Uh huh." Great, Star thought, another miserable romantic.

John looked to the floor. No one understood why his amazing transformation had led him to such moodiness and depression. They ascribed it to growing up. "Yeah. I can handle it."

"I don't know if I can, now," Star thought, almost out loud, just enough so John could feel it without hearing it. If this mess backfired, he was going to crawl into a cave. They sat there for awhile, silently, John looking up into Star's face when he could. When he got the guts. More looking at their hands and fingers touching, seeing what the feeling looked like.

"Love is supposed to be a good thing," Star said to the floor. "It never has been with me. I shouldn't be your introduction to it. And Scrap, he needs me. And I learned, watching him taken away, that I need him too. John, I need you as well. It's not the same. But I do need you. My family-"

"What?"

"They'll hurt you if they think something's going on. We're important, and things that don't usually matter matter. They don't like Scrap, and I have to fight to keep him. But I will keep him. John," he continued, "I can't say that life will be better for you as time goes by. But you are better than you were. And maybe at least you can make it better for someone else, if not yourself. By having been here, you can make a difference. All those guys on the team, you can make a difference to them. Just like I tried to make a difference to you."

"Why did you? I was nothin'."

"You was walkin' by, and I was bored. That's about it. Just being honest."

"That's ok. I'm glad you did."

"I'm gonna try to get your ass a college scholarship, too."

"You think I'm that good?"

No. "Maybe."

"If I have to go away, I won't see you."

"I don't desert my friends. If I did cheat on Hendrick with you, you'd always see me as a cheat. So would he. And that's what I'd be."

"I would like it, though. And I wouldn't tell."

"Don't sit around hoping for it."

"At school, I can't really say anything."

"I guess not."

"And these guys don't know. Nobody knows but you and Scrap."

"I'm pretty boring the rest of the week. You wouldn't like it."

"No you're not. I've been reading your sister's web page."

"She embellishes. She makes stuff up."

"It's got pictures of you on it. That's why I like it."

"I've never felt like I do about Scrap. I don't know what I'll do without him. No one can take his place. He'll be home in a few months. I need to say I'm still his man. He needs to know that, and trust me. You understand."

"I do," John acquiesced. "But I can dream."

"You can. But you can't afford college without a scholarship."

"I can afford the University of Missouri. And it's in town."

"But you'd rather use the money to take your boyfriend out to dinner."

"I'd do anything for you."

"Careful," Star cautioned, while plowing ahead like a bulldozer in a blighted neighborhood. "Or I'll hold you to it."

"Just hold me."

"Let's go outside. And practice."

"I'm tired."

"You need to practice practicing while you're tired."

"What if I do all this and nothing comes of it?"

"I'd say something already has."

John felt one step farther away. The only thing and the only one he'd ever really wanted, saying no. Saying never. He and Brad both had six months to change things. Both sentenced along with Hendrick Pardee. John was dribbling across the driveway in all kinds of ways; Star wasn't waking up fast enough to follow the bouncing ball.

Family dinner; or at least family meeting, all he knew was everyone was expected to show up Sunday at 3. Star burst in as the last one there, having stewed alone for the last week. He just couldn't think of what to say. Around the living room were Arielle in a chair, Lancer in another, O'Ryan and Mary on a Victorian sofa. He already felt under attack. "What the fuck is wrong with you people?" Star burst out.

"You know how I feel about 'you people'," said Mary, always one for protocol even in the grungiest of situations.

Arielle corrected him. "The correct phraseology is 'What the fuck is wrong with you *niggaz!*'" she said. She was slipping into her Lucinda Trampp mode, Lucinda being an outspoken ghetto character she created at age 15 that almost got her tossed out of private school.

"Arielle..." Mary admonished, her voice rising high on the "elle".

"Well that's what we is turnin inta," she said. She dipped into Lucinda when she was very pissed or very right. If she was both, it could be classic. She rose from her chair and punctuated herself with a z-snap. "And y'all is gonna be the laughingstock of every white mo'fo' in the city of Saint Louis if y'all can't keep y'all's names out of y'all's papahs. Now there ain't no time I open a papah and don't see one of y'alls personal lives written up in a way that is embarrassin' to this heah sistah."

"Ain't nothing more embarrassing than your family website," said O'Ryan.

"Ain't!" Mary pointed out.

"Can it, Mary," said Lancer.

"The sistah is just reporting what the sistah sees. And the sistah thinks if y'all don't wanna be reported on, the y'all should stop stinkin' up the joint with y'all's sleazy smarmy ugly shit. That's what the sistah thinks."

"Why don't you tell the sistah to shut her ass the hell up," O'Ryan suggested.

"I'll second that," said Mary.

"Star, do you have some issues to discuss? You look like you have some issues to discuss." Arielle took a steno pad out of her purse, poised a pen, and crossed her legs in her slinky red skirt. "I'm ready. And I'm pretty sure I'm on your side."

Star waited patiently for her to finish the intro, went up into his father's face. It took some effort, since Lancer was quite a bit shorter. "What in the goddamn hell did you do to Hendrick Pardee.?"

"What are you talking about?"

"I have spent five days locked in my house trying to figure out what the hell is wrong with this family. You did something in that courtroom. I wanna know when politics became more important than family. And when I became a pawn in your political career."

"It's not that," said Mary, and way too motherly. "Your father and I didn't think Hendrick was *appropriate* for you. Something had to be done."

"There wasn't anything that had to be done that I couldn't have taken care of. You don't know him, and you don't understand him. And obviously you don't know me, and you don't understand me."

"Oh, we do," said Mary. "And we know sometimes you need a little push in matters of the heart."

Star was towering over both of them, waiting for more.

Lancer sighed, caught, but not willing to give up his dignity or his priority as head of the household. "I had a talk with some folks at city hall. I told them what was going on, and they agreed this would be the best course of action."

"You'll ruin him. He won't get the help he needs." Silence from everyone, Star got himself more under control, looking down at Lancer's jet black greased up short hair and Mary's oversized red-framed glasses under a hairstyle that looked like she borrowed it from Ann Landers. Both nearing 60, they'd really held up pretty well. "I know what he did was horrible. But you weren't there! You didn't see what I saw. You didn't stand by me, and you didn't trust me. As long as I love him, Hendrick is family."

"How long will that be?" asked Mary. "We don't like jailbirds in our family."

"Star, there are a lot of dynamics to consider here," said Lancer, as close to patronizing as he could get without going over. If he was that close with prices he'd have won a refrigerator on *The Price Is Right*. "By doing it this way, we *were* standing by you. You'll understand later."

"This is simply a case of y'all salvaging y'alls career at the expense of one of y'alls own," said Arielle as Lucinda, who liked the various and repetitive uses of y'all. "And I hope y'all like oral sex, cuz right about now y'all is suckin' some big ol' African-American weenie."

"Arielle, shut the fuck up!" said O'Ryan, whose sense of humor went out with the Reagan administration. "You're not funny."

Lucinda fell to the floor, and Arielle just let it fly. "Look at him!" she pointed to Star. By far the smallest person in the room, she now carried much more self confidence than anyone had ever groomed her for. "You got the big man in tears, and he doesn't think he can trust his own mama. *His own mama*!" she repeated. "And you, O'Ryan, can slip off that ugly white horse you've been riding so high, because the next time, it could be you, or me, or one of our own kids. So Dad and Mama," Lucinda took it from there. "Y'all better git y'alls shit together and remember who y'alls chillun are, cuz y'all is too damned old to start this shit ovah when you run them outa the house."

Lucinda was brutal, brilliant, and honest, and that's why everybody hated her. There wasn't much she had to add. Lancer might have added an apology, but he wasn't wrong. Mary was caught between – she loved her son but couldn't bear to watch him screw up any longer. Star's bond with his sister grew that afternoon; everyone looked around at each other, grim faces bearing an accusation that perhaps the family name had become more important than the family itself.

Star was lonely when he showed up and a lot lonelier now. But he couldn't click the door shut and leave it behind – the league meeting was in three days.

Despite Lancer's commitment to bettering the city school system, he wasn't about to send his own children to that rat infested hell hole – and he used that term literally – until he was successful in raising the public school's standards and safety. They all went private to a school in the county where there weren't a lot of black kids. It was at a school talent show that Lucinda Trampp made her first appearance; the routine went on surprisingly long until the school officials could figure out a way to get her off the stage.

"When I grew up, everybody in my family was a queen. My sister was a beauty queen, my other sister was a homecoming queen, my brother was a drag queen, and I was a welfare queen. We was a royal family. By the time I was 23, I had pumped out four chillun of my own – Ima Tramp, Eura Tramp, Sheesa Trampp, and DaHosa Trampp. I was getting FS, AFDC, WIC, Medicaid, and I was making a helluva lot more money than them bitches on my block who was bustin' their patooties workin' for a living.

I was getting every acronym the gov'ment made up for us undeserving welfare broads.

"Then I got to figure out that the next time I had a kid, they was gonna add all of $50 to my welfare check. And I don't know about y'alls budget, but it wasn't worth me pumpin' out another baby for no lousy $50 a month plus sellin' another $50 in food stamps to that dude at the convenience store..

"So I was tired of havin' all these chillun. I wanted to start *chillin' out*. Get it? So the first thing I had to do was *get* the chillun out. I pawned 'em off on the foster care lady, an' I said to myself, 'Lucinda Trampp, you don't wanna have no more of these babies, not for fifty lousy dollars, and you don't wanna mess with birth control, and you don't wanna give up the *good* stuff, so what are ya gonna do?'

"So that's when I turned to Lesbian-*ism*. You know what that is, don't you? It's when you have the girls over to watch a movie, and instead of waitin' for a man that you know ain't *never* gonna show up – I mean, you *know* he ain't never gonna show the fuck up, and you're sittin there cryin' and wailin' and watching that phone like it's your lord and savior – now instead of eatin' a bowl of ice cream and pickles and pop corn with your girlfriends, you munch the carpet, you eat the taco... you know what I'm saying, don't ya?

"Well I tried that, and well, if y'all don't like Taco Bell, then y'all certainly ain't gonna like eatin' one of them fish tacos your girlfriend's been sittin' on all day – if y'all know what I'm sayin'."

There was a blackout – and thunderous applause. She had to pay for it by getting straight A's the next two and a half years.

CHAPTER 9

"Damn, you look like a white dude!" Star was really tired of hearing that, but coming from John Taylor, it was particularly stinging. John said it because he meant it.

"We're going to city hall," Star replied. "We're supposed to look like white dudes. We're supposed to act like 'em too. It's the only way anybody pays any attention to us."

"Then you're gonna have to take me shopping, cuz I don't got no white dude uniform in my closet."

"You can't go looking like I plucked you outa the Crips."

"I can," John smiled. "I can."

"You have nothing that-"

"Dudes my age don't wear shit that fits. It's too much being like everyone else."

"No, it's just a different way of conforming. Time for a trip to T.J.'s."

"T.J.?"

"T.J. Maxx."

"Man, I was just in there with my mama."

"Yeah but it's never ever the same place twice. And I ain't yo' mama."

"Then don't act like my mama."

"And I ain't gonna dress you like yo' mama's gonna dress you."

Star wasn't sure why he had the affinity for T.J. Maxx. He didn't like the service, the slow checkout lines, or the clientele. He wasn't overjoyed with the selection either. Other than that, there were memories. It's where he started his life over, and for that he owed that store a lot.

John came out of there wearing jeans to conform to his waist size, a tight black tank top, and a camouflage green cotton button down. After his growth spurt he needed new digs anyway.

"Fuck!" Star said.

"Fuck? I wish!"

"Look at you!"

John turned around to glance in the mirror. "I ain't the same dude."

"I like this one."

"Yeah, me too." John smiled. the transformation was complete, sort of. "Now you gotta git yourself something too."

"What?"

"Cuz there ain't nothing sadder than a black dude tryin' to look like a white dude. Except a white dude tryin' to look like a black dude."

"Chill, John."

"The problem isn't that he's dressing like a white dude, it's that he's dressing like a white dude who don't know how to dress." They met Arielle for lunch before heading down for the big league meeting. Star was bringing them both along for moral support, to try to talk the city government out of it, and on the other hand, to show off John Taylor.

"I'm dressing how I want to dress," Star was getting defensive.

"The shit needs to come off."

"I'll say," John smirked. He was sitting next to Star, conveniently his leg rested against Star's under the table.

"Ohh!" said Arielle.

"It's not what you think," he fenced.

"Oh, yeah. You is lying to the sistah." Arielle picked up John's eyes, wandering sidewise to Star time and again, roving up and down him like a cowboy checking out hookers in a dance hall. She caught Star's eyes, too, glancing off this new John Taylor. *Oh shit, and he's seventeen! Let's change the subject.*

"So what's the story on Scrap?"

John was all ears.

"I'm doing the best I can." Star put a thousand bucks in the prison treasury with his name on it, told them he was the contact if anything went wrong, had already been to visit a time or two.

"You think he's gonna get the help he needs?" Arielle asked.

"I hope so. I don't trust the prison counseling system. I think when he gets out we'll see what we can do."

"Think you can?"

"I have to."

"Why?" she was suddenly turning combative.

"He's my man."

"What if you can't?"

Star was silent.

"What if he can't be fixed and you waste another three years of your life chasing after it? What if this stint in prison just makes it worse, and the next time he beats the crap out of *you*? What if he snaps out of control and beats the crap out of O'Ryan. Or," she looked over quickly, "John is next on the list."

"Arielle, don't go there. Why are you going there?" Star felt his eyes bruising from being punched.

"Because it can happen. You take this time to take care of yourself, and *then* you see if you wanna take care of Scrap."

"I have to."

"Star, you can pick up any man you want to pick up. So no, you don't have to. *Don't fuck with the sistah, cuz she don't wanna sit around and heah none of y'all's bullshit.*"

"What are you talking about?"

"Just sometimes, when you lock up a dawg, it's for a reason," Arielle said. "It's because he poops on your mama's new carpet, or he attacks the neighbors."

"What do you want me to do?"

"Put as much heart into it as you can. If you find it's not happening, let it go."

"So you think I should dump him?"

"I'm not saying that. I'm saying you're throwing yourself into him, and forgetting who you are again."

"I do love him, Arielle."

"Yeah, and if my husband beat the crap out this hear sistah? You wouldn't care if I loved him or not."

John was eating this up with his burger, slurping it up with his shake; Hendrick needed a collar, or at least a lot of psychiatry, or if he was truly a mad dawg, he needed to be put down.

Star was right about one thing: Roof Howard couldn't play ball for shit. He was still overweight, uncoordinated, and homely. Too much TV, too many video games, and too much popular culture had ruined him like it had ruined most of America. But he felt better these days. He'd learned a game, he could get around, at least in John Taylor's driveway, and he felt finally that he was capable of accomplishment, if he'd just get off his ass to do it. At least, the decision was his, and now he knew it.

Nonetheless, putting him up against some dudes who really knew the game would just throw him back to the sharks; Star was afraid that putting him in a league would do him in. Yet it seemed there was no way out, if indeed his mother was going to administrate it.

John, on the other hand, would be pretty much done with it. He was a senior, and over the next summer would hopefully move on to college type pursuits, turn 18, and march headfirst into someone else's perception of the real world. Star realized things were just way in over their heads. He had picked John up at Bob Evans just to annoy Brad, to show Brad that he had a life outside of Brad, this whole thing subconsciously was done to piss off Brad for 15 seconds. So essentially, it was all about Brad. It wound up making Hendrick a nervous wreck over both Brad and John, wound up making John a new man, yet hopelessly in love with an older man; and it made the whole city start digging up affairs of the Bryan family.

For Star, the whole thing revolved around John Taylor and his small group of friends. It wasn't about keeping kids off the streets, out of gangs, or getting them into higher education. It was about hoops, and when these kids moved on, so would Star.

Well, not any more.

The last time the city formed a "let's keep the kids off the streets" league, a whole bunch of money disappeared from its treasury. Mayor Bosley, whose administration took on a tone of "sure I'm a sleaze, deal with it," lost a lot of prestige, and the kids lost their league. He lost the next election to Mayor Harmon, whose ran his administration on a policy of "I might not be doing anything, but at least I'm an honest man."

Honesty not being an effective form of government, Bosley returned the next time around to run on a campaign of "I'm sorry for what I did, and

68

I won't be as bad as I was last time."

Francis Slay ran on some other slate of goods, and Slay and Bolsey split the vote pretty much along racial lines, leaving Harmon out in the cold as a sitting mayor with 5% of the vote. It must have been humiliating. Slay became mayor, and apparently found something more important to do than attend the league meeting, which he canceled out on with thirty minutes notice.

Star, in fact, wasn't quite sure why the city had to get in on it to begin with – oh, that's right, Lancer needed some votes. That and it gave Mrs. Howard something to do. For some reason, she needed this. If it wasn't for her, he'd have stomped it out with one crush of a size 13E.

The ice between Lancer and Star was chilling everyone else in the room. John, brought as an example of the program's possible success, was frightened by it all, and was ignored after the first five minutes.

"What do you do, young man?" asked someone who didn't realize the condescension of calling a young man "young man."

"I'm a cook at Bob Evans, in Kirkwood."

It was the first Star had heard of it! "You takin' Scrapdawg's place?"

"I'm tryin'." All too honest, like it needed to be said.

So it came down to this. Maybe they could get six teams or so, and find some former college star to coach each of them. They could practice a couple nights a week after school and then play on Saturday afternoon. This would have the added benefit of keeping the kids off the streets three days a week instead of one, and provide role models of people who had somewhat made it in pro sports. Maybe they could do it for the girls, too.

Star wanted to mention all the drugs and sex and steroids he remembered from his college days, but he thought he'd better shut up. It just goes to your head, and ruins it.

Then, of course, a competing alderman brought up the race question. Was this only for black kids? Did we want to include some teams from the white areas of south city? What about the Vietnamese kids in the South Grand area? Could the city safely sponsor a league that was only open to blacks?

"You ain't gonna get any white kids traveling up to play ball in O'Fallon Park," said Mrs. Howard realistically. "Their mamas won't let them go.

And I don't know if I want Roof going up there either."

"Mrs. Howard..."

"I want him to learn to play ball, not become a drive-by casualty."

"Well," said Star, "what does the sistah think?"

"No one cares what the sistah thinks," said Lancer, trying to avoid turning a staff meeting into a weenie cookout.

"I care what the sistah thinks," said Star. "The sistah knows all," he whispered to the rest of the crowd, who had no idea who the sistah was, or why what she thought made a crows nest worth of difference. "Arielle here, she channels the sistah. And the sistah can't lie."

It didn't take Arielle much time to become possessed. "The sistah thinks that y'all's spending too much of y'alls time worryin' about who's white an' black and Oriennal, and too much time worryin' about gangs and drive bys and Mondays and Wednesdays and Saturdays and days that come in the same order week in and week out. Now do y'all want to teach some kids to play ball, which is usually the province of the YMCA or some or other church minister who really wants to get into some 15 year old's thangy-wangy, or do y'all wanna just use these kids to advance y'alls politics? The sistah thinks since y'all don't know a double dribble from a dunk, that y'all oughta leave it up to them's that do! And that's what the sistah thinks."

"Thank you, sistah," said Lancer.

"Don't you be tossing sarcasm at the sistah!" said Lucinda. "This sistah ain't seen any of y'alls programs turn this city around, and people are leavin' the city fastah than she can count." Oddly enough, Arielle pulled an abacus out of her purse and spun the beads. "It don't add up."

"Dad are you sure you want to sponsor this mess?" Star and Lancer were still pretty much at odds.

"I'm sure you will do a fine job," Lancer complimented his son.

"Don't say *you*!" Star shot back. "I don't have three nights a week to give to this. I have my own mess, thanks to you, that I have to mop up off the floor of my life. When I'm done with these guys, I'm done."

"I bet the sistah would think you're being selfish, wouldn't she?" Lancer looked to Arielle to support,

Althea Howard was duly noting the dissension with a look of "mm mm mm!" wrinkling at her brow. "Star," she said. "If you can do with my son what you did with my son, you have a gift. You owe it to—"

"Y'all gonna let Scrap help me coach the team?"

"Who's Scrap?" said some other alderman of importance.

"Scrap's doing six months for assault, and before that he did five years for possession and dealing. He's my lover."

"This kids like Scrap," said the Mrs.

"The city might not," said Lancer.

"This city might not like it that I'm gay, either," said Star. "You'll have 40 kids under the authority of a documented homosexual and his jailbird boyfriend. I don't think city money's going to support that."

"He's right," someone put in.

"Frankly, nobody gives a rats ass if he's gay or not," said Mrs. Howard. "The kids like him." Some folks looked at her like she had no business opening her mouth. After a lifetime of it, though, she wasn't about to be put in her place all that easily. "Look, I know you're thinking I'm some poor fat black bitch who's just trying to get her place on an island where she don't know nothin' about big city politics – oh YES YOU DO!" she said right into the face of an alderman who was planning to deny it. "You thought so the minute I walked in. I've always been the first three, and usually I'm the fourth as well. Now, I don't know what he's doing with these kids, but he makes a difference. I don't even think he tries to make a difference. He just does. Frankly, I think that's what makes him a man, and a better man than all the rest of you, who are expecting him to do it while you just sit on your asses spending government money calling sex chats on city cell phones."

Someone needed to kick her poor fat black ass out, but nobody dared.

Star turned to Althea, who suddenly feared that her small hegemony was slipping away. "You can do this," he said to her. "But not with the city. We can have black kids, and white kids, and Vietnamese kids, and when we get tired of it, we can send all these kids home to their damn mamas and not worry about any political shit going down here at city hall. Dad, you find some other way to bake your brownies. We'll do this on our own."

"So you will do it?" Lancer chirped. He'd lost, but he'd won. Star felt Lancer was driving another icy stalactite into his heart.

While the aldermen were looking to get feathers in their cap, for folks like Roof and his mom, Star was already the leader. Folks like John would follow that leader anywhere. Some bizarre sense of importance came over him, like he was turning into Plato's philosopher king. It was Plato's theory that the only person fit to rule is the one who, given the chance, would refuse. Yeah, something like that.

"What do you think, John?" Arielle asked, as only she would think to do it.

John was scared again; he knew he'd say the wrong thing, especially since everyone was already nursing an ugly scar now that it was decided that it was best to proceed without the city's blessing. "It's just a bunch of us playing ball," he said. "It's not really a 'program.' We just shoot. If y'all take the fun out of it I'll stay home and watch *Moesha* reruns."

"*Moesha's* gonna rot your mind out, boy," said Mrs. Howard before she caught herself.

"Basketball don't keep kids from snortin' coke or joining gangs or killing each other," said Arielle. "That's for their mamas to do. You oughta try teaching these kids to read. They'll find a way to play ball. Anyway, Star, I'll help."

Nope, Lancer didn't win. His kids found a way around him on his home court. The few other aldermen weren't that upset. It looked like someone was going to do something constructive, and they didn't have to be responsible if it failed.

For Star, oddly enough, it was that much closer to forging an identity.

Star and John riding home, Star played techno dance quietly over the stereo. He still looked at John with a bit of awe, never before having seen him in clothes that showed off his body to such a ravishing extreme. Not much earlier, John didn't really have a body to show off.

"Why don't you show me your place?"

"All right." Star knew where this was going, but he could handle it fine when he got there. He was in control. He'd bucked his father. He'd won. He'd let Althea Howard talk him into taking things to another level. He hadn't won, but at least it was apolitical. For a member of the Bryan family, that was as close as victory got.

John's green cammo shirt tucked smartly into his jeans, showing off the new angles of his body; the rolled up sleeves revealed the new muscles of his arms. It was open to the third button, and the dip in the tank revealed the top of his chest. He wasn't a squirmy little kid anymore, and Star had to be careful.

Star gave John a tour of his three stories, but no one was interested. Today the question would have to be answered. Would they have sex or not? It was the only question worth answering, though not one easily asked. If no one asked it, the rest of their lives would be interminable. Since it was not a question one could come right out and ask, it had to be slow pitched and swung at a few times until someone made contact.

"Hey, lemme show you something." John pulled off his shirt; the tank clung to him like Dido to Aeneas.

"What?"

"Look at this." John flexed a bicep, and it popped up strong. "Never had one before."

"Damn, boy. You've been training hard."

"I just noticed it. Feels kinda nice."

Star put a couple fingers on it, traced over it. John had never been touched like that before, particularly not by a man, not by a man he loved, and he was mesmerized. He watched Star's dark fingers run down his equally dark skin, down until they took his hand, fingers crossing across fingers, over his knuckles, palms touching, some kinda warm he'd longed for, and from this man, for months, finally radiating into him. He sprung up in his jeans like a bamboo tree.

Star led him to a couch in the extra bedroom on the second floor, sat him down. "We need to talk."

"We've been talking," said John.

"Not about this."

"No? Where you been bro?"

"I've been there."

"Arielle's right," John said. "You might not be able to fix him."

"Don't you worry about that," said Star.

"I have to worry about that," John dissented. "I have his job. And every night, I go to bed and I can't think of anything but having you there holding me. Anything, Star." He reached up, ran a hand from Star's forehead, down over his eyelid, his cheek, his goatee, his lips, for the first time, afraid, excited, and hoping that Star wouldn't toss him out on the street.

"I don't want no one else but you," said John. "But I've been alone all my life."

"I didn't have anyone at 17," said Star. "We could get in trouble. Big trouble."

"Who's gonna tell?"

"You."

"I won't."

"You'll let it drop. You'd tell Scrap. And I'd have to hurt ya."

"I know."

"I can't be your man."

"Just once, then." Finger tracing his lips, Star reached his tongue out, licked it, pulled it in for a soft bite. Almost like he was doing the guy a favor, almost like he was back in college again, he was 20, and the thrill of someone wanting him over took him, the thrill of watching someone fall to their feet to have him, him, him, the clouds in his mind, the same clouds that overtook Hendrick when he beat Brad to a cinder, the same Bacchic frenzy, his hand reached under John's tank top, played with a nipple, eyes looked deep into John's face, John lighting up, sensing things he only imagined but never before understood, yeah he's never, never, I'm the first one, what am I getting into?

Yeah, maybe he couldn't fix Hendrick. Maybe that was his justification. That, and Bacchus, urging him on. Out of control, he took control, pulled off John's top, studied him for the first time, knew that every place he touched him would send him into a frenzy, yeah, he would go there, better him than someone who would just use him for a cheap quickie and hurt him later.

Pushed John down, laid on top of him, held his arms up over his head, he's helpless, but feels so happily vulnerable, the door to the Elysium Fields opens as Star's hand pins his arms to a pillow at the end of the couch. Just that act in itself, convincingly erotic. Star laid a kiss on him. John kissed back, not quite knowing how, just trying out, learning how it felt; Star would give him time to explore it, all of it. A big neon 17 flashed in the back of his head all the way through it, exciting, foreboding, legal? Yeah. In Missouri, yeah. Whatever. Star felt curiously taken over, watching himself

74

act without reason, watching himself as if he were one of the spirits on the wall looking down. First time? He could swallow it. He hadn't let himself, even with Brad. He knew Brad was a cheat. Hendrick most likely positive. John was an angel. Star popped up, letting a white wad dangle off his chin.

"What?" he said innocently.

"My turn!"

John was more beautiful than he'd remembered any man. "Oh, yeah."

John showed his love to Star, tried his best to make all his fantasies become reality, all in one night, in one fell swoop, teased Star like a rocket ship waiting to launch during a rain storm, the countdown, again? Sometime, let's blast off! John shot one more time, he's young, he can, it's a good chaser to the first, look at his face! he's finally come together, his whole reason for life, finally come to be, his one, his only, his man, living out all the fantasies of one poor boy cleaning tables in Kirkwood, finally, the truth is out there, and now, it's in here! one small step for man, one giant leap for mankind, Bacchus slowly takes away the cloud, Star is left holding a bloody, dripping, severed head. 17 burning bright, Hendrick snapping John in half like his mother tossing out an emery board, his mother more disgusted by the minute, and Star caught with young cum dripping off his chin, smiling, saying "what?" as if he didn't know.

"What's wrong?" John, scared, sees something searing through Star's psyche, a comet too close to the sun, leaving dust, bringing catastrophe.

"Nothing."

"You sure?"

"I'm sure."

"I love you."

Who doesn't? "Please, John."

"I know."

"What do you know?"

"You love Scrap, and I need to shut up."

"Yeah." Maturity? But for how long?

"I'll wait it out," said John. "There's nobody else like you."

Thank God for that.

CHAPTER 10

The drive from Soulard to Wildwood was a long haul down Highway 44, then up the winding two lane 109; Star was afraid of what he was going to find when he got there, but he promised Brad he'd bring up some lunch and take care of a few things around the house that Brad couldn't get to, or in any case didn't feel like doing.

There was a lot of time to think; John gave him some new CD to play on the way, but all that R&B philosophizing about relationships was just aggravating. Everyone was so damned selfish; with all the me! me! me! going on it might as well have been grand opera. There was only one person he could confide this in, and that was Arielle, who would probably morph into Lucinda shortly after accessing the information.

Lucinda, familiarly, unhappily, and commonly known at The Sistah, originally came into being more out of necessity than contempt. Though she was initially conceived to comically disparage abusers of the welfare system in the underclass, she pretty much called things as she saw them in all walks of life, particularly, and eventually, at home. It annoyed everyone to no end.

"Yeah? Well when were we ever allowed to express our own opinions?" Arielle once said.

"I just thought it was a good hearted give and take," Star said back to her.

"Try disagreeing with that man. When was that ever tolerated? For a liberal political intelligent family, we were always very quietly punished for expressing our own points of view – sometimes for years. I didn't know what else to do. And I've completely lost the ability to speak my own mind around any member of the family. *So that's when the Sistah takes ovah!*" a wave of the hand in the air, the transformation came and went like a like a car slowly rolling through a stop sign, unaware that at 20 mph it was breaking the law.

It made a lot of sense, in a sorry sort of way. A lot of what Star took as good humored quarreling began to come clear to him as a very subtle invective to get everyone to toe the Bryan company line. That, and the catch-phrase "your father's career," to which all thoughts and opinions were forced to bow.

And Star could just hear Lucinda now: "What the fuck you doin' messin with some seventeen year old weenie? You know ain't nothin' good gonna come outa that, and you know in two weeks he gonna be ovah your sorry ass and you is gonna look like one sad little old man."

Maybe not. Life was like a minefield for now, and every relationship he'd cultivated was about ready to explode if he stepped in the wrong place. His mind cleared up now, focusing absent mindedly on the lane markers through Kirkwood and Fenton. There was nothing – nothing at all that could come good out of his experience with John Taylor. But damn! It felt good. He sort of wanted to do it again. It felt like it could work, except of course John was 17 and living in a new world, and once having discovered sex, was probably going to be taking whatever low road he had to in order to get it from every possible outlet he could find. Looking like he did, it wouldn't be that difficult.

Something in the family tie had recently given way, and playful banter in the form of serious discussion had morphed into ugly rivalry. Something had come in ahead of "your father's career." That something, in a way, was Althea Howard, or more devastatingly, John Taylor. If John Taylor was found out, "your father's career" would become extremely messy, the *Argus* would have a field day, and the *Post* would start running stories about how the guy who started the basketball thing was using it as a breeding ground for too-young lovers, not to mention a whole new take on the "how safe are our children" news stories that permeated television news like vampire bats hanging in a cave dripping blood from their wings.

The gay community would probably be very quiet.

The good thing about Hendrick Pardee was that he was locked up and could be left to rot for a few days while Star got his thoughts in order. For some reason, Star didn't feel that sorry for Brad. He should have, Brad was in a bad way. It was Scrap's fault. *I did try to stop it,* he reminded himself. It was so sudden, not to mention cracking his head against the wall kept him from saving Hendrick from his appointed round with as much alacrity as he'd have liked. Part of him loved Brad, part hated him, and part just liked being friends. Too much conflict.

And he was *really* tired of this "white dude" shit. Maybe it was something he picked up in Wildwood, unconsciously. If you're wearing Ralph Lauren and khakis, the soccer moms aren't so scared about picking up produce next to you in the grocery store, you're less likely to be stopped for a DWB – oh, and when going home, Mama wasn't going to accuse you of dressing like ghetto trash.

This time, to avoid all that, he decided to dress like ghetto trash. Ghetto trash with money, that is. He wore a black and red polyester shirt and black jeans that stacked up over some new black boots. To top off, the black scarf that was a present from John Taylor. Maybe a bit overdressed, but he looked damn hot, and part of him wanted to impress Brad as to what he had let languish in front of the TV for three long uneventful unconsummated years.

The girl at the 7-11 was more frightened than impressed; Star had to laugh a bit to himself on the way out. Coming down here so infrequently, maybe he didn't really belong. Maybe, if somewhere along the line, someone had let him forge an identity instead of saying he was too black, too white, or not enough of either, he might not be stuck trying to buy one at the ever changing T.J. Maxx.

Fuck! Not the best mood to go visiting someone who, maybe maybe maybe? You could have him back! Nah. People don't change. Bad news for Scrap, but maybe...

Brad was getting slowly back into shape. He was walking in pain, and a lot of time with a cane, his left arm in a sling – no one was sure yet how useful it would be in the future. Hendrick had kicked it pretty hard and pretty bad, and it might have to be replaced. It was all messy and indeterminate; in any case Brad wasn't going to be on the squash court for quite awhile. He didn't look much like the man Star had been so in love with not so long ago. Now, right after the John episode, Star didn't really want to go there. He didn't know if he would ever want to touch another man again. If being a stud had its downside, this must have been it.

Star sat on the couch, Brad hobbled over and laid down on his side, and pulled Star's closer arm over him.

"Aren't you seeing someone?" Star asked.

"Sort of." Brad changed the definition of "seeing someone" to suit the moment.

"I'm sure he doesn't want you sitting like this."

"Well he isn't gonna kick the shit out of you, is he?"

"I don't know," Star joked. "I haven't met him."

"Would it bother you if you did?"

Maybe not. Maybe it would close up the whole thing. "Not really. Bring him over."

"Nope. I just want us to be together."

"I brought over some Chinese."

Brad played a bit with Star's hand; there was a time Star would relish this, and for the sake of convenience he brought that feeling back, let Brad kiss his fingers a bit, and closed his eyes, waiting for some or other bomb to drop.

"What are you going to do about Hendrick?"

"I don't know."

"I've missed work. I'm behind on everything. I can't use the gym. I can hardly walk. And I don't know what's gonna happen with this arm. He did it, and you were right there."

"I was. I wish he hadn't-"

"Do you? I'm so nicely out of the way."

The pitty potty, and it wasn't a good idea for anyone to hog any sort of potty wasn't a with all this Chinese food that was about to go down. "It's awkward," Star said. "If you don't want to be friends any more, I'd understand."

Since Brad was currently sucking on Star's index finger, that probably wasn't what he was thinking. "You wanna?" Eyes up, that cutesy little smile meant to entice but that just annoys.

Star ignored it. "Yeah, I'm hungry."

"No, not *eat*. Well, not eat *that* shit."

"No, I don't wanna."

"You sure?" Brad turned around and put a hand under Star's shirt. You sure look good in this. Bout time you stopped dressing like a white guy."

"Bout time I stopped dating one, too," Star said.

"I don't know," Brad said. "I think this white guy can make ya pretty happy."

"You could, but you didn't. We each have our men. Let's leave it at that." It was killing him to say it, because it'd have been so easy. And if it weren't for John... messing with two guys while Hendrick was being warehoused, that would be too much. That was more choice than impulse.

"I've been talking with my lawyer."

Yep. The sack of Mantua by the Austrians, burning up the only copies of 12 Monteverdi operas. Some things, people can never recover from. "About what?"

"About what to do with Hendrick Pardee."

"Pardee of the first part? Or Pardee of the second part?" Star tried his little joke, but he was afraid of where this was going.

"About getting some compensation from him."

"He's already doing six months."

"What do I get out of that?"

"Satisfaction?"

"I'd rather get that from you." Brad's hand was still running around under Star's polyester; he did sort of remember what worked and what didn't, from the days he cared, and Star wasn't quite ready to pull him out of there. Star remembered that hand, all the bumps and curves and how it felt, the calluses from the squash court, and he liked it.

"What do you want?"

"I'm not sure I'll ever be the same. And when this heals up, I'll probably be in pain all my life. I think he owes me something for that."

"He's worth about 50 cents, and I'm sure he's had to use that for protection in prison."

"He'll be working again. I don't want him to forget this and think he can do it next time. Every time you have a friend over, you'll have a pit bull at the door."

"Yeah." Brad was probably right, but Star still wasn't sure where this was going. More and more sure, though.

"Of course, *you* have money."

"Yeah. But I ain't the one that beat the shit out of you. Though I'm gonna."

"Well if you were with me again, I probably wouldn't want to be suing any friends of yours."

Star was still being friendly, because it was Brad. "That sounds like 'African-American mail' to me. I gotta be your lover so you don't sue my boyfriend. You're desperate."

"You do still love me, don't you?" Brad's hand down to Star's belt, Star got up slowly so as to not break any more of Brad than was broken already.

"Shit, does the damn thing even work after-"

"Yeah," said Brad. "And it *gets* worked. Just not as good as you could."

"Well, Scrapdawg, he ain't around for now, but..."

"But what? He's givin' it up to every nigger in the joint."

"You can shut up right about now."

"Oh, suddenly you're turning PC?"

Somehow the "n" word was particularly grating; Brad's use on the assumption that Star wasn't black enough to care raised his heartbeat and brought back about 15 years worth of family issues. "You're gonna have a very hard time getting money out of *anyone* you call a nigger. And if say it about one of us, you say it about all of us. I'll testify you said it, and you're gonna be stuck with nothing but a bunch of west county bigoted white folks to lie and say they never heard you say it."

"I don't mean it. I'm just using it to get to you."

"Well it's getting to me really, really bad. I am black. Very, *very* black. Dark enough that most black families wouldn't admit to having me. But it looks good on me." Star said it as much for himself as anyone else. "And don't you play that *there's white niggers too* game on me," he added. "I'm not going to ignore it for your sake, or my father's. I know what's going on in prison. I don't know if he's strong enough to deal with it or not. It's not your place to torture me with it."

With all the papers trumpeting Hendrick's sexuality, doubtless someone in prison knew he was gay. Maybe he would do what he had to in order to survive. Maybe that *was* what he had to do – or what he wanted to do under the guise of coercion. It worked last time, and he would just as easily revert. Maybe for Star, prison survival was John Taylor. Certainly it wasn't this wreck of a man crumpled up on the couch and mixing up a Molotov of love and blackmail. "You saying if I don't come live here again, that you're gonna make my life hell? And if I do live here again it's gonna be the same hell it was last time? I'm gonna track down your dawgboy and tell him what kind of a mind you have, and you can heal that arm up all by yourself."

"He's not a dawgboy," Brad asserted.

"He has to be pretty pathetic to hang around this kinda crap. I was pathetic. My sister brought it home to me. Waiting on you to love me. To change your mind! It's not going to be a condition now."

"Star!"

"What? You want to legislate emotion? Maybe in Utah! One wife is plenty for me."

"I'm sorry. He's good. But he's not you."

"Then maybe that's something you have to live with. Or... without." Star would have left in a huff, but he was hungry, so he broke open a carton of fried rice and started shoving it behind his goatee with a wimpy plastic fork. "You're not gonna sue Scrap."

"Yeah I am."

"Brad, that wasn't a question. It was a statement. If you do our friendship is over, and *that* you can't get back in court."

"What are you defending him so much for? You might try living your own life instead of his."

Ouch. "I will, when I find one I like." He looked around the big home that used to be his own. Brad never did let him put his name on the deed, even though he asked. It hadn't really been redecorated, but yet there was nothing here that showed off Star.

Being who he was? Out in the driveway with the kids and the ball. For once, just being himself and not having to work to be liked. Okay, he was in on the league. Just out on the city. But a big part of him, the part that still had longing, decided not yet to reject Brad out of hand. Soon, yep. If someone was served, sued, or drug through any more criminal gymnastics, maybe. Definitely. Maybe.

For now, if they could just stop talking and have sex, everything would be fine. For awhile, put the baggage away, and just go to it like they did...

82

well... uh... years ago... maybe the few times before Brad didn't give a shit any longer...

It'd be hard now. He couldn't very well move Brad without breaking him, and all that smashed china that used to be the bones in Brad's elbow, that was because of the man he purportedly loved now.

You can just hold me. That's about all I can deal with.

Call your boyfriend.

Sorry, I'm out of ideas on how to get you back.

I thought we were friends.

Don't go.

Okay, this afternoon sucked.

Next wasn't looking better.

TAKE CONTROL! A little voice was screaming at him. Take control. Everyone else would be let down. It wasn't that easy.

Star wasn't enamored of passing through all the security and suspicion of going into a prison. His kind of lawyering didn't usually scope him behind bars and the process made him uncomfortable. Now he was toting Brad's garbage, John Taylor's ecstasy, and whatever new hell Hendrick was going to throw at him from his cell.

It always seemed worth it, at the beginning. That glow that came from his face – the same luminescence he noticed the first time they ran into each other at T.J.'s would always shine for Star when he first looked into Scrap's eyes. His whole being was pumped up, being next to Star. Star was having trouble figuring out if Hendrick was desperate, or part of him was too comfortable readjusting to this short stint of prison life. It wasn't quite the same as the state pen, but men were still men, and criminals were still criminals. The stories, the society, too much like home for him sometimes.

"You ain't found nobody else, have ya?"

"No."

"I wonder all the time. I can't think of you with someone else."

Star laughed a little. "That's why you're here."

"It won't happen again. Ever."

"Are you getting the help you need?"

"Not really. No. No one's talkin' to me much."

"So we'll have to find something for you when you get out."

"Things are happening here."

"What do you mean?"

Scrap looked away. "Things. Things I can't control."

This wasn't hard to believe. Star wanted to take Hendrick's hand, but it was impossible. "You someone's boy?"

"Yours."

"In here."

"I get scared. You don't know what it's like."

"No, I don't." Good excuse for John Taylor, at least. "Did you put up a fight, or just let 'em at ya?"

"Star..."

"Dawg..."

"You can't-"

"I'm not blaming you for it, I'm just asking."

"Don't ask, cuz I don't know." Looking away, like there was solace on the floor, before someone randomly stepped on it and quashed it.

Star sighed and shook his head.

"Don't be mad at me." More of a plea than a demand.

"Well we gotta get you some help. I can't bring you back if you're gonna pummel anyone who comes over."

"That was your ex."

"He may never be the same again. He wants to sue your ass for busting him up. I'm trying to talk him out of it, but I don't know if I can." That whole ugly afternoon was rearing its head, including a bad gastrointestinal reaction to the fried rice. "He wants to do it to get at me. But if he does, I don't know what we can do. If he doesn't heal up the same, he's lost a lot, and because of what you did to him. Maybe if you're getting some help for it the court might be more lenient."

"You think I'm nuts, Star."

"Yeah, to a point."

"It's just love. Maybe a bit too much sometimes. That's all it is."

"Rein it in, boy."

Scrap said "boy" to himself and smiled. "They ran some tests on me when I got here."

New subject, and equally ugly. "You still a dawg?"

"Yours." Hendrick took some time. Star could almost read his mind, but was hoping he was mistaken. "I'm poz, man. You know, Rashad, he probably was. His eyes all bloodshot an' everything." Star stayed quiet. "You knew, didn't you."

"I assumed as much."

"We played safe."

"Yeah, my mama drilled it into me. I can't enjoy sex worth a damn after that woman. I don't know why I bother."

"Star?"

"I love you."

"Will you keep me? After all this? I'm not sure anymore."

"I'm thinking a lot of things over," Star said. *You don't know the half of it.*

"What's that mean?"

"I don't know. Just that I'm thinking. You know when I met you, it was too soon."

"Oh please don't."

"But I thought we could make it work anyway."

"Please don't leave me here, not knowin'."

"I found you before I found myself."

"Star, please." Almost crying now.

"Scrap – I do love you. But things can't..."

Behind the glow of his face the fire burned, hot with fear, hot with anger. "What are you tellin' me?"

"I don't know." Star was honest. He didn't. His voice conveyed that.

"Star, you're all I have in the whole world."

"What did you have before me?"

"Nothin'. My job. Workin' and goin' home. Scared to do much more."

"John Taylor's a cook now."

"Aw, fuck. Why doesn't he just practice witchcraft and assume my identity?"

"People still need to eat," Star rationalized.

"*That's* what you're doin'," Hendrick said.

"Doin' what?"

"John Taylor. You got eyes for the man. He's clean, and now you know I ain't."

"I am not messing with John Taylor." It hurt to say that. Lying to the one you love, about that very love, sentenced to a physical hiatus.

"It don't matter. It'll be someone. Look at you. You're handsome, and you're big and strong, you're everything someone can want, and it's stupid of me to think I can hold you from behind these bars."

"Awww God."

Hendrick smiled. "I used to make you say that."

"You will again."

"That's the worst," Scrap pulled out of his misery enough to see a blade or two of reality. "See, I have time to think. Tryin' to keep you all to myself is what made me lose you. So you don't worry about me till I git out. Then you see what you want."

"I wanna do right by you, Scrap."

"You just said you gotta do right by yourself first. But there's no point in me comin' outa here if I can't be with you when I do."

They looked deep into each other. Those eyes, deep, deep, deep, transcended looks, muscle, heart, soul, luminescent eyes burning like hanging Chinese lanterns swinging their candles behind translucent paper, and like Linda Blair in *The Exorcist* had written *help me* deep within, and Star knowing this blood dripping misery would be on his doorstep all too soon, forever. How many lies? How much truth? What said just not to hurt? What was reality, and did that matter? Nothing, for a few more months. Plenty of time to think, and plenty of time – well Hendrick had given him tacit permission – no, that doesn't make it right. What does? Something has to. Only goodbye. Star wanted to hold Hendrick – not kiss him, not make love, not nothing, just hold him, and fall asleep. "When you get back, we'll see what we can do."

I love you.

I love you.

U r all I have.

The drive home from city jail was a quick one, at least. Star stopped into Clementine's bar, sloshed down a couple beers. That was about all he could take. *Please, please, don't hit on me, don't ask me, don't talk to me, just let me be invisible.* Clem's was dark enough, and Star was dark enough, he came close to it. Still, he cut into the space deeply, and people noticed him. Big handsome-featured man like he was couldn't remain invisible in a crowd looking for that very commodity. *My boyfriend's in jail for beating the crap out of my ex, because I stayed friends with him. Now the ex wants me back, and he wants to sue the pants off the boyfriend. To ease my pain, I'm boffing a 17 year old kid I picked up out of Bob Evans in Kirkwood that I taught basketball to over the summer. The basketball thing took off, so boffing the kid could have political ramifications all over the city and really set back the progress of gays and blacks everywhere, given the right detractors.* That story would make just about anyone flee, if he was lucky. Someone else started confessing his life to Star before he could even *get* to the boffing part; it was dull, alcoholic, and defensive. But for a few minutes, it threw the spotlight off him onto someone else. At least, he realized, *his* dilemma was fascinating.

What if Hendrick was gone? I could tell Brad to fuck off, do John when I felt like it, and – no, Hendrick just feels right – focus focus FOCUS on the law career, the league, Althea Howard, and... and... oh, the family.

CHAPTER 11

John was next on the list; Star was going to sit him down and have a long heart to heart, and send John away disappointed, or some such nonsense, until one day John showed up at the door with a four foot high carved wooden giraffe he had purchased only moments before at World Market in Kirkwood down the street from Bob Evans. He was making a bit more money and wanted to give Star something for all he'd done for him—and because he was thinking of Star 24 hours a day.

That of course made sex mandatory, and breaking it off out of the question.

"I know you like this kind of stuff," John said.

You have no idea. "Thanks, boy!" John smiled. The boy thing worked. It had a whole different context than anyone would imagine. Not ownership, not condescension, not race, just affection. "You can call me boy, too, if you want."

"Ya do like it." John smiled. "Boy."

Star wanted to ask how John could afford it – it had to be at least 75 or 100 bucks – but he knew better; Mary Bryan always taught him to say thanks and shut up. He learned that the one time he didn't say thanks and he didn't shut up. "I do. Let's put it upstairs. Second floor needs some sprucing up."

"I'll spruce you up!"

Star picked up the giraffe and started carrying it up the steps. "You got some wood of your own?" *Hendrick says I can have you until he gets out,* he wanted to say. That is so ghetto! So Jerry Springer. But... so nice.

A guy who's had it for the first time in his life certainly doesn't want to wait for his partner to find a place to put down a wooden giraffe. He took Star's hand, laid a kiss on him, confident it was all being returned, confident of the eternity of such fleeting impermanence.

There was a certain freedom about all this for Star. John was clean, new, fresh, eager, whatever love he had was untainted, so far, by the idea that it might be anything less than perfect and perpetual. Besides, that little goatee he was sporting felt so good scraping across Star's mouth and his body. *Buy me a giraffe and I'm yours for the day*! He'd have a whole herd for afternoons like this, for John's young perfect body, just to look at him and soak up the belief that the world was good, when he knew better – that at least for now, Jerusalem was all his before two competing religions came in and to kill, rape, torture, and reclaim a damaged prize.

"I had no idea that shit could feel so good," John said in a burst of honesty. John, sweaty, wet, spent, and so beautifully debauched, limbs sprawled exotically across and over the edge of the bed.

Star smiled at him, reveling in his euphoria before the ghost of Agave came back to drip her son's blood over the cum towel. That and – shit! – go get tested!!!!

"You know I did all this for you," John said. "Figured if I got myself looking good, you'd notice that we had something."

We do, for a few months. Now isn't the time. Don't ruin it for him. Star, too used to taking the world on his shoulders, making it right for everyone, at least making it tolerable, and bearing the responsibility when it all came crashing down. But with John rubbing those shoulders, that seemed like something he could put off for at least a week. "What you say we try this again, and then figure out a place to put that giraffe?"

"Oh yeah."

Alas. Then again, if you're goin' down, might as well party like it's 1999. *Next time, we talk.*

John was still moody at home; when he wasn't with Star he was either doing things that would gain Star's admiration or pining away in fantasy. He worked out a lot, he bought clothes that showed it all off, his grades were good – although the basketball scholarship was probably not happening. If he could make a team, it would be to a college that didn't care enough about basketball to reward people with money. And if he went away, he would leave have to leave Star. *Get a life, John.* Star had to encourage something to move John's life along.

You want me to leave?

I want you to put yourself first. We'll always be friends.

I want more than being friends.

You do now. You don't have to make your mind up on all this.

Forever.

Scrap's getting out soon. He wants to come back.

I don't wanna hear about no Scrap.

There was no hope for John, except perhaps to divert his attention. On an animal level, and even on some sort of emotional level, Star didn't want to give him up. But he'd been raised in a political family, and in some part of his mind he knew he had to break it off without John opening his mouth to a bullhorn like Althea Howard.

How how how? Divert.

Whatever happens I will always be here for you, John.

Me too. You might need me more than you think.

John, more than anyone, had led Star to his own self-redefinition. It would be a shame to kill the messenger.

"I want in on this." Lancer was pissed, annoyed, mad, and pacing around the floor. Mary was supporting him.

"Your father feels like you've left him out."

One more *your father* from that woman and Star was going to turn into a supernova.

"This one's mine," Star demanded. "I started it, I finish it, and I say where it goes."

"I want the city to be part of it. The city needs it. The mayor needs, it, and my career..."

"I don't give a damn about your career!"

"Yes, you do," Mary changed his mind for him.

"Okay, then, I do. But I wanna play ball. I like throwing it, I like tossing it, and I like the fact that I can make someone better at it. If I was better myself, I might have 50 million dollars in the bank. If I was just one tiny bit better." Rarely if ever did he let himself think on that for too long. "I was the best man on that team. I got us into the NCAA. I was talkin' to the NBA. I look at the standings every morning and I realize I could have been part of it! Then I close up the paper and to go work. Don't you take it from me."

90

"We never knew you felt that way," said Mary, who after being married to Lancer for about 37 years had managed to appropriate all his emotional responses, or at least manage them.

I didn't either, Star wanted to say, but any reach for humor at this juncture would be frowned upon. Somehow, things had escalated into *not funny* for no good reason. "Dad, you really don't care about those kids. I'm not trying to save lives or keep people off the street. I just like playing ball. You're not about playing ball, you're about symbolism."

"We are not about symbolism," Lancer crashed.

Star wanted the symbol suspended. "In the family where I grew up, everything was about symbolism. It was about being exemplary, because our family symbolized so much more...! Because everything we did had ramifications for black St. Louis." More pensive, shaking head. "I didn't want shooting baskets with John Taylor to suddenly have ramifications for all of black St. Louis."

"What's going on with you and John Taylor?" Mom, all knowing, or at least conveying the appearance thereof – Star hated those fucking glasses of hers, but it was never so clear why until now.

"What do you mean?"

"Hendrick's locked away, and you're spending your time with John Taylor. You're not shooting baskets. You're *socializing*."

"You're not shooting baskets either. You're accusing."

"Yes, I am. I'm your mother. Lancer said he saw something at the meeting."

"What?"

"He said-"

"Dad, speak for yourself?"

"Sorry, I've forgotten how." Lancer chuckled a bit at this trifling disgrace.

"Try it!" Star looked at his father, losing respect by the second.

"Your father said John Taylor was looking at you like a hyena ready to stalk and mount his prey. And you enjoyed it."

Star was silent. Stunned.

Lancer finally spoke up, almost as if he'd a mind of his own. "I'm a politician. I notice things. It's my job to pick out my enemy's flaws, and in this case, you're playing the enemy. Oh, I didn't want it to be that way," he headed off any protestation, his voice diving slightly into the contours of a Baptist minister. "But when you align a loudmouth bitch like Althea Howard against your own father, I have to play dirty."

"Wow," said Star, shaken just a bit, and quiet, but they had no NO no no evidence. "You're not nearly as euphemistic as mom."

"That's why I do all the talking for him," says Mary. "It makes him a lot less abrasive. Sometimes I even moan for him during lovemaking."

Star spoke quietly, but firmly. Legalistically, perhaps, as if he knew he was going to have the last word. "Hendrick is my boy. You can think what you want. When he comes back, he works with me. Althea is going to run it. I don't know if she can, but she wants to. If she can't we'll find someone else. The city can pump money into it, and you can grandstand all you want. You can take credit if you want. But if your slimy political cronies lay a hand on my boys, I will take you down. If it starts getting involved with race, politics, or percentages, you're out. I don't need you. And I don't see why you need me."

"Star..." Lancer wasn't sure.

"This is family. This one here is all about family. Do not fuck with the family, Dad."

Silence awhile. "Let's see if he can swim," Mary said.

"I can swim."

"Star, we don't know *what* you can do," she said candidly. It was annoying having someone so much shorter than him wield so much instinct. "You gave up your life for love. Now you're doing it again. I know we seem controlling and domineering, but it's only because we want the best for you – and for ourselves, Star. We're selfish people just like everyone," Mary admitted. "But sometimes, that selfishness can help others. That's all politics is. Helping someone and getting something in return. At least your father is trying to help the right people."

"Now, you can help me."

"How, son?" Lancer seemed a bit more conciliatory.

"Support me. Scrap, John, Brad, Althea, Arielle... support me in what I choose."

"Star," Mary went up to him. "I will. But not if what you choose is stupid and self destructive. You can't blame us for that. Self destruction comes from the inside."

"Funny," Star said. "I thought it was the white folks."

Both his parents laughed, which was a good sign. "Let Hendrick go, Star," Mary advised. Threatened? Advised. Whatever, Star wasn't sure. "Everyone you're involved with is going to take you way way down."

"Even you?"

"Not if you're strong. You might be six-five and God knows how many pounds, but you are out of control. It's going to take your mother to tell you."

"And my sister."

Star felt about 16 again, he sat down on the couch, head in his hands, slowly looking up as his goatee scraped across his palms. "So where are we?"

"We know where we are," Lancer said. "Where are you?"

Wheels churned, Star the lawyer came out of nowhere. It was a trick. The support, the attention, the love, all to convince him they were right and he was wrong. And about what? He forgot. If only Lucinda was here...

Scrap's my dawg, John's my best friend, Brad's a bloodsucking viper. Maybe he always was. He's sucking more than usual, and these days he's sucking away the dawg. Everyone is sucking up everyone else, and soon there will be nothing left to suck.

CHAPTER 12

"Are you fucking John Taylor?"

"Arielle!"

She sopped up some lentils with a wad of injera bread. "Are you *fucking* John Taylor? How many ways do I have to put it?"

"Well I'm not actually *fucking* him. But the groundwork's been laid."

Arielle sighed. "Star!"

"How does everybody know?"

"How does anybody know anything around here? It makes sense, that's how."

"How does it make sense?"

Because you aren't teaching him basketball, and you're out together all the time."

"It's just till Scrap gets back."

"Does he know that?"

"He should, by now."

"You're playing with lives, Star. You said you'd make them better, and you're double-dribbling them all the way down the court."

"How does everybody know what the fuck I'm doing with John Taylor!"

"It's our business to know, and then to keep it quiet. That's what this family is about. Dad told Mama, who called me in a tizzy, all of which was extrapolated from some eye contact the two of you had at the league meeting. You looked at John the way you looked at Brad. *You* don't look at people that way unless *you're fucking them*!"

Arielle was dressed in some sort of West African ceremonial garb as they sat in an Ethiopian restaurant in the University City Loop. Although well past its heyday, The Red Sea had been there for years. The Loop was a classic success story of urban redevelopment. Near the city, but *not* the city. Soon the U. City Loop would extend into the city, and simply be called The Loop.

Arielle looked like she was screaming racial identity. Actually she was working on some sort of cultural program for her kids' school. Hearing the word's *you're fucking them* coming out of this dress seemed sacrilegious.

"All right," Star was defeated. He knew he was wrong on the John Taylor thing, but to have to admit it publicly was shameful.

"You need to get everybody out of your life and start over."

"Even you?"

"Not me, you dummy. I am on your side."

"Sometimes you don't sound like it."

"I'm on the side of truth. You can either hear it now, or hear it when it fucks you in the ass."

"Hendrick likes that kinda truth," Star smiled and scooped up another fingerful of lentils.

"When I was younger, and I had the biggest tits in the class, and I was the hottest ho sistah out there. I could get any man I wanted," Arielle said matter of factly, but loud enough to be overheard by several who were all too ready to agree. "The problem is, when you're a hot mama like me, you have a lot more to choose from, and your chance of choosing poorly is magnified because everyone wants to get into your patootie. It may sound conceited, but it's true," she said right to some yuppie who was... well, using this speech as an excuse to stare at what he considered a couple really nice patooties.

"Star, look in the mirror. You can get what you want. You don't have to just take what wants you."

"Scrap's my man."

"Fine, rescue him." She shook her head. "This is hard to watch."

"Arielle, I feel like everyone's on top of me. I don't like it. I don't know how to get out."

"Try standing up. You're taller."

Star wasn't ever quite sure how he came about to be the way he was; the looks and gait of a man who could get anything he wanted; the ability to take anything he wanted, yet never sure of what he wanted and always a slave to whatever horrible events were controlling his life.

His mother could say what she wanted, but as far as he was concerned his family had been raised with very little sense of cultural identity. Lancer and Mary had enough money to spare their children the ignominy of the St. Louis City Schools, and so sent them private, insulating them from many of the ugly facets of city culture both black and white. A man like Hendrick Pardee, raised in the ghetto and largely salvaged by basketball, was as foreign to the Bryan children as someone raised in the ghettos of Soweto. A young man like John Taylor was lower middle class and largely uninteresting to the Bryan mind set; John himself seemed to be struggling with having too much money for the ghetto mentality, yet not enough to leave it. Star was of his father's rather conservative opinion that folks who complained that they wanted to get out of the ghetto shouldn't hang on, at all costs, to the ghetto mentality.

Being gay wasn't that big an issue with them for some reason, and he kept his early promiscuity well hidden – so he thought. Mary was cagey, O'Ryan nosey, and Arielle just intuitively knew everything, so known events were unspoken and swept under the rug as long as Star was their famous son taking Saint Louis University to the NCAA.

Finally he was just tired of himself and of being led around by his dick or whatever pleasure was in store. Perhaps it was a rebellion against his upbringing – and perhaps, due to his parents' strict instruction on how he develop his own mind, he never really had the chance to develop his own mind. It was too easy – not to mention compulsory – to let someone else do the thinking.

Shacking up with Brad seemed natural. Why his friends suddenly wanted him to assume a black identity he'd never really had much to do with confused and astounded him. The interracial aspect was seen as largely sexual, or an ugly way of social climbing; the fact that they related to each other intellectually and the sex was good seemed to be over most people's heads. Anyway it made for boring gossip.

While Arielle went on to teach African culture to schoolchildren, while Lucinda continued pointing up hypocritical truths of the welfare community, and while O'Ryan followed his father into politics and civic planning, Star's choice of a white boyfriend plus moving out to Wildwood pretty much divorced him from the chance to acquire any racial identity whatsoever. Who cared? He never had one, and thus became reviled for achieving a veritable racial nirvana – being a man before color. But in world without hate, a color blind world without walls, where no one pays attention to what anyone else is, how will we hold on to what we are?

In white walled Wildwood, Star found his peace. He looked in the mirror and just saw a man. And what a man he saw! That goatee made him look dangerously sexual, then the Ralph Lauren wardrobe took it down a notch. Take off the shirt, and... well, never mind, Brad didn't care.

Finally, Brad left him stranded on an emotional plank, never quite pushing him off into the choppy waters of solitude, but never commuting the sentence while he was out playing squash, watching TV, or "working late at the office."

Star was miserable, lovelorn, lost, and after giving up everything of himself to become The Creature Of The White Lagoon, setting out on his own was the hardest thing he ever did in his life. Thank goodness for T.J. Maxx, for Hendrick, John, and even Althea Howard's basketball league.

It was, then, as Arielle said. Stand tall. Take control. Think with the head on your shoulders. You'll lose a few friends, but maybe get a few more.

Nothing good, other than an orgasm, could come out of sex with John Taylor. Find a way out.

Hendrick gets another chance. If he fucks up, he's gone.

Brad needs to be *Gone With The Wind,* sent into burning Atlanta and shot if he tries to escape.

Oh! The family! They wouldn't like this at all.

Oh well, maybe it wouldn't last, and he could go back to trying to fix everyone else's life and leave his own be. Maybe, though, fixing lives was its own reward, if he could do it without asking for anything back

Time went by. Hendrick was due out; John was more hopelessly in love than ever. When Star wasn't around, John went dormant, waiting in his room, thinking, dreaming, still working out and shooting hoops with the sole purpose of impressing Star, the very qualities that anyone might like in him disappearing under an all consuming love. Star noticed it, and it was no fun. John had to go, but gently, since by now taking away his only reason for living might induce him to stop altogether. It seemed that bad; John's father even gave Star a sly call to ask "what's wrong with my kid," and Star said he'd have a talk.

"He really loves you," said Mr. Taylor. Star's heart jumped to his throat. "I mean he looks up to you. You've changed his life around."

You have no idea.

That short conversation set things in motion; Star wanted to transition back to being friends, and if he hadn't done enough damage, salvage him to be a good boyfriend for someone else – someone who might even be near his age. John wouldn't have to hide, he wouldn't be accidentally ruining people's lives and careers, and perhaps he would shut up. Since the entire Bryan family knew, Star had to get out from under it, no matter how good being under it felt.

He closed his eyes for just a moment, dreaming of the hard young body, the lips like a waterfall on his own – stop! Scrap it! So to speak. He still loved Scrap. That wouldn't placate anyone, but it would have to do. Just because this particular temporary betrayal had Scrap's approval didn't make it any less heinous.

Star threw 35 cents at Arielle and suggested she call someone who cared.

"What?"

Star was a bit afraid of her candor, but he liked the idea that they were seeing each other more often. "You need to find John a boyfriend."

"I don't see where that's my job."

"I haven't done very well with it," Star said. He felt a bit awkward making this proposal, but he'd rehearsed it 1,000 times. "You know a lot of young folks."

"So you want me to get some black boy to stand up and proclaim his homosexuality in the midst of an African culture class, and in between a lecture on Nelson Mandela and the lack of women's rights in Kenya you want me to just post the very simple question: 'do any of you cool brothas-into-brothas wanna hang with this dude?'"

Star wanted to ask what the women of Kenya and Mandela had to do with each other, and why they were being ramrode into the same lecture. He didn't. "If anyone can…" he said.

"Why don't you just go to Magnolia's?"

"Too old. He's 17."

"Maybe at 17 you shouldn't be introducing him to the gay lifestyle," said some very Christian white man at the table next to them.

"It is way too late for *that*, brotha," said Arielle. "And don't you be eavesdroppin' into a conversation that ain't none of your ass' business."

"When I see two adults planning to introduce a young man into the homosexual lifestyle, I *make* it my business," he sniffed. "And it's hard not to overhear with how loud you people get."

Such conversations weren't supposed to happen in the Central West End, one of the few places in the city where folks of all races and lifestyles came together in harmony, or at least politely ignored each other.

The 'you people' made Arielle's significant hairdo stand on end, being trained from the age of four that no one – absolutely no one – was ever to be identified as such.

"Why don't you go back to protesting abortions in front of the doctor's office?" she asked.

"A boy of that age isn't old enough to make such choices."

"If you were at all up to date, you'd know that such choices were made for him – unlike religion, which is a choice thrust upon us at an age where we're too young to understand it and too scared to refute it."

This was going to get uglier and uglier, and Star didn't want to get thrown out of the Coffee Cartel. He simply followed Arielle's earlier advice. He stood up and walked over to the man in question. "Do you have something to say?" asked the man.

"No," said Star. "Just stretching. And you're stretching my patience."

Behind the very Christian white guy sat Darrock Ndlele, reading a paperback copy of William Faulker's *Pylon*. Young, smart, and confident, he'd taken advantage of the Cartel's reputation as a hangout for gay guys who weren't old enough get into the bars. Most of them were hideously self-aware – and aware of little else. They were annoying, pretentious, and obsessed with hair, clothes, and satisfying their sexual interests while making sure the other party walked away unhappy and carrying their baggage. To accumulate all this hypocrisy by the age of sixteen or eighteen seemed to 19-year-old Darrock quite an achievement, and energy better

99

spent behind a book. Sadly, this combination of confidence and disgust had kept him a virgin, a condition of which he was rapidly tiring. On the other hand, anyone with any education knew not to interrupt someone reading Faulkner, because chances were more likely than not he was in the middle of a very long sentence. If he lost his train of thought he'd have to go back 15 pages to regain his place.

For all Darrock knew, Star was selling off some 17 year old like Mr. Bumble walking Oliver Twist through the streets of London. Whatever. Star looked hot, and Arielle definitely more fun than a latte. "Who you got for me, bro? Sorry, I've been lost in New Valois."

"New who?" Arielle asked, over the head of their interloper.

"It's New Orleans," he said. "Faulkner called it New Valois."

"Yep," said Arielle, dipping slightly into Lucinda. "Whevener I needs me some money, I flies me down to N'awlins and calls myself 'da big easy!' Now I can have some easy values in Valois. My brother Star here needs to fix up a friend of his. And fast."

Star and Darrock shook hands, introduced themselves. Darrock had thick features, broad nose, dark skin, hair in cornrows falling off his scalp in braids, dreds, or whatever the popular term was on any given Saturday. It was impossible to moniker, Star thought, but it looked interesting. He looked like a man in control of himself, whose hair was an expression of himself instead of a mating call. His tongue was pierced, his lower lip was pierced, his body thick, good shape, but not necessarily gym toned. His hormones had been raging for years, but we wasn't about to give it up to any of the insipid Barbies he'd been watching drink French Sodas for the last year or so at the Cartel.

"I really do come here to read," he joked.

The man in the middle packed up and stood up, rising up to Star's shoulder. "You win," he said. "I'll leave it up to the Lord."

"Did we win a Camaro?" Arielle asked after him. "I've always wanted to drive a Camaro." She didn't, but it was all she could think of.

Star didn't carry a picture of John around. He thought it might be dangerous, and he never really had any reason to. He just thought about it because John made him hard. Well... and giving him up? A sacrifice for the betterment of mankind. Shit! "Darrock, you are going to be one lucky

100

cuss – if you can land him."

Althea Howard wasn't overjoyed with what had become of her life. She'd had to devote a lot of it to keeping Roof under control. He was definitely a mistake on her end, and despite her best efforts, he seemed determined to grow up to become entirely useless.

"If that music tells you that's how it is on the streets, then maybe you should stay off the damn streets," she'd tell him.

"I just like the beat."

"That's all it is, is a beat!" Turning out fat and uncoordinated didn't help, and being a thug was Roof's only way out. He wasn't very good at that either, so he just tried to look like one, an endeavor at which he was somewhat more successful. Be it as it was, Althea had enough of his shit, and was glad he finally found a purpose in learning how to play a better game of basketball. True sports, for the love of the game, made a difference to him – a good thing, since if he had to play it competitively, he'd suck, and whatever self esteem Star drilled into him would swoosh right off the court down the toilet in the locker room.

Althea managed, through all this, to wind her way through nursing school and land a decent paying job at a hospital, eventually finding herself a shift supervisor at Barnes-Jewish, not far from where they lived. That was enough. She worked, came home, watched TV, ate heartily, and talked on the phone. It wasn't much, but it made do. Same with Roof. She certainly wasn't going to be able to live vicariously through his accomplishments.

The league gave her something to do, as well as the fact that she could sit in one spot, eat, make phone calls, and slowly meld the whole thing together by barely leaving the house. Star had almost forgotten about this; since the league reminded him of John Taylor, and since John had to go, he was losing interest in the league.

Suddenly, Althea became another solider in the battle with his father, and she unintentionally laid a war plan for a much more gruesome combat. But oh, was she excited! Six teams. Six! She organized three teams of black kids and then started probing the new ethnic communities that filled in one or other pockets of south St. Louis. All in all, a team from Dogtown, one from the bordering municipality of Maplewood, another in Richmond

101

Heights (just to the north of Maplewood), a group of Bosnians, a team of Mexicans from the Cherokee Street neighborhood, and some Vietnamese kids from the Asian community in the South Grand area.

"I didn't know Vietnamese kids played basketball," Star commented.

"They don't. That way my team has a fighting chance," she said.

She'd lined up some places to play, talked a few do-nothings into coaching, and basically discovered that folks who like doing what they do often do it for nothing, particularly if there's the political payoff of giving to a minority community.

Worse – or better – than that, with two of her teams being outside of the city of St. Louis, the City of St. Louis really couldn't share much in whatever payoff there would be. Lancer couldn't say it was his idea, and he certainly couldn't toss city money into the Maplewood treasury. Even Maplewood wasn't so good at that. At least *this* wasn't Star's idea.

"You'll still coach my Dogtown boys, won't you?"

Star felt like a video camera was documenting every move he made. It was an enforced morality worse than religion, and it was going to kick him in the ass for the slightest misstep. "Sure I will."

"And what are you going to do about John Taylor?"

"What do you mean?"

"You know what I mean."

"No, I don't." Star was getting angry; all this fame should have brought along a little fortune, he hoped, always in vain.

"Roof said that-"

"Roof?" his voice skyrocketed into sopranoville.

"Roof. We all know that John's in love with you. John's broke with it, and he can't talk about much else. It's not because you buy him milkshakes. You should know better, Mr. Bryan."

"Well, it was only *your* son I promised not to fuck." He wasn't sure if he could get away with that or not.

"John's a delicate boy. He's different. You need to turn him loose, and let him down easy."

"I know. Scrap's getting out soon."

"Another winner." The whole gay sex morality was annoying to her, but she tried to wind her way through it and at least make sure that as few people as possible got hurt. Too many black guys had AIDS because of idiots like Star.

"I can't help it, Althea."

"You can. And when you learn that, you'll finally be able to call yourself a grown up. If you act ghetto, and you traffic in ghetto, ghetto is what you become."

"I know that. I was raised on that. And I still don't know what I am." Enough of this. "You did good on the league."

She was proud, and for good reason. "Yes, I did. And I'm counting on you."

"I bet those Vietnamese kids are gonna kick the shit out of Dogtown."

CHAPTER 13

Star had never seen this reclusive, distant John Taylor everyone was talking about. Like Carrie's hand reaching out of the grave, John came back to life only when Star was in the picture. After that he went back into zombie mode. But Star had heard enough about it, and knew from his own experience with Brad what it can be like to become dependant on another man for a complete package of emotional sustenance. At 17, it was easier, and more intense.

Turning him over to Darrock might pay off in the long run, in the short, this gut wrenching and enforced shifting of allegiances would terrify John. Star figured the best way to get himself in a mood bad enough to carry this out was to visit his mother – or whatever she chose call herself at any given moment. Star finally realized that she'd ceased being a mother to him long ago, and instead had set herself up as some sort of media patrol, trying to keep him in line with his father.

Maybe it was worse. Maybe she wasn't on his side, but she did what she had to in order to shut him up. Maybe with Lancer, her life was a living hell. Maybe. None of the kids – well Star and Arielle, since O'Ryan hadn't shown a friendly emotion in several years – seemed to realize until recently what all they'd gone through growing up under the tutelage of Lancer and Mary. In the process of rewriting their childhoods into misery, perhaps they needed to re-evaluate Mary's married life.

Maybe, but right now Star needed a mother, and this was the closest thing he had. "I come not to praise Caesar, but to bury him!" he announced. Some black provocateur once rewrote the Bard from the slaves' point of view. It didn't work. Star wondered if redefining Mama would make much difference now.

"What is it exactly you want from me?" Mary wasn't thrilled with his intro, nor his request that she speak to him on terms with his own morality.

"I want you not to judge me."

"You walked out on a perfectly good relationship-"

"It sucked!"

"You walked out on a perfectly good relationship, took up with some piece of litter you found in a parking lot, let him spend half a year in jail while you cheated on him with someone who sees you as a father figure, denied your own father even a small coattail of your successes, and now you ask me not to judge. Someone needs to. Better me than the *Argus*."

"We took the league out of the city." Damn! They needed to redecorate, and give these memories to the Goodwill.

"You *what*?"

"Althea Howard took the league into Maplewood and Richmond Heights. The Board of Alderman doesn't have jurisdiction, and frankly, it can kiss my ass."

"There's a line of people out the door waiting to do that," Mary said. "You've seen to it. We did not teach you this kind of promiscuity."

"Well then maybe it shows I can do something on my own. Sometimes, though, I *don't* know what to do. And that's why, every now and then, I want a mother to talk to, and not a political adversary." A lump welled up in his throat; he forced it back for the time being.

"Star," Mary took his hand, and he looked into her eyes and realized how much he hated those red-framed glasses. "Speaking as your mother, it *is* my place to judge you. I've had the job of judging you since you were about three days old. I don't know why I should stop now, when you need it most."

"I need compassion."

"*You* do? But no one else does? You've had your life given to you on a platter long enough. You rode through college on a basketball scholarship."

"I worked my butt off for that."

"You got everything you wanted."

"Mom, I just want to find some way out!"

"You want to find some *easy* way out. And you want your mama to do it for you."

"No, I don't."

"Well good. Because I can't break it up with John Taylor. And I can't break it up with Scrapdawg, though God knows I'd like to. All I see is you're

105

going to break John's heart, run back to Scrap, and break mine. But if you don't set John free, it's going to came back to haunt you. He's underage, you're a lawyer, and your father-"

"Seventeen is legal in Missouri. And fuck my father's career. I don't give a fuck about my father's career."

"Neither do I," Mary knocked Star across state lines. He walked away, and looked back at her across a theoretical Mississippi River from a theoretical Illinois. Long silence. "I've been second to it myself all these years. But I love your father, and often, showing that love is showing him political support."

"The family shouldn't be political."

"It is, when all you know is politics. A disagreement becomes political, and you become an opponent. I think you know what you have to do. You have to get rid of them both. Buy them out if you have to-"

"Mama!"

"What kind of lawyer are you?" Her disappointment was deep; the kind of disappointment only a mother who loves her son can bear and yet still love him all the same. "If it takes money, it takes money. Be glad you have it. Too many black folks use a gun for their talking when money does just as well."

"I love Scrap."

"I love your father, and look where it got me."

Star looked. He couldn't see a thing wrong. Was she unhappy? Did he have to go years back and find the deleted articles of *Pravda*? "Are you happy, Mama?"

Mary looked around her place. Quite a nice place. For a brief second, it flirted with her. Maybe she wasn't. "Yes, I am. Lancer is a good man. He's just a pompous ass most of the time."

"You always take his side."

"I know. Being pompous makes being right annoying, doesn't it? Your father has his faults, and I have mine, and if you and Arielle would admit to having a few as well, we might all get along again."

"You think Dad was always right?"

"Absolutely not! But he and I both agree that you're a mess. You're stringing people along, you're lying, and you're throwing this league in his face to get back at him for some real or imagined ancient insult – there is such a thing as family loyalty. It means putting the family first."

"Family as a legal term," Star countered.

"Yes. Not you, me, Arielle, or your constipated brother. Just family. And family says you turn John loose and leave Scrap on the scrap heap."

"Mama! I love Scrap! Maybe it's time for the family to be loyal to that!"

"The family can't be loyal to something that's going to destroy it. Right now, everything you're doing is going to destroy it. So, if you want to stay in it..." It was as if Aphrodite had suddenly turned into an Amazon. "If I tell you want you want to hear, there's no point in you dragging your ass over here."

"Nobody in this family tells me what I want to hear."

"You are too smart, too handsome, and too public to be carrying on like this. It's not always a picnic living with the *Post*, the *Argus*, the *American* and the *Riverfront Times* breathing down your neck. It's the price we pay for being black and influential. We've been black and influential before it was hip to be black and influential. We were country when country wasn't cool. We've had it good, but the white folks think we're uppity niggers and the black folks think we're a bunch of Uncle Toms. All we have is each other."

"What about the Vietnamese folks?"

"They're not influential. So it doesn't matter."

"Althea's made a whole team of them."

"I didn't think the Vietnamese played ball."

"They will when I get through with them."

"Good. Then go out there and be black and influential. And remember, if you screw up *your* life, you screw up mine."

That was a sad, self serving battle cry, but it did put Star in the requisite bad mood to do the dirty deed. He toyed with just having Darrock over and pressing a few buttons on his remote, but that seems cold, heartless, and calculating – just like the entirety of last six months. Yep, he did love John. But not like that. Ok, like that. Whatever, it was impossible in this political climate.

Maybe it was lust. It was watching John's face screw up and watching him shoot up in the air, and it was being loved. Being loved is pretty addicting. But it always felt bad because it wasn't Hendrick. It just never felt bad enough. Time to get his own life back on track, and any wreckage left in its wake could go out with the trash on Monday morning.

There were two options: have sex and then break up, or just break up. He chose the second, but when John showed up, looking hearty as he always did, he veered to the first. It wasn't hard for John to look good in Star's presence. It was the only time he bothered. Chemicals and lust combined to remind John he was still alive, and that the reason for it was right there in the room.

So what was one more outing? Star remembered a few folks in his early days... "you said you'd always love me, you said this, you said that..." What does a *you said* matter if it's not going to happen? "Sure I said I'd always love you, now do I have to spend the whole wretched rest of my life with you?" *When I said I'd always love you, I meant I'd always love you. But since I don't love you now, what I said then isn't binding. I can't love you just because I said I would while blinded by the assumption that it was actually going to happen. You don't have to be a lawyer to figure that out.*

John looked good... he looked stunning, as usual, that deep wet lip to lip kiss as usual, that goatee scraping over Star's lips as usual, across whatever else they scraped across on their way down, up on the second floor in his bedroom, the giraffe keeping watch outside, identity didn't matter, history, future, it just all seemed irrelevant once passion stationed itself as king of the roost. Star looked into John's bright eyes, so different from when he first met him at the restaurant. "Damn I love you!" John said.

"You show it good," Star said back.

He watched the clock after they were done. He didn't wanna play wham bam and then start in on things. It seemed a lot harder now, after all that energy spent. He wasn't sure how much he had left. Slowly, he got up and put on a pair of sweat pants. Orange, they said Tennessee down the side, made a jarring color contrast against the curves of his torso. Old, from K-Mart, but they were comfortable, and in any event, people in Tennessee seemed to know their basketball.

"Those look so dumb," John said.

Star caught a glimpse in the mirror. Bright orange wasn't his color. "I thought I looked good in everything."

"Or out."

He had to get John dressed. It was too vulnerable. Still, the jeans were too provocative. It was like dressing the cast for the wrong ending. He rummaged through a drawer and found another pair of sweats. Brad's? Maybe. Tossed them over John's head. "There ya go."

"What?" John wanted Star closer; the life force wasn't the same if they weren't actually touching. *You can't be sure what Star is thinking, if he isn't touching me, he could be thinking anything.*

"Scrap's getting out soon."

"I know."

"He's gonna have to live here."

"I don't wanna talk about it."

"John, we have to."

"What you mean? You love me. What's he gotta do with it? He's got a place."

"He can't make it on his own."

"*I* don't live with you. Why does *he* have to."

"You got your parents."

"So you're just gonna get rid of me. I love you."

"I know you do. I love you too. You knew this was coming."

John felt a chill wrack through his body, and pulled up the blankets.

"I met a guy named Darrock," Star said. "Me and Arielle met him at the Coffee Cartel."

"Who the fuck cares?"

"He'll..."

"He'll what? Do you like I do?"

"No... he... wants to meet you."

"Oh. So some other guy's just gonna step in for you. You're a smart mutherfucka, aren't ya?"

"Yeah, I am." Star went to lean over John, wanted to look at him again, didn't want to see him hurting so badly. "I'm sorry."

"Yeah, just use me and throw me away like yesterday's garbage."

"John, we talked about this. I can't let this go on."

"Why not!" John screeched it out, losing control. "Why not?"

"There's so much going on. It's not just me and you. It's the family, it's the-"

Not much made sense to John. It was him and Star, and the rest of it didn't matter. Love was supposed to be all consuming, all important... hearing about family politics, family battles, getting sneered at in the *Argus*, setting an example for the city and not fucking one of the kids that you were coaching.... it all made no sense.

"So what am I?" he asked. "Nothing?"

"There is too much at stake, John! For both of us. If I love you or I don't, this just can't happen."

"*If* you love me?" Maybe a few tears, but if they made Star feel bad, worth the embarrassment.

"Oh, stop it! I know I can't say anything right."

"I did everything for you." John pulled back the covers, trying to hold back the chill. It wasn't cold, it was just emotion. Killing him. "This hair, this goatee, all these muscles I worked up... there was only one reason... only because I thought it would matter to you... that you would like me more. I lived my whole life not bein' shit. I don't even know what it feels like to be someone." Tracy Chapman echoed in his mind. *Fast Car*. Be someone, be someone, be someone...

"Well..."

"Well, there's no reason to keep it then."

"There is. You've turned yourself into quite a man. I'm 30. You're 17. You'll get tired of me soon anyway."

"I can't think of anything else! How could I get tired *of* you! I'm tired *from* it. From thinking of you night and day, making my self look good for you, getting you presents, giving you everything. I gave you stuff I never gave anybody. My heart, my... tongue... my..."

This was getting gruesome. "I wish it didn't have to be that way."

"It doesn't. You're just chasing after bad. After trash. You can change it."

"No I can't. I love the man. I'm sorry."

"So I was a stopgap lover in the mean time."

Well, yes. "I'm sorry, John."

"No, I don't think you are!" John heated up a bit. "We could be something! You and him will never be anything! Look what I did with

110

myself, and look what he did! He'll kill you. If he'll kill Brad, he'll kill you."

"John, here's the scoop," Star wanted to take this boy and run away, but he knew even in the best of circumstances... the 18th birthday, a house in the country by the lake, John's obsessions would do them both in. "I was wrong. I can't change it. But I have no choice. You have no choice. You can meet Darrock if you want, or not. He's 19, he's smart, and he's kind of hot. In an African sort of way."

"What the hell are you talking about?"

"He's Nigerian."

"I don't give a fuck! You think you're gonna walk off from this scot free. You ain't gonna pay nothing for it."

"I hurt."

"Oh... you're such a big man now!" Taunting! *If I call you names, you'll realize how much you love me.*

"Big man!" Star sliced back. "Everybody knows. My family knows. Roof Howard knows. Roof Howard's mom knows. You told the whole world when I told you to keep your damn mouth shut."

"Yeah," John threatened. "I could go more public. I could tell the papers, and I could tell the police that you took advantage of a boy who was too young to take advantage of. I'll tell 'em you took me at sixteen. Then maybe it wouldn't be such a good idea to dump me."

"You won't!" Almost mean, but too shocked for any real derision.

"I will." Last chance, and on top of it.

Losing it. "If you do, I will take you out!" It was loud, and stacatto, hearkening to part of Orwell's *1984* where authorities convince lovers the only way out of hell is to have them torture the other.

"Star!"

"John! I'm sorry."

John settled back into his oblivion. "I don't know what to do without you."

"I'm not leaving you."

"If I can't hold you."

"I'm always your friend. That's all we were ever supposed to be. I didn't even know you were gay when I tripped your ass at Bob's."

"I didn't either," John laughed despite his best efforts. "I don't want to

111

go back to being alone."

"Come meet Darrock."

"What am I, the baton in a four-man relay?"

"I'm handing you off to a good man."

John got back up, hugged Star as hard as he could. "We can still do this, right?"

"Long as Scrap don't see it and beat the shit out of us."

John let go and shook his head. "That's why he's in. Well that and because he did it to a white dude. This guy speak English?"

"So you are gonna meet him."

"For you."

"Well keep the muscles, and the goatee."

"For you."

"You have no idea."

"What?"

"How good you're gonna look in about 5 years if you look this good now."

"So you're really fuckin' up letting me go?"

"Probably. Definitely" Star was starting to feel that albatross that Hendrick hung on him so long ago. He couldn't live without it. The closer it came to the release date, the closer his heart pounded. John became an impediment, albeit a sexy one, to reality. Somehow, he'd have to atone for it. Maybe doing six months without would have been a better way to prove his love. Maybe Hendrick could have fought someone off in prison. It's doubtful he would. Society accepts so many excuses, hides so many realities, then complains that so many people have HIV.

None of this seemed excusable, and everyone in his life, the major, the minor, and even the normally indifferent, thought less of him. Even his mother, his sister, and his brother... well how O'Ryan *could* think less of him at this point was doubtful. Taking Hendrick back into his life wasn't going change popular opinion.

John pulled Star back to bed and held him like Leonardo DiCaprio clinging to that flimsy piece of furniture at the end of *Titanic*. Maybe by morning, Star would be gone, and John, if he was lucky, would be dead. It wouldn't matter, and it beat living in freezing water off the coast of

Newfoundland.

CHAPTER 14

Star sat on his bed and analyzed. Legs on the floor, hands on the legs, mind all over the room, brains splattered among everyone, and everything oozing out inconsistency. Life as he knew it was about to change – it was as if he could almost see that white albatross perched on his window, cross-culturally communicating with some of the African spirits so cheaply represented on his second floor.

They couldn't be "real" art – not from T.J. Maxx. If someone could carve a face out of a block of wood in Accra, then pack it up and ship it from Ghana to Kirkwood where it retailed for an incredibly smarmy $9.99 – considering how many hands it passed through on the way – it was an insult to whatever it was supposed to represent, not to mention the original artist.

Was it bad luck? He's seen friends buy a glow-in-the-dark Virgin for a buck ninety-eight. Tacky! As if the spirit of the Virgin Mary could be contained in a hollow plastic shell.

At least he knew what she represented. These anonymous wooden heads he'd accumulated meant absolutely nothing outside an artistic realm. Maybe Arielle or Darrock would know something more. Maybe he had to get rid of a few that were inadvertently slinging bad luck in his face – maybe they'd summoned the albatross hither in the form of Hendrick Pardee to dangle from his neck and pull him down into emotional and financial quicksand.

He could feel it – the anticipation of finally having his man beneath him. The release of love, passion, sex... The loss of respect that came with the acquiescence of betrayal, and the acceptance that mom was, indeed, right.

This thought looped through his brain for hours. Bad enough he was a lawyer – now he couldn't even bill himself for wasting his own time like he could do with a client – a client that deserved his focus more than these white birds and black magic.

Besides that, these Ghanaian spirits might be the wrong ethnicity for Star and his family. He might have come from Angola, Zanzibar, or who knows where? It would be like a Greek displaying French art and saying it was still his heritage. As it was, when the Africans got rid of their common white enemy, many of them turned back to killing each other. Ethnicity mattered.

Then there was the issue of rewriting his own history – of suddenly realizing that things weren't as they seemed to be, and that he'd gone through his entire life with the wrong self perception. No idea now how to have replaced it or what could have been done differently. Worse yet, how his biggest inter-family battle was conveniently won for him off the chessboard by Althea Howard inadvertently knocking over an onyx king and shattering it by including pawns and bishops from Maplewood and Richmond Heights. He hadn't even talked to Lancer, but he was getting a feeling there was no need to – ever again. Well, that feeling had to go.

How something as small as this extruded into such a major ordeal was outside the comprehension and manipulation of a lawyer... why was it so simple for Althea?

Now everyone's reputation rested on a few nights of basketball changing kids' lives for the good of the city and the media. The NBA didn't help its progeny; it just exploited its players until they were either too rich or too drugged up to be of any use – or they went to jail. Maybe these local kids didn't need to change their lives. Maybe they just wanted to play ball and have fun.

Maybe Roof was an anomaly, in that he *could* be changed. John was a basket case waiting for a shining suicidal moment. Pity that such prime beef suffered from mad cow. Pity Darrock would be the rancher unwittingly infected. Just a petty terror inflicted upon the unsuspecting by someone with more money and a more important agenda.

Star stretched his fingers long across the keyboard. His hands practically dwarfed the keys, covering them, casting shadows under the lamp that burned light over the side of the computer. He logged onto the Bryan family site to see what garbage Arielle had recently unearthed, and

115

on whom. Maybe her reporting would get folks to clean up their act. More likely they'd hide it deeper, and risk even greater embarrassment upon having it announced.

Star read the latest with awe, dated April, 1832....

My name is Fawn Bryan. We took our master's first name as our last, because we can't spell the last. I am just learning how to spell myself. But I thought it was important to write things down. We are free Negroes in Virginia in a time where there are no free Negroes in Virginia. I should tell you how this happened.

My husband Mack Bryan twice saved the master's daughter. One time he took after a white boy who was attacking her. The second time she fell into the river and he swam in to save her before she got swept away. He risked his life to safe her both times, and we thought he was going to get in trouble for running a white boy off the property, but Master Bryan, he said we were doing the work of God, and he said we should be free. She never listened to her father, and that's why she got in trouble.

He gave us a small plot of land, and me and Mack and our children are working the land. And he gave us some of his slaves to help us work the land. Now I know some people are saying what are these Negroes doing with slaves? I say the same thing, but I know in my heart it was the right thing to do. We can treat them better than the white people. And we can't say no or set them free. That would be an insult to Master Bryan. And I don't know what will happen the next time his daughter gets in trouble. We can hope Mack is there. We really don't like to go back on the plantation, and have people look at us the way they do. It is very hard.

Already both the Negroes and the whites have cast us out.

So we will do the best we can, and try to be honest people, and stay away from those people who think no Negroes should be free, especially here in Virginia. It is going to be hard. But I wouldn't go back. I will write more as things happen, and better, as I learn how.

Fawn Bryan, April 16, 1832

Apparently nothing could bring the family together quicker than history. Arielle promised 182 more pages to follow, as she was diligently entering Fawn Bryan's diary into the computer and contacting the Smithsonian Institution to display and protect the original document.

Phones rang, cells buzzed, and everyone wound their way to Arielle's place for an unofficial impromptu, her house a bizarre bastion of African art and dress where no one had visited in a long time. Arielle lived in University City, not far from the fabled University City Loop, culturally eclectic, one suburb over from St. Louis itself. They had a nice sized house in a pretty decent area; there were other parts of U. City that still needed some spruce-up and education.

Her two children were running around with toy planes; her husband, as usual, rendered submissive upon being surrounded by so many of the Bryan family. No one was sure who was to blame, or not to blame, or if any blame was to be placed, or even where this thing came from. Under discussion was the existence of the document itself, where it was found, where it was going, and worse yet, why it was hidden and never brought to light.

Star had largely taken to junking his Ralph Lauren wardrobe, now wearing it mostly for clients who thought his prices demanded he put it on. He wasn't sure for whom he was plying this current repartee – certainly not himself – *never* himself – and more probably as a memorial to John Taylor's preference, but his combo of gold jewelry, black cotton, and a bright red silk scarf tied over his nearly bald head was a completely different heart and soul than could be found in the khakis and pastels of the Polo collection.

O'Ryan was already on the couch, staking out an expensive divan next to the fireplace; he looked a lot like Arsenio Hall trying to talk people into calling 1-800-COLLECT. If only he could adopt Aresnio's sense of humor. Arielle herself had taken to wearing her teaching costumes at home, and had over the past few months accumulated a moderate collection of ceremonial attire from Afro World up on Natural Bridge. Deep maroon and black draped and wound over her body, with a headdress to match. It seems a bit excessive just to wear around the house, as if she was recently cast in a passion play as Saint June Cleaver of Lagos. Husband wasn't much less, but lighter colors. It looked better, just out of place... more like a political statement, but what a nice family portrait it would make.

"What you people spend on clothes!" Mary sighed.

"Despite her best efforts, all of Mary's children turned out black!" Arielle sighed back.

"Worse than that, you said 'you people'," Star shot from the foul line. "You're ruined for the evening."

"Ninety eight percent of Nigeria can't afford what you have on," Mary admonished.

"Why don't you just hoist a flag for the Olympics?" said O'Ryan from his seat.

"Why don't you just shut the fuck up?" Arielle said. "Who gave you the right to treat us like the shit you are!" It was incredible how O'Ryan's sense of superiority made him impervious to such verbal attacks. She was going to have to mutilate.

"Whoa whoa whoa!" Lancer stepped in between them with his arms out, as if O'Ryan might decide that Arielle's outburst demanded the importance of rising from the couch. Arielle used that as an excuse to grab her father and face him with a deadly glare.

"I want to know where that came from and why you didn't tell me about it!"

"I want to know where you found it and why you thought to put it online for everyone and the *Argus* to get their hands on!"

"It was in some trunk I stumbled on in the attic looking for old clothes and toys for the boys! I want to know why you didn't tell us about it! Our whole identity is bound up in this book!"

"I'm glad it's somewhere," Star said. "I haven't been able to track it down lately."

"Where did you find it, Arielle?" said Mary, trying to inject a fair scent on a foul breeze. She was a bigger politician than Lancer, only on the domestic front. But her diplomacy was all too one sided, and no one had realized it until recently. It was all to keep shit from flinging up in her face. "Because I've never seen it either."

"It was a family heirloom in a trunk," Lancer said, trying to diminish the whole enterprise. "I forgot about it. I forgot about the trunk. It's just been passed down through the family for 140 years. We take it, and we store it. I don't know what the hell is in there."

"How could you *forget* about it?" Arielle put in.

"Maybe everyone isn't as interested in our past history as you are," Mary said. Peace at any price? No one could really figure her out, and it was destroying a lot of love.

"We've been called Slave Owning Niggers far too often in our lives," said Star, way too oversized, falling all over a leopard-print covered bean bag. "It would be nice to have known this. *But* for politics...we might have."

"*What* but for politics?" Lancer felt himself being unnecessarily exposed. "Politics made your asses what they are today."

"But for politics a lot of things!" Star shouted. He might have stood up, but it was too hard to untangle his limbs from the beans. "We might have been happy and expressed our own minds, and knew about things you tried to hide—or rewrite."

"I don't know what you're talking about."

"You tried to hide this for..."

"I forgot about it!" Lancer said with enough determination to make everyone think he actually had, were it not for his background.

"How!" Arielle demanded. "An early nineteenth century document about slavery written by a free black woman? And you forgot?" Her *forgot* reached into the heavens of operatic coloratura.

Lancer looked from her to Star, trying to just walk away from it, or at least ply his trade of dancing around it. "It's that, Dad, or talk basketball," he threatened.

So Lancer did the next best thing. Rather than play ball, he played guilt. "Why have my own children turned against me?"

"Maybe *you* can answer that, O'Ryan," Arielle suggested.

"No, I can't." he said from whatever sovereign nation he ruled by the fireplace. "Because *I* haven't."

"That's because you don't have a mind of your own," she retorted. "Or you do, but it doesn't conflict." She turned back to her father, whose face seemed more calculating than contrite. "We're all grown up now, father," she said, addressing him like the village idiot. "We're no longer extensions of your political career. Now are you going to tell *me* about this, or are you going to have to tell... the sistah?" she threatened.

119

"Oh stash that whore in a closet!" said O'Ryan. "Nobody likes that bitch, or you for creating it."

"And that bitch don't like nobody," Mary put in. "She uses truth as the devil's poison. Lancer, why don't *you* tell the truth. You're not out for votes."

Lancer felt boxed into a corner, standing in the middle of the room between all three children and a wife who was slightly wavering in support. Even Arielle's children slowed down, and her husband crept back up to the arch dividing the living room from the dining room. An athletic man, full head of hair, mustache, faithful as far as anyone could determine.

Lancer was on display; they all looked at him like he was a mechanical teddy bear behind plate glass at a Famous Barr department store Christmas display. Arielle had just pushed the start button. "Fawn and her husband had slaves," Lancer explained. "She didn't set them free. She said she couldn't, but maybe she could have. She could have let Master Bryan give her the slaves and set them free." The words *Master Bryan* sounded painful on their way out. Nobody was sure of his last name. "Instead they worked her land until she died. Almost thirty years, and she never... let them free. Well you know, Arielle. You read it. It passed down, and it just got stored in the trunk. No one thought much of it. It was just always in the trunk. Someone brought it here from Virginia. I looked at it once or twice and put it back. I didn't like what it had to say. I almost threw it out, but it was too old, and seemed bigger than I was. All I could do was hide it."

"It's a document." Arielle sat down, astounded with the information that it was almost taken to a dump. "Most black families have no history whatsoever. Kids don't even know who their own father is. And you were going to throw it out."

"It's a mark. People see it, and they hold it against you."

"They already do that," Arielle said. "White people have their shit. They don't throw it away."

"They don't have to," Lancer said, almost as if he had just discovered this, and it hurt. Almost like it was a lesson he should have taught his children 20 years ago. Maybe he tried, but they were too rich to care at the time. "We have to. It's the way the world is. It's dogged me all my life," Lancer was pensive, more sympathetic than he'd been in years. "We went from slaves to masters. How much better would *we* have been, and how much better can we ever say we are?"

"Damn!" Star said. "We might have to pay our own reparations." It was the lawyer in him, not thinking.

Arielle wasn't ready to drop her fists. "No, it's the way *you* read it," she said. "You'd destroy our heritage for politics. And you know you can't even do *that*. Once people stop thinking of you as black, you lose your seat on the Board of Alderman."

"That's the city's fault," Mary said. As usual, taking Lancer's side in some odd sort of way. "They want white people or black people. Being a leader is something you try to do, in spite of being white or black. But being a leader is not why you get your seat. It's just being white or black in the right place at the right time. You just try to help the city in spite of all that."

"No one's blacker than you are," O'Ryan said to Arielle as if she had no entitlement to her own race. "Or trying harder, at least."

"I'm learning about it," she replied. "Maybe you should too." Her demeanor changed to that of a TV anchorwoman. "I'm trying to teach kids not to be ashamed of themselves, and yet integrate them into a multicultural society with the ability to access a broad ethnic and racial heritage in the face of disparaging attacks by members of the Caucasian or Mongoloid races, or just plain ignorance by other members of their own. What are *you* doing, O'Ryan? So Fawn wasn't perfect," Arielle said. "She learned to read."

"I was ashamed," said Lancer.

"It's an 1832 mentality," said Arielle. "Either you oppress or you be oppressed. She's not going to be able to adopt our 2001 mentality ethic any more than her owner, who at least was kind enough to set them free and set them up. That in itself is amazing. I'm not sure black or white entered into it. She had a chance to advance. She got out, and she sure as hell wasn't gonna get no white boys to work that land. What did you expect? She treated them well. They were fed, clothed, learned to read, and didn't have to worry about having half their family sold away. In any case, I got it, I'm keeping it, and I'm showing it around. You've hid that trunk long enough. I think it needs to go to a museum before the pages rot out. It's a huge contribution to America that you chose to keep from us and from everyone who could learn from it. I don't think you had that right."

"After the war," Lancer went on, "what I hear is that Fawn and her family – our family – weren't ever very well accepted. Not by the whites, and not by the blacks. That's why they left Virginia. The black folks didn't want to see them prosper and the white folks resented it. They'd burn you out, or they'd make up some kind of story and someone would be lynched at a picnic. So they came here, where nobody remembered, and someone put that diary in a trunk. The trunk's from 1865 as well. My grandpa had it for awhile, his father before that, and I wound up with it. He said I should keep it, so I kept it. I shoved it in a corner when we moved here and that was that. We can trace our family back to 1832 when a lot of people can't get back to last week."

"So everything in it..."

"Is probably from 1865."

"Good!" Mary said. "Now we can be a family again, and stop all this fighting."

"I wanna see," said Star. "And no, we can't stop fighting until you all accept that I'm seeing Hendrick Pardee and that the basketball league will go on without St. Louis aldermanic supervision."

Mary sighed, almost like a cry of despair. "Hendrick! I almost forgot. Oh, and tomorrow!"

"Yes, tomorrow. Six months."

"Hardly. You've had your interim delight."

"Scrapdawg!" O'Ryan said with a bit of jovial, yet derisive, sarcasm. "Let's have a coming *out* party. You bring the beer."

Star reached up and yanked off his headscarf. Sometimes it was damned uncomfortable, and he wasn't in the mood to make a statement. He shoved it in his back pocket, where it glowered with anger. O'Ryan was a little scared, but he knew that Star wouldn't beat the crap out of him in full view of Arielle's children.

Star chose to bypass his brother's ugliness and go straight to the electric transformer. "Tell ya what, Dad." Never before had so much *fuck you* been put into the word *dad*. "You sponsor a team, and you can crow. Crow all you want, just buy them some t-shirts, and pay for a few dinners. It'll be good for you, and we can keep everyone else on the board out of it. And y'all deal with Hendrick. If you like Brad so damned much, go meet him for dinner. Go drive your asses out to Wildwood and have yourself a party with Brad. He's blackmailing me into coming back to him. If I don't, he's gonna slap me with a lawsuit the minute Scrap gets out."

"He is not!" Mary said, still wishing for the best from that loser.

"He is! I'm a lawyer and I know such things."

"Wait!" Lancer brought it back to himself. "I guess I could sponsor a team."

"Yeah, you could," said Star. "Keep the city's ass out of it. Here's the deal." The lawyer in him came back, and he was ready to negotiate, or better yet, lay down terms. He had to win this one, because he couldn't handle Hendrick if no one at all was on his side. He was lost enough on that as it was. "You buy a team. You keep the city's aldermanic ass out of it. You keep race out of it. You be nice to Scrap." To O'Ryan. "*You* be nice to Scrap." Back to Lancer. "And let me look in the trunk. I'm having an identity crisis. I just want to see things. See if I can put it back together." Such sorrow, coming from such a big man, seemed out of place. "Then maybe we can all get along. Again. Like we use to. I think, like we used to." They thought it over for a while, and doubted it.

"There's nothing in the trunk but old shit," Lancer said.

"Old shit is good," said Star. "I don't like the new shit."

"Like Scrap?" said his brother.

"What could you possibly have in common with him other than sex?" Mary asked, jumping on O'Ryan's wagon.

Ouch! "He don't have time for nothin' else when I'm done with him," Star replied.

"Fine," she said. "If it means that much to you, we'll include him. We won't like it. John's a much nicer boy, but he's too young. He's clingy. You just don't make good choices."

"I have to live with them a lot more than you do."

"Get your ass a woman!" pumped O'Ryan.

"One day I'm gonna punch your ass," says Star. "If I wasn't bigger and stronger and better looking and had so much more to offer the world, I might have had a complex because of you. If you can accept *that*, mama, you can accept Hendrick Pardee." Back to O'Ryan, who looked smug as usual. "You useless piece of shit. What gives you the right to hate me so much?" He'd looked smug since they were kids. And why? Because he was straight? Prejudiced black folks were really annoying. O'Ryan wasn't going to answer, particularly in front of his mother. Stroke of genius on the dad thing. The rest wasn't going to change.

"Just for today," Mary said. "Let's leave our resentments at home."

"No," said Arielle. "Let's get them out in the open. That's why we're here! You people are stupid! Yes… you people! Just a little bit of honesty crossing your lips and you all fall apart. The sistah is tired of your hypocrisy and your self degregating ways!" she said with a deliberate mispronunciation. Anger and African ceremonial dress didn't go together well. It seemed unbecoming to the fabric.

Star was starting to let go… It wasn't going to matter all that much, soon, if he was going to spend the rest of his life with Hendrick in a cocoon. Tomorrow afternoon, it was time to go to prison!

It was hard to sleep the night before. He stayed up reading the diary online, which Arielle was dutifully typing and posting. She was pretty deft at such things. He so much wanted to see the real document, but she wasn't about to let it see the light of day with her father around, and she was afraid after 170 or so years that the wrong touch or drop of sweat would destroy it.

Then again, his own sweat mingled with an ancestor's hand – to touch something she had created, touched herself, and poured her life into – it might mean the world.

One o'clock rolled by, two, then three, Star cruising the net looking at news, law, porn, an e-mail from John Taylor that maybe they could be friends… no time for that drama today, it could play itself out later.

Finally he fell asleep exhausted, thinking himself into a stupor. Noon tomorrow. It was easy, getting out of prison. They gave you back your clothes, your keys, and your chocolate bar if it wasn't out of date, and set you loose. No parole, no probation, it was part of the deal Lancer worked out behind the scenes. Teach everyone a lesson and move on.

Meanwhile, Star's financial side was kicking into full gear. He had closed up Hendrick's apartment, figured they might as well live together. Too many nights alone as it was, dreaming of that hard body next to him. He tried getting some insurance for Hendrick, who would need a lot of it given his HIV status. No point in sending him back to Bob Evans to fight it out with John Taylor. He'd scrapped most of Hendrick's furniture; they'd talked during his visits about what could stay and what could go. Most of it could go. Most of it wasn't really furniture.

He hadn't told anyone Hendrick would be living with him; that was too much of an argument he didn't want to add on to what was already boiling. Maybe he'd never have to, and people could just figure it out when it was too late to protest.

Morning on the appointed day... his skin was tingling with lust, longing for the feel of his man again. Over six months it'd been a handshake, if that. To have unlimited access... that would overpower all the guilt, misery, and insanity he had been reveling in for so long.

The drive wasn't far. A few miles to the city jail, the white bird flying along beside him. Where where *where* in his forgotten high school lit class did that damn thing come from? This bird wasn't going to slow the car down. He flipped it off – gave it the bird, as they say, alienating a driver next to him who didn't understand. Damn, and he was getting hard, too! Too many conflicting emotions, the biggest being "what the hell is wrong with you?"

Star wasn't so sure if he should go in, out, or what have you. Either way, at noon, Scrap would be coming out the door. Being the alderman's son, best to keep a low profile on this one. He jawed into a double jumbo jack from Jack In The Box, tossed down some French fries, and sucked a coke up over his lips, all tossed back gracefully while driving around the blocks near the prison.

Hendrick trusted Star to be there; if he'd come out with no Star waiting for him, he'd probably turn right back in – right back to the burning barn everyone seemed be running to for safety.

CHAPTER 15

Still in the prison mentality, physical contact seemed out of the question. Star looked over at his passenger while the daytime sun cut through the car; Scrap put his hand in between them on the seat as a tentative invitation. Star finally grabbed it and held it tight, feeling every callous, knuckle, the pulse of blood through his fingers. Star smiled, even laughed a couple times, looked over to his friend's face. Nothing looked like that. Nothing in the world. The radiant eyes, the curve of his cheek, the partial beard always on his face, the way his lips curved up in that innocent smile, so unique, so telling, saying that no matter what he'd been through, no matter who did what to who, here he was, home again, home at last, home forever.

Star wanted so much to bend over and kiss him, but not here, not in the daylight. He just let feelings wash over them both. Let the bird fly along, let Mom and Dad and O'Ryan and Arielle and John and Brad bray like wounded donkeys. He took Scrap's hand to his mouth, kissed it, couldn't wait, didn't care – damn, everyone knew anyway, from John Taylor's big mouth and the *Vital Voice* spreading its stories of goodwill.

"Got ya back," he said.

"Yep," Hendrick replied. "Ya got me back."

So hard to concentrate on the road, and not look in his eyes, the short drive seemed interminable; Star was nearly shaking by the time he got his man home. So many emotions – they hadn't gone away, just rolled together into one new one.

Star took Hendrick up to the bed. Nothing much yet. Couldn't just go to it. It wasn't like either of them had been deprived – just of each other, and just of the sanctuary that they'd learned to appreciate – the refuge that two people in love deserve with each other, and that people out of love only wish they could have, and why so many confuse love with safe haven, and why a bad lover is one who won't offer it when it's well within his grasp.

He ripped off Hendrick's shirt, tossed off his own. They fell to the bed,

Star on top, he grabbed Scrap's hands and held his arms over his head onto a pillow. He'd rehearsed this so many times in his own head.

Looked deep into his eyes, deeper, deeper, in for a kiss, a long one, powerful, tongue crossing the threshold into Scrap's waiting mouth. Star let out a deep sigh, a relief of tension from waiting for this moment ever since they were pulled apart in the courtroom. This is what made it worth all, his chest bare heaving against his man, lips locked for as long as he dared, no time limit, no guards, no family, and just for awhile, the bird off his neck locked in a cage. Just for a short while, so he had to let this short while last as long as he could, before it was time to clean up the sports page that invariably wound up under spilled bird seed and albatross crap.

Finally, resting his head on Scrap's shoulder, significantly enhanced since he had little to do but pushups and fend off or acquiesce to various prisoners. His arms and shoulders were cut like glass, but hard as diamonds. It was a diversion, and a source for pride in a place designed to knock it out of you. Still, the muscles reacted to Star's fingers caressing them, running over them, savoring the delight he had missed for so long, watching Hendrick's face glow as he touched sensitive spots, their eyes locked with a deadbolt, speaking thoughts there were no words for. It *was* worth all that.

"It is so good to see you!" Star said quietly.

"Yeah. Back with my man."

"Back with my dawg." Star was so tired, he rolled Hendrick over, grabbed him tight with one arm, and fell asleep. Somehow having a huge hunk of flesh beside him made it easier; Scrap followed suit. So went the afternoon for both of them, the first peace in a long time.

Star woke up first, watched Scrap sleeping off six months of laying there with one eye open, hoping for now the man would find a bit of solace, a bit of recovery, taking him in that car was like picking him up in a helicopter off a burning building, leading that horse out of the burning barn, hopefully it wasn't still screaming to go back. Eyes came open slowly, realizing they weren't looking at dirty socks, angry men, a new sterile paint job. City jail being redone, it wasn't so pretty from the inside anyway. Heart realizing life was his to do with as he wished.

Star bent over, kissed him gently, ran a hand over his face.

"We got a hard road ahead of us, Dawg."

"Where we goin'?"

"Git you back together." Should he bring it all up so fast? Wasn't sure. Sex seemed like it wasn't a good idea. Not quite yet. Wasn't sure why. He so wanted to. "Scrap, you okay with the poz thing?"

Embarrassed. "Think so. Not really."

"What isn't wrong with you?" Star asked with a small laugh, more out of fear than humor.

"Not much," said Hendrick. "If it wasn't wrong before I went it, it probably was by the time I got out."

"We'll take care of it. Counseling, too," Star said.

"What?" Still clinging to each other, Star's peace was slipping away; he'd waited too long for it to be this shallow.

"You gotta git your shit together."

Hendricks eyes became frightened. "I got you."

"I'm not enough," Star said. It slammed down on his partner like a car trunk on a kidnapping victim.

The lights in Scrap's eyes were flickering, like a candle about to go out, gasping for what little oxygen was left. "You're takin' over my whole life! I'm not gonna go tell some stranger what all's wrong with me."

"It's no secret," Star said. "You're half the man you can be. And I think you're quite a man as you are. Imagine!" he hid as much sarcasm as he could. He wanted it worse than he could *imagine*, and maybe worse than Hendrick himself. Having him here was da bomb. But definitely a fixer upper to diffuse before it exploded. It was just as well he was done decorating his condo.

"For you, then," Hendrick acquiesced.

"For you," Star said. He washed his open mouth over Scrap's eye, his cheek, his lip. "You can't go kickin' the shit out of any more white boys."

"Who cares?"

"I do. It's not over," Star affirmed.

"Why not? I done my time."

"Brad's arm is permanently damaged. He'll be in touch."

"You've been talking to Brad?" An unnecessarily raised heartbeat.

Star rolled back on top of Hendrick and drew out a kiss. "I had to, to tell him what he's been missing."

"Just don't show him."

"Aw, Scrap, I'm so sorry. About John and all."

"Shit, everybody knew it. I didn't have a choice in jail. You did. It was gonna happen anyway."

That was bullshit, but Star didn't want to get started on it. "Well from now on, then. And John's gonna be around, here and there. You don't touch him."

"Why would I want to?"

"I mean don't kick him down any stairs. John's a mess. He doesn't need you making it worse." Star couldn't believe he was having this conversation. His mother seemed so right, but his body, heart, and soul were at peace. Nothing felt like this, nothing looked, talked, sounded, smelled, tasted quite like Hendrick Pardee. And he knew Hendrick had a true heart. He just needed to exorcise a few demons. He wasn't sure if a psychologist was up to the task. Or if Hendrick was. Who knew if either of them would pursue that seriously?

Hendrick got up after a few minutes, went outside the room. "Nice Giraffe."

"John gave it to me."

"John?"

"Yeah," Star said offhandedly. "Don't toss it down the stairs either!"

"Will ya shut up about it?" Star saw a bit of anger flash in his man's eyes already, like a coal stoker in a locomotive fanning the flame. "It ain't so funny anymore. And I don't trust John."

"I'm fixing him up with someone," Star assuaged him. "He'll have a new man to cling to and I'll be outta there. That's how that works."

"That's how what works?"

"People who can't tell love from obsession." Star rose from the bed, and his mass filled the doorway, then finally imposed itself between Hendrick and the giraffe.

"John's a fucked up dude," said Hendrick. "I spent more time with him than you did. He never learned how to grow up. At Bob Evans. He was always whinin' about something. Never wanted to do his job right."

"Well, I grew him up," said Star. "I made a man out of him."

"Apparently."

"He's a different person, Scrap. He's gone from nerd to stud. But his heart is still lonely, and he doesn't know how to be alone. He's just as scared as you are."

"You don't know what it's like!" Hendrick said, exhaling an emotion Star couldn't figure out.

"What?" he went to his man, hand around the back of his head, trying to pull him in for a hug. He needed it.

Hendrick resisted this one. "Growing up black."

Star just about puked on the floor. It was like someone had ratcheted his guts open with a crowbar. "Growing up black? I did! And I am!"

"No, you didn't, and no you aren't! You went to private schools, you had money, you had culture, you didn't deal with drug shit, all your friends goin' to jail, and worryin' about getting your head blown off walking down the street. You didn't deal with prejudice about being on the down low. Being scared half your life! You didn't have none of it! And you wonder why I am like I am, and why I'm trying to hold on to you. It's because you are all I have. I'm just scared all the time. We all were. The coke made it go away, but I can't do coke any more. And you won't let me hide from anything. So I'm just scared," he settled down, his blood pumped slower, muscles relaxed, accepting his fate. "Just a scared little dawg."

"You don't need to be."

"You don't get it!!"

"And if I did," Star said, "what use would I be? You can follow me and stop being afraid, or stay where you are."

Hendrick let go, picked up that giraffe by the neck, put it back down. He wanted to snap its neck in two. Not because of John, not because of Star, just because. Something hurt. "I don't know how."

Star the lawyer took over a bit. "I can't protect you from it, if it's in your heart."

"You can," said his dawg. "Don't let go of me."

"You really are a dawg, ain't ya?"

"Yeah." A tear formed in his eye, the fire behind them was being smothered out, the smoldering choking smoke that was left just as

130

dangerous and destructive. "When you called me dawg the first time, I figured you knew."

"I love you." Star said. He'd wanted to say that for so long. "But you can't live like this. Neither can I."

"Fine, then I'll leave."

"This all you want to do with your life?"

"What else is there?"

"Enjoy it," Star said, though the words fell false on his heart. He hadn't either, in such a long time. "A journey of self discovery."

"Why do you love me?" Hendrick asked. Folks who don't believe in it fault those who do. "No one else has any faith in me."

"No one else can see you like I can."

"They see the real me," Hendrick said. "You just make shit up that I'm something better than a jailbird."

"Do you love me?"

"Yah! I do."

"Well here's your choices. You can doubt me and walk out that door, or you can trust me and stay here. If you stay here you do what I say to get your head together or I'm gonna shackle your black ass to a cargo boat and send it to pick chocolate on the Ivory Coast. I'll get more use out of the hundred lousy dollars I'd get for selling you back into slavery than I can dealing with this shit day after day."

"What? You bastard!"

"Fuck you, dawg!" Star's anger was boiling over from a lifetime of stolen identity. "If I ain't black like you are, who gives a rat's ass about what happens to you? I don't have to be a ghetto slumboy to be as black as you are, and fuck you for defining me out of the race. Just fuck you."

"I didn't mean that."

"Oh, but you did. I haven't betrayed my community because I've had an easier life. It hasn't been so easy, growing up with my family. I don't know what the hell to do with them, or if I should ever speak to them again. They are fucked up, boy. Really really really fucked up, and they hate your ass as well. I have gone through hell every minute you've been gone. You're not going to compound it getting out."

"This is such a shit-ass conversation to have just getting out of jail."

"Freedom sucks," Star said. "It means you can't have everything you want. It means you're free to make something of yourself, or if you'd rather, take yourself down with as many people as you can along with you." Silence awhile; Hendrick was right, it was a shit-ass conversation. "And it means you got yourself a big guy to hold you whenever you need it."

"How about now?" Star was just big enough that it made a difference. Scrap could hide his face in Star's shoulder, and maybe he'd never have to look up and see the world and the bleak path that lay ahead of him. Maybe it would be good not to live in fear and anger. Right now he hated everyone, himself included, except Star, and that by a trifle.

With his eyes an inch away from Star's face, his lips brushing against Star's goatee, down his neck, down back into the bedroom, Star kept thinking AIDS, issues, what have you, but he couldn't say no any longer. It felt like he'd never been touched before. Nothing quite felt like this one, deep deep in his heart, this was where it was.

Not John, not Brad, not countless others, Hendrick was an entirely different kind of being, and more beautiful than any he had ever seen, in ways too deep to believe it was true. Hidden far too deep behind the man all too many people assumed they knew, Star could see through to the reality.

Behind the HIV, the mental illness, the unchained innocence, making love brought out the real man, the one where it was love, not just put this here and put that there, not just *look ma I got me a ball player!* and not selfish, just a way of saying I love you that words were never intended to express.

It was a way finally to stop the fire in his eyes, or restoke it to burn more kindly. Or just another biscuit to the dawg to keep him from biting. A nice biscuit. "Fuck man!" Star said. "There just ain't nobody like ya!"

Scrap smiled. It was nice to see. "Don't forget it."

"Remind me. Soon."

White bird took off from the window, just for a short time, probably on his way to get a ball and chain. Maybe Star could put up a feeder and the doves would chase the albatross away.

He looked to Hendrick, spent, lying on a soft bed, luxuriating in being free, not wearing anything, and altogether content. It was like Star had set the timer back on a bomb and bought himself a few more days. "Good way

132

to do it," he said, just about aloud.

"Yeah, it was."

"A man's gotta be good at something," he said. "And ya know," he said, "your turn to hold me. My life ain't been so good either." Hendrick's arm drew across him like a curtain of sweat closing on a soccer ball. Warm sticky flesh surrounded him, and Star was pinned to the bed. Hendrick couldn't just lay there and not be a participant. It had been so long since they were together without guards watching their every move, holding wasn't enough for now. Things were okay, and hell could wait.

Hell was just beginning for Darrock Ndlele, who was about to be saddled with a rebounding and obsessive John Taylor on top of his own raging and unpaddled river of hormones. Overwhelming his need to save himself for the right man was a desire to know what it all felt like, to feel someone, kiss him, hold him, as well as read the complete works of Faulkner – deciphering whatever language that was would certainly aid his future as a linguist.

For once, thought Darrock, he wanted to keep the brain from ruling. Maybe for once let the body talk, live out the romance, just have another young guy he could be with and not be known forever as the guy with the funny hair at Coffee Cartel that *really* came there to read, instead of the rest of them who brought a book as an excuse to scope out guys. It wasn't so much the book as the Faulkner that gave him away as smarter than everyone else there. Intelligence was perceived as patronizing by people unwilling to access their own, and was a greater barrier than Darrock ever realized.

Star wasn't so much disgusted with John as with himself, and what he'd turned John into – or what John turned into on his account, at least. Though if it wasn't Star, it would be someone else; John was just "tetched" a bit that way, chances are him and Scrap should have gone to therapy together, where they could kill each other off and let Star go back to Brad. Such ugly alternatives for such handsome men.

Not black enough? Perhaps he was *too* black! Dark enough that black folks with lighter skin would ostracize him if he weren't 6 foot 5 and a whiz with a basketball. That bald head, piercing eyes and goatee made him look

133

demonic to some, but those who were really scared would cower rather than attack. His new wardrobe of red and black didn't help matters any, but the tough look on the outside bolstered the weakened support system underneath. In any case, he didn't feel comfortable taking John to the Cartel in his own car, and was hoping anyway that John could ride off with Darrock into the sunset. Something had to break so John would refocus and not think about blabbing the truth to the last person in St. Louis who didn't know it.

The Cartel's smoking area was finally closed off from the non smoking – it was two separate kingdoms entirely, though the smoking area was larger and more comfortable. First off, it was farther away from the rudeness of most of the folks who worked the counter, and second it accommodated large numbers of young people, including gay boys not old enough to get into the bars, the residents of a new generation who determined they were somehow immune to the consequences of smoking and barebacking, unlike the millions of their predecessors who were leveled by both.

Besides that, none of the furniture in the place seemed designed for a guy of Star's proportions, and he was afraid of the chairs outside, although the day was too nice to waste it indoors.

Darrock was already there, eyes in a book, head in the clouds, hair dangling off the back of his head, a red colored French soda nearby... he saw Star approach but as was his way, couldn't acknowledge anyone's presence while still in the middle of a paragraph. With Faulkner, this could lead to some awkwardly slow acknowledgements.

Darrock smiled, hoping his slice of heaven wouldn't be far behind. "Where's your boy?"

At home tormenting a giraffe, Star wanted to reply. "He's coming." This was too weird. Matchmaker and sanitation engineer all at once, with a load of family pressure to boot. Why they were gunning for Brad, after all that misery? Since Brad was blackmailing him with love, it made no sense. All a matter of appearances; on the outside Brad was solidly middle class with a good job. Just right.

Then again, Star wasn't sure how much happier he was now. But he loved Scrap, the rawness of it, and it was worth the chance. He couldn't help thinking that he'd never see his family the same way again, or that the process of forgiveness would take years, and that maybe they weren't interested.

"Darrock, John's a different sorta dude," Star said.

"So am I. I could use something young and stupid."

"He's not stupid. He's just a little hurt."

"*You* did it to him, didn't you? Now I'm supposed to pick up the pieces. I get it."

"Are you sure?"

"Look at me." Darrock let something other than self confidence slip out from between the pages of *Absalom! Absalom!* He stretched out, threw his hands behind his head and then down over his face. Folks were watching, but from a distance. Not only was he intelligent, he was interesting. Fascinatingly intimidating. "I can have these guys," he said swinging a finger around the morass that had accumulated outside the Cartel. "I've been holding out. I don't really want to hold out much longer."

"You be careful," Star warned. He remembered how he was at 20. The flood gates opened, and several were injured as the water came rushing in. "Don't go runnin' around with everyone you meet. It's hard not to, once you start."

"Maybe for you," Darrock said.

"Ouch."

Darrock waved his book in Star's face. "I'm not like everyone else, and fuck anyone who thinks I should be." The hair was amazing, so were the biceps. The shirt yellow, bright, sleeveless, that made the very act of lifting his arms one of cursing at The Lord's Prayer – Darrock was definitely Darrock, and not some kid you'd find trying to be like every other kid. "I don't want someone like everyone else."

"I know what it feels like," Star said. "I don't fit in anywhere. And places I thought I fit in I don't any more. Like home."

"So we're two puppies trying to jump over a fence."

"Woof." Star didn't find Darrock particularly handsome, on the other hand, *wow*.

"You want a piece of this?"

God no! Well yes! Well no! Darrock was stable, smart, and moral. Of course not! Well, and he was 19, which made him entirely too old.

John came from around the corner, had some sort of smile on his face that he couldn't seem to wipe off. Maybe from seeing Star again, maybe from the chance at starting fresh, whatever it was, it was nice to see a smile different from the lovestruck variety.

"That him?" Darrock saw Star's eyes point in John's direction. "That's a nice lookin dude!"

"I did that to him," Star said. "Last year at this time he was a dweeb. Ain't that right, John?"

Star got up to hug him, a minor societal infraction in the West End, if at all, particularly at the Coffee Cartel whose underground purpose, whether intended or not, was to promote this sort of toleration. "This is Darrock."

They shook hands, John sat down, Darrock put Faulkner away, thankfully coming to the end of a chapter; trying to process that and John at the same time would have overloaded the circuitry. At least John was speaking English.

John didn't know what to say, or what he was supposed to say. "You readin' that?"

"Trying to."

John had gone a bit baggier since Star dumped him, a bit out of laziness, and a bit because he liked it better. His arms poked out of a black sleeveless fleece shirt, you could see a good deal into it when he lifted them out. "You got all sorta of things, don't you." Pointed at Darrock's piercings, his hair; he had no idea what to say, other than talk fashion. He'd never been in this situation before.

Star felt awkward just staring at this particular set up. "Sounds like I'd better find something to do," he said.

"Well wait," said Darrock. "We don't have a flow going yet."

"I didn't bring you together to talk Faulkner," he said. Why not call a spade a spade? John was looking over Darrock like he was examining prime rib at the meat counter, except that his mother did the shopping and he wouldn't know good meat from botulism. It was the first time in a long while he'd felt the weight of depression, oppression, and suppression off his mind, unaware it was simply transferring itself across the table to Darrock.

"Thanks, man," said Darrock. "If this works, we'll owe you."

136

"Something has to," Star said. He pulled up Darrock's French soda and sucked a wad out through the straw. It was almost as radical as licking beer off Hendrick's chest. "See? We share everything. Y'all take care."

He felt bad, but wasn't sure why. Maybe because he wasn't letting nature take its course, he was shaping it to his own needs. Raping the land; letting the land rape its own. It wasn't pretty, though fantasizing about the two of them sent him home faster to Hendrick. He didn't have to stay there and help them navigate their way through love. No one ever helped him.

Well, that sculptor did. That was probably his best chance at it, ever, but he was too good to be tied down. Spread the wealth? Now everybody's broke.

Darrock was definitely different. John was just a normal guy. So John thought. But here someone different, more educated, older, better, not to mention African – was talking to him and drinking him in with an agenda of his own.

Both were lonely, both not particularly picky at this point who filled it. Darrock wasn't going to admit that, but he was getting there rapidly. Looking at John as the answer to everything. John was still reeling from being dumped by Star, but he could rebound for the right smile, the right touch, the right kiss. As long as he could live for someone other than himself. All he needed was one of Star's T.J. Maxx spirits to shoot Cupid's arrow at him, quickly. It was too confusing for Cupid, of Greek descent, to be urged on by spirits from Ghana. He started shooting randomly. It hit one of Darrock's metal studs and glanced off, hitting both men at odd angles. Darrock couldn't hold back any longer, and John's heart was bleeding.

It was a dreadful moment, more because of the battle and anxiety leading up to it than that actual crossing of the threshold. Star walked Hendrick up to his parents' doorstep almost like having a dog on a leash. He didn't even need to bring Hendrick other than to present him to his parents as a gesture of defiance. His victory would be pyrrhic if they didn't respect him; anyway how could he blame them? He'd lost most of his own respect in the years of pining after Brad. Once again he was letting his life go down the tubes for something marginally resembling love.

Scrap followed a pace behind, their fingertips lightly touching as they walked up to the door.

"I want to see what's in the trunk," Hendrick said.

"What's it matter to you?"

"Because you're the only black family who's got one. Only white folks have a trunk."

"Anyone can buy a trunk," Star said.

"Not with stuff in it. Y'all don't know what you have. You got all that white shit everybody says they want, and it don't mean a thing to you."

"It ain't white shit." Star was getting impatient.

"You go find me one family north of Delmar what's got shit in a trunk they've been saving since 18fucking32. Niggaz can't remember what they did yesterday, let alone 170 years ago."

Silence on the drive. Star was thinking more of family dynamics, not pre civil war history. It was weird, though. Old shit, with the name Bryan on it. Bryan because someone who owned them was named Bryan. Yet Master Bryan's generosity the only reason they had what they had now. So maybe so, maybe it all went back to the trunk.

"I'm sorry about John," Star said.

"Don't matter."

"Yeah it does. I coulda waited. It was selfish. If I loved you-"

"Yeah," Hendrick said. "If."

"If I loved you, I shouldn't have done it. But I can't wipe it off now."

"So you're saying you was wrong?"

That was a harsh word. Star just about whispered. "Yeah. So, please forgive me. Anyways I set him up with some Nigerian fuck we met at Coffee Cartel."

"Poor guy."

"Get offa him."

"You the man who was on him. No one asked ya to climb aboard."

"No one asked you to kick Brad's elbow into 14 pieces."

"That didn't give you the right to fuck around with John Taylor."

"Nope. John was hot, and he wanted me. That's why I did it."

"That sucks."

"Yeah," Star said. "If I was some ugly fat dude you wouldn't look twice at me."

"Fourteen?" Scrap's face screwed up with a touch of pride.

"I dunno," Star said. "I just made it up. You're gonna be named in a civil suit, so I wouldn't get too high on how many pieces, or what ya done. It was worse than me. Our hearts can heal. Brad's arm's fucked up for life, and thanks to you."

"When are we gonna start havin' fun, Star?" Innocent question, no easy answer.

Star turned onto his parents' street and pulled up into the drive. "How's about we work on the HIV, the lawsuit, a bit of anger management, and the fact that my family hates you? Oh, then it's basketball season. We need to teach a bunch of Vietcong how to play ball with Bosnians."

"Don't we get no niggaz?" Scrap was amazed at all this multiculturalism.

"You get this one," Star said back. "It's the only one you need. Look, there's 15 year old kids from Bosnia that can whoop your ass into the ground with a basketball."

"Well don't go fuckin' any of 'em," Henrick said. Always worried, always concerned. When you've got the best there is, you can't let go.

"Is your cell still empty?" Star said, slamming the door. "They're gonna need it for me when I'm done with your ass."

"Pound it!"

"Boy, just be good. Now heel, dawggy, or stay outside."

That shut Hendrick up way too quick for Star's sense of decency. But maybe a few well placed commands would keep him close by, and docile. Too bad he didn't learn it before. He might have saved Brad's bones, and all the misery in between. Heel. Heel! Damn!

CHAPTER 16

"Good afternoon, Mr. Pardee." Mom was too nice.

Hendrick looked to her with envy. She had a past, even if she married into it. "I just wanna see what's in the trunk," he said, with a bit more innocence than Star could remember.

"Just a buncha old shit," said O'Ryan, who for some unexplained reason was on the couch watching TV.

"Don't you have a wife to cheat on?" Star asked.

"Yeah, I do," was the reply.

"Boys!" Mary was over the constant squabbling. It was keeping her up nights.

"Were not boys," said her older child.

"You act like it! I shouldn't have to be afraid to have more than one of my children in the room at the same time."

Star and Scrap walked past the TV. News. Arielle. Her husband. The book. "Does she ever take that damn thing off?" Mary wondered half aloud. That same African wrap-around, and her husband tagging along with another sale item from Afro World. "Your father should be on there," Mary suggested.

"He hid the damn thing, I don't think so," Star combated.

"Can we for once stop fighting?"

"I dunno." He bent down and kissed Mary on the forehead. "I love you, Mom."

"If she does the sistah, I'm going to throw a brick through the TV," Mary laughed. She hadn't heard those words in a long time, even from the sainted O'Ryan Bryan. "It wouldn't be beneath you to say that every few years," she turned on him. While she was throwing darts, might as well hit as many triples as she could.

"Did you know she was gonna be on?" Star asked.

"Now Star, that would imply she was speaking to her father. I'm just waiting for a *Wheel of Fortune* rerun."

Well this should give the *Argus* a field day. Slavery, costume, literature, and the Bryan family, for whom that newspaper's disgust was all too gleeful and consistent. A few close-ups of the writing, and then the address of the family web page for folks who wanted to read the whole thing. Great, now everyone would know everything about everyone else.

"Do you think it should be published?" some reporter asked her.

Arielle was on her couch, her husband quietly acquiescing by her side, her kids firmly held in place. "I think everyone should read it."

"What can we learn from this?"

"I guess that God created us all equal. And he gave us the opportunity to do good and to do wrong. That good people can do wrong. And that being white or black doesn't have anything to do with being good, or being wrong. But don't y'all use this as a way to run us down," she said, dipping a bit too deeply into Lucinda Trampp, and almost daring someone to do it. "Fawn was a good woman. She was just living under a different set of rules."

What a prologue to going through the trunk. "There's nothing much in there," said Mary. "Nothing really."

Scrap held onto Star's hand while the two of them sat up in the attic. He was afraid to open it up for fear of being disappointed. He vaguely remembered seeing this growing up, packed under a few blankets and other castoff items. No one bothered with it. It was part of the landscape, and there was too much stuff on top of it to move, even for a curious child. A few choruses of *"that's not for you!"* and the kids were poisoned from their curiosity like an East German seeking freedom under a rain of bullets.

And old picture in a frame, preserved pretty well by being kept in darkness for 150 years. "Who's that?" Scrap asked.

"I dunno," Star said.

Scrap leaned over and gnawed on Star's ear.

"What you doin' that for now?"

"We're alone."

"Not with this bitch looking on," Star said. He meant it. "Maybe that's Fawn."

"Maybe that's some slave lady."

141

"Looks like she's dressed too good," Star said. Museum pieces all, here... stuff folks bragged about, if they had a family history. A couple hair ribbons, jewelry, suspenders, a doll, an iron, some shoes, a schoolbook. A couple more photos of people nobody knew. "This is neat," Star said. He turned a page or two, afraid the book would all fall apart. Surprised Arielle didn't snag it along with the diary. He looked back on the pictures, and there were no names. Could have been anyone. Fawn? Mack? Who knew? He just looked at it, taking it all in. What would have been so off limits? The book, of course. Without the book, it was marvelously benign. And almost meaningless, except that it was his. "Well, that's where I come from," Star said, more talking to himself. He felt his hand being squeezed a bit tighter. "That's the primordial ooze of slavery from whence we arose."

"Spooky."

Star looked at Hendrick, trying to see if that glow in his cheeks and his eyes would still shine in the dim light. If it did, it would be love. He half hoped he wouldn't see that torch burning behind Hendrick's eyes. Yet there it was, lighting up the attic on its own. "Spooky," he said. Damn! It would be so easy to turn away, if it wasn't what it was. "We gotta get you to a doctor and get this HIV thing going," Star said.

"Where did that come from?"

"Cause this is all my life, and so are you." He had no idea, the mind just went from the 1830s, and precious things, and a light burning in Hendrick, to a life with no electricity on a plantation in Virginia. So it all made sense.

Star looked in for a long time. He didn't want to close the trunk. Something about it was fascinating, but gut wrenching at the same time. Just like Hendrick. All these lives boiled down to a few artifacts in a box. People lived, had pictures taken, and they were still forgotten.

"Hey. At least y'all weren't slaves."

"No," Star muttered. "But we sho' nuff is fucked up." He closed the lid. Well, he could revisit it, but maybe not.

He took Hendrick's hand and led him back down to the land of the living. Through the door, the hand-holding a statement of defiance, not so much to his mother, but that damned O'Ryan. Nothing he could do but... well... kill him! And that wasn't about to happen. Just something! Anything! Just to see him contrite.

"That asks a lot more questions than it answers," he said. Scrap was silent. He was holding master's hand, so he didn't have to talk. "Who are those people?"

"We don't know," Lancer said. "I don't know how to find out. Can we just leave the box alone already?"

"O'Ryan, you should take a look. Might change ya," Star said. He still didn't have the courage to look in his older brother's eyes at a vulnerable moment like this. So many of his moments had been vulnerable, O'Ryan just picked away at it. So did Brad, so did all of them. Maybe it was time to stop being so vulnerable. "Why don't you display the iron?"

"I don't want him to talk me into using it," Mary said.

"Well why not? What are we hiding the iron for?"

"I have issues with that whole box of crap," Lancer said. "I don't want to keep looking at it, and I don't want it to keep being thrown in my face."

"Who's gonna throw it in your face? The *Argus*?"

"Or my daughter. It's almost better if we don't have a past, for all the shit I've taken for it over the years."

"Well, you shouldn't have hid it from us," Star said.

"Didn't we just have this fight last week?" Mary walked in between them. "Now can it, or we're going to leave you alone here with your brother."

Everyone was very quiet, as Star and O'Ryan both realized that would be horrific. And the tragedy of that realization, even more so.

Star wasn't worried about all this. Hendrick was there, and there for a reason. It was too "in your face" for no one to address it. Mary took a deep breath and just spoke her mind. For once, hers, and not veiled as her husband's.

"You seem to want us to take him into the family, so okay, you're in. But I have enough trouble with what I already got, and I don't want any more from you. Especially if you're planning on breaking my son's heart."

Star was ready with a reply. "Scrap's got HIV, he's gonna have to get a job, and Brad's gonna sue him for beatin' the crap outa him."

"Well that's a walk in the park," Mary responded. "We're lucky we live so close to it."

Star hugged Scrap from behind. "No," he said. "It isn't. But he's mine, and I'm gonna take care of him. You can help me or not. Being that he's got trouble in every corner, I hope you'll help."

Hendrick was looking around helpless. "It's okay," Mary told him. "We talk about you like this when you're not here, too. We've fought about you, and we really don't think you're good for him. So, it's up to you to prove us otherwise. Or," she said happily... "I'm going to lose respect for everyone! Because if you blow this one, Star, it's an arranged marriage for you."

Only one word to respond to that bit of artillery: "Basketball."

Sunlight blasted its way through the windows of an old and underfed gymnasium donated by the City of St. Louis, it silhouetted panes and frames on an old wooden floor. In this gym, it was probably the best heating system available. Star looked around to six groups of teenage boys provided by hunter/gatherer Althea Howard, beaming as the woman who brought all this together.

Looked like she got them together by nationality. A team each of Vietnamese, Mexicans, and Bosnians, and three teams of black kids, one each from Maplewood, Richmond Heights, and Dogtown.

"Anyone here speak English?" Hendrick was curious.

"Probably the Vietnamese," said Star.

Then there was the media. Waiting for him to say something inappropriate, as always. The *Argus*, the *Vital Voice*, the *American*, the *Post-Dispatch*, what? How did this get blown into such a big saving-the-world parable? It's a basketball game! Something's missing! Star looked around the room. It would be too good to be true, just to see him look up from the bench with the Dogtown boys. John Taylor. The whole reason for any of this, and he'd outgrown it. He'd moved on to Darrock. Ok, so he was pushed on to Darrock.

"Those Bosnian kids are gonna kick y'all asses," Althea warned the team from Maplewood.

"Yeah," Star agreed. "White folks from Europe know how to play ball." So hopefully no one spoke English. They were hinging on his every word. Althea laid into them all that they were part of a major happening – a social experiment, an opportunity to learn from the best, and most importantly, with a wry smile, her reputation. "We beat out big city brass to give you this chance! You screw it up, and you fight city hall."

144

It looked motley, young guys trying to look tough by conforming to whatever fashion was pointed out in the trendy malls and magazines. Bad hair, oversized clothes, holes in the wrong places. First it's a $2 t-shirt torn accidentally, then because it looks sexy someone charges $75 for a shirt that's hand-torn at a factory in the Emirates.

Soon it all didn't matter; they were all required to wear "Lancer Bryan for St. Louis Alderman" shirts as part of the program. Heck, it was free. For a brief moment, the sun glanced over dozens of bodies of vulnerable young male flesh as each team changed into a different color Lancer Bryan jersey.

Lancer glanced over at Althea, and gears turned as if part of a malfunctioning invention in a children's movie. She sure had some skills. Maybe he could harness them somehow? Maybe she was just a bitch who did this all to spite him. Maybe Lancer wasn't the center of the universe. Nah, she was just a bitch who was getting far too much praise for an accomplishment his own children took away from him.

Star looked over at his mother with amazement. Amazed they were here, and amazed that...

"It's self serving," she admitted, "but he's taking an interest. And he's putting money into it."

"He's trying to piss me off," Star said, looking away to the back of the gym, still searching out some faded elixir of that Bob Evans busboy.

"He did, didn't he?"

Star looked around at the guys enjoying the smell of new cotton hugging their chests. Some big war wound scar on a Bosnian, quickly, almost embarrassingly quickly, covered up before Star's eye could register. The shudder went unspoken between them. Maybe life here wasn't so bad.

"Let your father have his victory," Mary cajoled. "They're not old enough to vote, and their parents probably aren't registered."

Where's John? He should be here. He doesn't have to play. He should just be here. He'd still be cleaning up carrots at Bob Evans if I hadn't-

"It's about the shirt." Star talked to the crowd in terms he hoped they'd understand. He felt like he was in some kind of movie in a scene where it was his time to reconstitute his life. To make it meaningful by instilling some kind of pride into a group of kids that didn't realize the hero he might once have been. To meet that hero himself on the rebound. But he had to tell the truth. "It's about the shirt because my father bought and paid for those shirts. He had them silk screened with him name on them. So if you don't give me 100 percent, you're shaming my father's name. And trust me, you don't want to carry my father's name around if you grind it into the dust. So I don't care if you stink, you suck, or you can't throw the ball two feet in front of you. As long as you give that 100 percent, that's where the pride comes in. At least my pride."

Some kid from Richmond Heights looked him in the eye, silently asking the obvious question. "Because you signed up to spend 3 days a week with my ass over the next couple months. So if I don't like you-"

"If you don't like me, I can keep my ass at home." Smart alecky brat.

Star chucked him gently on the ear. "And these guys can find it and bring it right back here." He wasn't sure who understood and who didn't. He picked up a ball and threw it at a surprised Bosnian. Admir. The wounded. It bounced off him onto the floor.

Scrap took up the slack. "That what you're gonna do when someone throws you the ball?" He tossed it back again. Screw the gay angle, screw father's pride, screw all of it; some kid left war and misery to come to America and play basketball in a purple shirt. He challenged Scrap all the way to the basket and looped in a shot over his head. One, two, three, it teetered on the edge of greatness and dropped in.

"Just remember," Star said. "You can be a man and do *this...*" and he scooped up the ball and swooshed it back through the hoop. Lucky, it always worked when he was trying to set an example. "And you can be a man and do *this*." He scooped up Hendrick and laid on a kiss, once again, nothing but net. A pity O'Ryan didn't come to support. A pity gay men couldn't be affectionate in public without having to make a point at the same time.

Photo for *The Vital Voice*, wincing at the *Argus*, gossip for the family website, and for a small time folks might stop yakking about long gone Fawn. But it didn't seem right sloshing through months of teaching kids to grow up if he couldn't do it himself. Besides, Hendrick, most days, was too kissable to pass up. The sun beat on his face, the eyes glowed, screw the kids anyway.

"Everybody thinks I'm gonna make men out of you," he said. "That's yo' mama's job. I'm here to teach you to play ball. But a better man can play a better game of ball." He was talking in sound bytes. He had to, it seemed, with so much media pressing *record*. Getting in one on one with someone, learning his heart and soul, and shooting a few as an afterthought, that's what would have made this all good. Maybe once everyone left and lost interest, he could throw out the script.

What he needed was someone to focus on. A new John Taylor. Someone to personalize it so it would make a difference if he showed up or not. What about Admir? Nah, he'd been through enough already. Some kid from Dogtown was looking at him with that glazed over fifteen-will-get-you-twenty-but-I-won't-tell-anyone young unfathomable lust ... nah, enough of that too. Maybe he could do it for Scrap. At least they'd have something to do besides sex and jealousy. Anyway, it kept Hendrick off the streets.

"You always talk to the kids that way?" Lancer was curious. Now since they were wearing his name, he owned them all.

"It works." His family had gotten along for an entire afternoon. Then again, they let Lancer manipulate behind the scenes and come out on top. "You shoulda tried it with me."

Star was quiet on the way back. He was afraid to comment on any of the guys in case Scrap would get jealous, and he didn't want to talk about his father's t-shirt stunt.

"Those boys from Maplewood must be serious if they're wearing mint green," Scrap hazarded finally.

"They're not in his ward, so they get the ugly colors."

"Looks cool on Tyrell."

"Tyrell looks cool in everything."

"Great."

"You started it."

Sex was difficult in some ways. Always something in the back of Star's mind about HIV. Where did it come from? Why does it matter? Sometimes he felt like he was trying to be heroic, telling the whole world it didn't make a difference, telling himself, but sort of unsure when Hendrick became more important to him than he did to himself. Sort of like Brad, mounting ever so imperceptibly onto a throne that pushed Star into subjugation. Just to keep the peace. Just like his... mother!

147

Brad was important again. The lawsuit was in the mail when they got home.

CHAPTER 17

Just like Admir, Darrock's father inadvertently advertised the brutality from his homeland every time he changed clothes. He did it in front of John – inadvertently – as he inadvertently did it in front of everyone, and then suggested people stop complaining about America. Still, he convincingly juxtaposed his freedom in America with a loud disapproval of homosexuality, which he believed should be punished everywhere, including the purported land of the free. He didn't know what was going on so close under his watch; John and Darrock learned to be quiet and disinterested, a difficult feat for Darrock, now that for the first time he had reason to be otherwise.

Faulkner was hot. Never this steamy before, but Darrock had never read it with someone breathing and drooling down his neck with wet ready lips. The steam of a Mississippi summer rolled off the pages cinematically, enveloping him in a southern ennui, humidity supplied from above.

"Those aren't real words." John's first mistake was trying to make sense of Faulkner's prose.

"You just get into the psychology of it," said Darrock. John's breath wasn't making any of this easy.

"What you reading it for?"

"I just do. It's one of those things I can't explain." Gorecki's 3rd symphony emoted a classically defined misery in the background. All in all, a very odd culture for John, who was usually immersed in people who shared his own tastes to the disdain of anything else. *Who cares? Let's have sex.*

"We just did."

"Well I'm into you, Darrock."

"It'd be a real turn on if you'd take some of this in." No idea... Darrock was always looking for someone who could appreciate his bizarre notions of entertainment. He threw another novel in John's direction. "Here. Start it, and we'll talk."

John flipped through a few pages. "It makes my eyes swim."

"Dr. Seuss would make your eyes swim."

There was no point in continuing. John wouldn't leave him alone until he closed up the book and opened up his pants. Sometimes it wasn't a bad thing but sometimes he just wanted to read. Darrock turned on a very loud box fan. "You'd think someone who was tortured for being different would have sympathy for someone else who's different."

Darrock was as annoyed with himself for giving in to John as he was for giving in to father's intolerance. John was too "of the people" in too many ways. He couldn't appreciate Darrock's brain as much as his cock. He didn't want to take the time, which furthered the insult. But Darrock had waited too long for this. He wasn't going to walk away. Just it seemed nothing could convince John they had a thing goin' on unless the thing was actually goin' on. Sometimes he wished Star would have offered up himself instead of this leftover protégé.

Slowly he laid down over John's waiting heart, pushing him down on the bed, pasting his lips with a deep kiss, letting his lips slide over John's, letting his tongue relax inside of John's mouth, and just for awhile forget that he was stuck between the two extremes of closeted love and closeted hate. He behaved like one of those guys at the Cartel that let everything roll off him like spilled coffee onto the floor. It was easier to do that than to drown his potentials in a life of pent up sexuality and pasty Nigerian politics.

John felt good, John would drive him crazy, John cared about him in a way no one else ever had, and at this point, so delicious, so near the edge, that took precedence. Sometimes Faulkner would go through his mind, or whatever it was he put aside to satisfy John's momentary craving. Sometimes he felt guilty, feeling his flesh so spoiled after his own father's was ravaged half a world away. Who could say which world was more real?

Darrock tried hard to keep quiet under the whirr of the box fan. It was like walking through a wet wonderland, still so new, still scary; John seemed almost tribal sometimes, with his proletarian tastes and sexual appetite. He was one of the masses, perhaps, in a way, Darrock's connection to the popular world, and a way for him to determine if he wanted to join. No one was sure what would happen if there was that dreaded paternal knock on the door – the same knock that took his father away that night in Lagos. So far, so good.

Arielle connected through this molasses to get to Darrock's father. *Talk to my African Studies folks*, she said.

I have nothing good to say.

That's why need to hear it. Too many of them think Africa is like Los Angeles.

Dad stripped off his shirt for a quick lesson in African reality. *Don't complain about America. You got TV, CD, movies, cars, three meals a day, and you call yourselves poor. You call yourself oppressed. It's so easy, in so many worlds, to overlook what we do to our own.* Yet he would disown his own son if he knew Darrock loved another man.

Some felt betrayed after a lifetime of pretending the grass was always greener and that all the faults of that continent were on account of South Africa. But they'd never actually seen Nigeria face to face.

"I doubt it was ever Alex Haley's paradise," Arielle agreed. "But it's something to work for."

Fawn Bryan was making an annoying case for conservatism. For the "I told you so" right wing, and for the folks who argued against reparations.

Mack and I often talked about freeing the slaves. We know that just a quirk of fate made the difference for us. Just a white girl falling into the river when he happened to be walking by. Just a white man who for once believed he was saving her instead of attacking her.

You never realize how much work it is to run a farm until you have your own. We need the help to survive. We couldn't afford to hire hands, as they do in the north, I hear. And they need our protection. We're still not free as Negroes in this world. We still can't go where we want to go. We still can't be part of their world. And we don't really want to be. But as it stands, we're on our own for the rest of our lives. The names we must be called by black and white, I'd hate to hear.

Sometimes I do wonder if it would have been better to keep things as they were. But then I think, now I can read, now I can enjoy having a husband and family. I can promise our own slaves they will never be sold or their families split up. In Virginia such liberties aren't meant for everyone.

I suppose we will always be cast out. No one will forgive us, and no one will ever understand.

Once we talked about letting them go, and working together on the farm as equals. Mack says he doesn't trust anybody that much. We laughed. We just enjoy our good fortune. Praise God.

"Fortune!" The radio talk show host who lived across from John Taylor was having a field day. "They laughed. Ladies and gentlemen, they *laughed*!" Slavery has nothing to do with race, it has to do with humanity, he pointed out. But only because he was a bigot. White folks called in to agree, and black folks called in to make him take it back. He logged on to the Bryan family website and picked up tidbits as fast as Arielle has typed them in, pitching out fastballs of vitriol and aiming for the head. Lancer would have edited; not Arielle.

Fawn's diary spanned a couple decades. She didn't write a lot, after all, it was hard work running the farm. She seemed gentle, awkwardly thrust into a position of authority, but not sure she deserved it and not sure it was proper of her to use it. Still, she was unwilling to share or let go. There may not have been a lot of choice. Over 150 years later it was still haunting family relationships and city politics. It was ridiculous. It was history. You can't blame me for what she did in 1850, Lancer said. It's ridiculous.

And the talk show host said the same thing.

The past chained everyone as much as the present. Star looked over all this, hunched over the computer, clicking back and forth among pages on the website. He let his mind go back to the old trunk. He held things she held, touched things she touched. If only he could ask why. He scurried back and forth through the diary looking for that answer. Wasn't sure Fawn knew it herself.

Star wasn't sure if he should call Brad or not, now that they were legal adversaries. Still in blackmail mode, he could probably get Brad to drop the suit with a declaration of love.

"Why're *you* in on it?" Scrap was curious, looking over the letter that Star handled like a hot potato.

152

"Because I have more money than you. He said I didn't do anything to stop your ass from kicking his."

"You were smart to stay out of the way," Scrap laughed a bit.

"It doesn't matter. The truth won't make a difference, it's whoever's lawyer can twist what happened."

"Nobody was there."

"*You* were, that was enough," Star said.

"Can't you lawyer your way out of this?" They were on those same steps where Brad's insult took its untimely injury – Star curled about three steps up leaning on the rail, Hendrick hovering over him a bit higher.

"I do wills, estates, that kinda crap. Not sure I can dig myself out of a hole."

"What happens if you lose?"

"I dunno. But my dad put you in jail, so he owes me one."

"Your dad put a bunch of high school kids in mint green." Scrap still couldn't believe Lancer sold out the county ball teams.

"He owes me two." Star got up from the steps, leaving Scrap to languish on his own. "Dammit!"

"What?"

"Just one more piece of shit thing I have to worry about."

"It would never have happened if he hadn't come over," Hendrick put in.

"It would never have happened if you'd controlled your temper!" Star said, losing his.

"Whose side are you on, man?"

"Mine, boy." Star swirled around the other side of the steps, looked his man deep in the eyes. "This ain't gonna take a dollar out of your pocket either way, and you know it. You ain't got the dollar to contribute."

"Show me the money!" Hendrick felt righteously debased.

"You have no idea how much I do for you!" Star said. "None!"

"I thought that's what love was about."

"So did I," said Star. "But even John Taylor got me a fucking giraffe."

"That's because you were fucking John Taylor and cheating on me."

"I cheated on you because you were in jail as a precursor to putting me into this predicament."

"And you said you're no good at lawyering." Scrap laughed a bit. "We've done some shit to each other, haven't we?" He got up with a grunt. "I suppose we ain't finished."

"We screwed Brad up for life," Star reminded him. "That ain't cheap."

Hendrick took umbrage. "I just did six months in Roachville!"

"Brad's not after justice. He's after revenge."

"He's after your cock."

"I tried to be friends," Star said.

"You shouldn't have. It's different if you know he don't want you no more, but you knew every minute he was plotting to get you back. And you still went over and over and over. I didn't know what else to do. It was go after him or after you."

Star turned around and felt like knocking Scrap to the ground, using one of those secret basketball moves—that everyone sees but the ref— to save the score. He began to wonder. The public appearances, the gay basketball duo, the demands on his family, just for show? Where now was the light that shone his face? He searched in vain, as one looks for a holy grail that's been kidnapped by the infidels. That was the light that kept him coming back. If that bulb went out Star would be very hard pressed to go to TJ Maxx for a new one.

Well, he'd get over it eventually. They'd fought before. And the suit was on, whether Scrap stuck it out or not.

"I could fuck Brad three or four times, and he'd drop it." Ka-ching! Someone just installed a 200 watt light bulb in *his* head and yanked his chain.

"You wish." Hendrick was joshing, but scared just hearing it.

"If it saves me a quarter million that I don't have, it's a pretty judicious couple of fucks."

"You wouldn't really." Scrapdawg wasn't looking his master in the eye, and his tail stopped wagging.

"No, not really."

Yes, really.

Star shared a receptionist with other lawyers, so it was easy enough to close the door and say take a message. Being unavailable for four hours

154

could cost him some money, but substantially less than a quarter million, substantially less then the time it would take to defend himself against a case of battery and blackmail.

The drive out to Wildwood seemed interminable. He didn't even call Brad, he figured Brad wasn't going anywhere. Besides, if he was the suit would have much less merit. Many guys talked about the "drive of shame" *after* an unsavory sexual counter, but never *before*. Never on the way. He wasn't even sure he'd be able to perform.

Well, it *was* Brad. He still wanted Brad, it was a good excuse, and dammit if he hadn't let Hendrick into his life so quickly after, it wouldn't matter to anyone who he slept with. Except Brad. Except John. Three on a string. It was a great recipe for athleticism and self-loathing.

This wasn't sex. This was saving his ass, which he wouldn't have had to do if Hendrick... A tight black muscle shirt let out the big knobs of his shoulders, the cut of his biceps; Star walked out of his car on a mission. A couple missions. Basically, enough sex to get Brad to sign out of the suit. Somewhere along the line, sex stopped being fun.

You have to move in first.

On the cusp of orgasm, hands tied, camera at the ready, sign the paper. Take over his mind when he can't think. Whatever it took. All's fair in love and war, and this being both, he couldn't go wrong.

Brad spent a lot of the day hanging around, computer, TV, eat, repeat. Computer was a window into pornography, typing this and that fetish into Google, "hot blond jock," "sucked his cock," "dirty teen feet," he wasn't finding quite what he wanted until the doorbell rang and he threw his body in to "walk" mode to answer the door. Odd, because people didn't just "show up" in Wildwood like they more often did in the city. Not so odd, because the back of his mind expected this.

Star, left hand over his head on the door frame, right hand in his pocket, head cocked downward, cock headed upward, tongue crossing deftly over his lower lip in time with the opening door. Why waste time?

Brad was different, after John, after Scrap, after... far too many men, he just seemed delicate and weak after the taller and the bigger. But this wasn't about that. It wasn't about comparing partners, it wasn't even about "what the fuck is wrong with you that you're using three guys and don't

155

really like any of them?" This was about... well it had to be about love. Sex wasn't going to cut it. Brad had to be convinced that Star was coming back, not just coming and going.

But sometimes, just sometimes, love and sex can blur in the eyes of a person who's using one in place of the other. Star ripped off the buttons from Brad's shirt. Sue me for 'em. He whirled Brad around and pulled it off with one hand, just like he'd done with a basketball on the Billikens' home court so many years ago.

Brad looked back in confusion and wonderment.

"I thought you wanted this," Star said smugly. He dropped Brad's shirt to the floor, it lay like a dead seagull on a beach in Portland.

It was the smug that got Brad moving, turned him on, triggered something of an attitude Star had years ago, when we was 25, when he owned the world rather than carried it, they both remembered, both forgot, *how could we let this go?*

Why did you?

I don't know. But I've missed it since you left.

I missed it longer.

The moans, the passion, the biology taking over humanity, looking at Brad so turned on and having spent so many nights wanting that, needing that, not having that, and now, suddenly, to be manipulated into it...

Still it felt good, it felt different, the more delicate touch, five different fingers passing over an insatiable male quest for variety, the memories of the past, the savings galore! Star barrels down the interstate of plummeting self esteem at full throttle until he sees the backup far too late to stop comfortably, and screeching to a halt screams out "oh Jesus" as everything in the back seat crashes to the floor while the passenger in the front just about rams his head into the dashboard.

Brad was stunned; he was taking that same road and saw no logjam up ahead. He was ready for the best ride of his life; he'd gotten his man back even though he had to stoop lower than a rat in a sewer to do it.

Star felt those rats running over his legs, his back, his arms, sticking their whiskers in his mouth. "Man, I can't."

"Oh yeah you can."

"Oh fuck you." He was disgusted with himself, but it was easier to take it out on Brad. "I'm not gonna betray him for you. I'm not gonna betray myself for you."

"Star, I love you."

"Enough to dangle a court case over my head? I can't love you. Not under these circumstances." It was bad enough he might see part of his own face in the rear view mirror.

He put his clothes back on, jeans snug over his legs, black shirt hugging his torso. Brad didn't deserve what was in there.

"Star. It is so wrong to leave a man all horned up like this."

At a door he knew he would never cross again. To him, finally, Brad looked pathetic. And criminal. The love switch had finally shorted out. He shrugged, and started to pull the door closed, this time for good. "So sue me."

CHAPTER 18

John became fascinated with fluid dripping off the male body. Sweat dripping down eyes, nose, arms, neck, droplets like beauty marks calling attention to the already beautiful. He watched Darrock in the shower whenever he could. He fantasized about cum and drool dripping down his face, but was scared to ask D to act on it.

Physicality was difficult as neither of them often had a place to themselves. While Darrock's father wouldn't allow him to entertain a woman with the door closed, he didn't really think twice about him shutting it with a man in the room. In fact, he was hardly interested, because in his world homosexuality was the province of other people and would never disgrace his own family. It didn't happen in Nigeria, or in the Little Nigeria that was their apartment in the West End.

John lived in a marginally more tolerant universe than Darrock, and was always throwing it in his face. His parents knew he was emotionally unstable but let him express himself as long as he didn't do it criminally. He didn't understand the need for silence, the need for covering tracks, the need to say no if there was a chance someone would find out. *This must be why I never bothered before,* Darrock thought to himself.

Father was getting suspicious, because two young guys shouldn't be that quiet.

Radio, Darrock said. Mozart. Rock music. Something to cover it up.

It's all white dude music.

We can make our own black dude music.

Darrock on the floor propped up against the corner of the room, head lolling to the side, arms bulging out of his yellow muscle shirt. John, always horny, always wanting, didn't understand that in his mind sex was a substitute for security. He pictured Darrock in one of those Nike ads on TV, droplets of sweat flipping off his head as he swirled his dreds and bent down to take off a shoe.

He bent down to take off the shoe himself.

"What are you doing?"

Don't go anywhere. One shoe, then the other, then the socks. *That is so much better.*

Than what?

Than anything?

He dug his hands under the yellow cotton, pulled it up slowly, Darrock, resigned, raises his arms while warm fingers caress his sides on the way up, he flops 'em back down, leans lopsided and looks up, eyes wide under falling dreds. He knows what this does to John. He knows what it does to most people. He's managed to infuse more sexuality into what looks he had than most who were more blessed could ever hope to achieve.

"Let me try it," John stands back and looks at his prize.

"What?"

"You know. The face thing. I wanna see what it looks like on you."

"You're a perv, John.'

"I am not, bro. I just wanna see it on you. Ain't you seen pictures on the net?"

"Actually, no."

"Oh, I have. It's hot." John felt older, suddenly, and more important. He had a fetish.

Darrock saw an unusual shadow creep under the door. He ignored it, but it worried him. At the moment he felt he owed John this chance more than he owed it to both of them to look out for their safety. A knock on the door could begin his torture.

The shadow of his father, scars on his back pressing up against the door, listens with growing anger as John watches semen drip down Darrock's face. He'd seen it with Star but it never got his brain going like it did now. Better than water, better than sweat; here you know something happened. The results are in.

"That's cool shit!"

"Shhh!"

"Oh, what? Darrock, dis bro is tired of having to be quiet."

"Get this offa me before he sees it."

"He ain't gonna come in." John took his eyes close to Darrock's face,

159

then he moved back for an overall picture. "You look soooo good. It's like you're mine. It's like I love you. You know that?"

"Yeah I do." Darrock was getting scared, and he wasn't sure why. They'd played around before with father in the living room watching TV. Perhaps he was getting too suspicious.

"Well here." John threw the yellow shirt over Darrock's head. "Wipe it off."

"This's my favorite shirt! Get a towel," he whispered.

"How can I do that?"

"Just go get one. You don't have to make it a worldwide broadcast. You shoulda got one before we started."

John put on his jeans, put on his shirt, left his feet bare. Darrock, shirtless, wiping under his eyes with an index finger, tracing over the top of the cheekbone and the side of his nose, getting a big wad hanging over his upper lip. He exhales heavily and shakes his head. "John," he says. Part love, part exasperation.

The door opens to the figure of Mr. Ndlele filling in the frame like a dark cloud of evil in a Tolkien novel. John's euphoria doused by an open flame and all his thought processes coming to a halt. Father's eyes are burning him down. Darrock instinctively turns to the wall, but it's too late to hide what's going on. John would have been proud, a new layer of sweat was forming quickly all over his body. No running, no lifting, just sitting in what suddenly became a very hot room, John's issue on his face turning to tears; he knew what would happen, it was only a matter of time before the same torture that wracked his father would fall upon him in this free land.

In Nigeria differences of opinion were not settled by quiet negotiation – those in power settled it by inflicting pain and prison on those out. Darrock for awhile believed in this. He deserved it. Not for being gay, but for disappointing his father. His accomplishments, education, and classicism were swept away in one swing of his father's hand; across the side of the head above his eye, across his mouth, his father beat and bloodied him with Darrock's silent acquiescence that he had that right; an unseen corner of a Lagos prison in St. Louis' Central West End. His father had come here to practice his own beliefs, and anyone else's be damned.

Darrock could only take so much. Apparently this was never going to stop, and his endurance was failing him. But he hadn't grown those thick muscular arms for nothing. They needed to be more useful than just to make eyes pop at the coffee cartel. Finally he acted, before it was too late, to save his own soul and his own life. Family or no, respect or no, this was self preservation; finally, he became the Israel that's just had enough of a world opposed.

As his father pulled back for another blow Darrock finally summoned the courage to move out of the way. The unexpected, dad's strong hand grabbed his forearm and snapped it back. It hurt, but it didn't break. Dad wasn't letting go. Darrock did the seemingly impossible; he took his free hand to whack his father across the face, a knuckle catching just under an eye, stunning him so that for a brief moment he let up on Darrock's arm. Now D could break free. He pushed his adversary to the ground and hurled a chair at him with all the brute force he could muster.

"I've been good to you," he cried. "I didn't deserve this."

"If I ever see you again, I'll kill you." The phobia was deep, imported from the old country.

"You don't have to bother," Darrock responded, heaving, crying, bleeding. "I am no longer your son. To think I ever felt sorry for you. Or I ever believed you came here looking for freedom." It was hard for him to talk. His mouth was bloodied, but he had to say it, had to talk to this man one final time. Maybe it was the fear of this pain, of knowing that finding any kind of love would lead to the ultimate disengagement with his family; maybe it was this, rather than his love of Faulkner, that kept him so aloof for so long.

Not much time to decide: what to take with him? The only think that would buy him time would be killing the man that had so recently planned to kill him. Darrock; breathing hard, put a hand to his face, felt his own blood mixed with his recent escapade with John. Quick look in a mirror. And his father, a wounded monster stirring from the depths of hatred.

He'd had enough of tolerating bigotry because *someone was raised that way*. Darrock at least had to buy time to put on a pair of shoes. He bent down quickly and laid more blows on the man on the floor, no longer his father but just the adversary, just another monster out of Beowulf, Darrock landed blows enough to keep him lying in the corner, to answer blood with

161

blood and hate with hate. Darrock got a few things together and left.

This was not a time to struggle, to panic, to cry; it was a time to move. There would be time to think later. All he could think about was Coffee Cartel, Star Bryan, John Taylor. Fuck John Taylor. He got me into this. Where is he anyway? Whoaaaa! Where was he? In this state John's image morphed with his father's, both standing over him for very different reasons.

Someone at the Cartel could take him to the hospital down the street. Or he could walk himself. He just didn't want to be alone. Somebody might recognize him.

Dude, what happened?

Can you take me to emergency?

What happened?

Please. I know it's only 3 blocks.

I'll get my car.

At the hospital, they ask for insurance. Darrock has a card. His father's policy.

Darrock waiting in the emergency room alone. They'd given him some pain pills and bandages to stop the bleeding as best they could, and left him there. It was an emergency, but one that could wait. He flipped through his cell phone trying to figure out who to call. Who might care, and who might be a friend "in case." John's number showed up. Where was he? John disappeared and Darrock didn't even see it. Oh, here's some guy from the Cartel who wants to fuck me. Yeah, not now. People who want to fuck you find medical emergencies selfish.

Star Bryan. He's a lawyer. He knows John. He's responsible.

He's at the office. He's pissed at himself, pissed at Brad, and charging a client out the wazoo for marginally good advice, trying to focus. He couldn't think of anything else other than Brad. Kissing Brad, touching Brad, leaving Brad, still wanting Brad in his life through all this and then when he finally took the opportunity to have Brad he has to walk away at a much higher cost than perhaps had he never gone in the first place. The call from the Barnes-Jewish emergency was a welcome relief. He told his client to come back, and said he was obliged to take care of something personal. He headed down 40 to Kingshighway, around the curve of the exit ramp and into the morass that serves as a parking megalopolis for Barnes-Jewish.

Emergency room parking might have been easier, but it didn't dawn on him until he was meandering around the garage. Star was so distracted; Darrock's distraction was welcome in that someone had it worse than he did. He was sure the parking garage, charging for time, made most of its money while people were looking for an empty spot, or looking for their car on the way back.

He hadn't seen Darrock in awhile, and John was too bound up in his new love to give Star much of a narrative. He just remembered the hair, the muscle, the intelligence, now seeing him mangled by his father's hand made Star wonder about his own growing up, and if the same thing had been done to his heart.

Not now.

Not the time for self pity or self reflection. Darrock was in an exam room on a table with a small bag next to him. A couple books, a cell phone and charger, a couple personal items, and a clean pair of underwear. Not a lot – all he could grab before his father would regain consciousness and start marauding again. All he had in the whole world. He was staring into a page of FitzGerald but not reading.

"Darrock..."

"I didn't mean to call you, honest. I didn't know who else to call." He brought Star up to speed. "I don't still have splooge on my face, do I?"

Star looked over the blood, bandages and bruises. "Yeah, he does like that, doesn't he?" A short pause. "Huh. You do."

"I don't know where to go."

"Where's John?"

"I don't know, bro."

"He knows you're here."

"I don't know what he knows. My dad appeared in the doorway and I looked to the wall. I don't know what happened to John. John shoulda stood up for me. Stood up with me. He put me in this position. He made me face my father with cum dripping down my nose and he walked away."

"John's 17. He was scared."

"I'm 19. I'm scared. But I fought."

A techie came in to take a couple readings. "Hey, you're that basketball guy, aren't you?"

"I don't feel like it today. Yeah. You play?"

"A little."

"You should help."

"I wish I could."

So do I. "Is he gonna live?"

"He's been beat up pretty bad, but he'll be ok. He's a strong boy. But yeah, I'd take him somewhere to rest up."

A couch at the Coffee Cartel.

Darrock showed Star his bag. "This is all I have in the world."

"We can go back together and move you out civil-like. I'm a lawyer don't forget."

"Yeah, but my dad's a Nigerian. They don't pay attention to laws. They bring that shit over here. Besides I don't wanna go back through that door. I don't know if I can."

"You have nothing."

"Basically. Don't have John, either."

"He'll be around."

"Sometimes when the stakes are down you learn who loves you and who loves themselves. These stakes were grilled, burned, and eaten by a dawg." Darrock began to cry, quietly. "Fuck I don't wanna do this."

"It's okay, man."

"No, it isn't. I got no time for it. I gotta start a life over on the street. You tell me."

"I'll find a place for you."

"Tonight?"

"Tonight you stay with me." Bad idea. Really baaaad idea. No choice.

It wasn't a horrible idea. Star had three floors and things were pretty well picked up, so if Darrock needed a place to rest in quiet, that would be the best thing.

"No friends?"

"I'm the Faulkner geek. All my friends are livin' with their mamas who don't want some beat up Nigerian taking up a hospital bed."

Most likely right. The place for Darrock was home with dad.

For a brief moment, Star forgot he lived with Scrap.

A key in the door, an accusing brow reminds him. "Where you been?"

"Oh shut up."

"Who dat?"

"Scrap can you just not talk to me?"

"Look, if you bring in some beat up nigga you can at least have the dee-cen-cee to tell me who he bee."

"It's John Taylor's boyfriend."

"Great."

"Be glad he has one, it keeps me out of his ass."

"Star you know just how to say the right thing."

"Scrap, right now the right thing for you to say is no-thing. This kid's got the shit beat out of him by his father and all you can think about is petty jealous faggot bullshit."

Short silence. "Oh."

"Darrock don't you have any-"

"They're in Lagos. My family does not know I exist."

"Your dad doesn't send money home?"

"They're the ones that turned him in."

"I don't know what to do." At least he shut up Hendrick, and that was in itself a notable accomplishment.

Broken, bloody, and bandaged, Star put his arm around Darrock and led him up to a second bedroom. Darrock hugged him tightly. "You go to sleep and we'll figure something out," Star said quietly.

"You might be the only one left who cares."

"No. I'm sure I'm not."

"I don't wanna see him." It wasn't the same Darrock that was so sure of himself at the Cartel. It wasn't the same Star, either, who corralled him to dump off an unworkable love interest.

"Go to sleep."

"You've been a motherfucking barrel of love today." Scrap's pissed, and more to the point, scared.

"Been a hard day."

"So you keep me out of it."

"Because I don't want to deal with your issues on top of everything else."

"My issues? What are my issues?"

"Whatever you decide they are at the time," Star said. "If I ever have dealings with another man you have issues. Between this and Brad I just don't-"

"What about Brad?" Issue primo, now that it was brought up.

"I talked to Brad today. About the suit."

"Did you see Brad?" Hendrick's ready to pounce.

"No, I said I talked to him."

"I called your office and they said you weren't there."

"So obviously I was out fucking Brad." What better a way to deny the truth than by simply reporting it.

"You said it."

Star tried to calm down, but it seemed useless to keep a cool head while the nukes were curving towards his culture and history. "I need to deal with this problem," he said, pausing for effect every couple words, "without you... accusing me... of being a cheat. For once."

"Well it's a perfect excuse to bring John Taylor back under my roof."

Star took a pause. Half his face screwed up and lights from the lamps reflected the metal that adorned his face. "*My* roof?"

"Our roof."

"Scrap, you live here by the grace of... well... me. It's whoever's roof I deem it to be."

"How long is beatup boy gonna be here?"

Darrock slept peacefully, or dozed off in lucid dreams; it felt good to do nothing and not be hit. "Until I figure out what to do with him."

Star picked up his land line and took a swipe at John's number. Thankfully John was home. "I need you to come over here."

"Well, okay." That was an offer he wouldn't turn down.

"Now."

"Is he there?"

"There's a lot of hees here," said Star. "Pick a he, and he's here. This

166

ain't a matter in which you have a choice."

"Why not?" John sounded more frightened, like he was going to get in trouble with someone and he wasn't sure who. The more men, the more trouble.

"Because I said so. If you're the man I know John Taylor to be, you'll come join this party." He hated dipping into "motivation," but it seemed necessary. He'd have to remember that line for the league.

CHAPTER 19

John came up the walk, not used to this. Usually he'd get a kiss, a roll in bed, kind words. Star didn't seem mad, but he could tell Star was keeping Scrap in a quiet corner by brute willpower, like a tank terrorizing a small town that recently tried to overthrow the government. Hendrick glared at John with all the loathing he could to take away every vestige of Star's welcome.

"You need to see Darrock."

"Man, I didn't mean to run away."

"You're all he has, John."

"I saw his father, and... and... and I never seen anything like that before. So I got in my car and I went home. And I've been wondering ever since."

John hadn't been to Star's place in awhile, not since they ended what never was and never had hope to be, and memories came flooding back as he walked up to the second floor, past the giraffe—*why did I drop so much money on this fucking giraffe?* Under the cold lights of Hendrick's icy stare. "This isn't about you so leave him alone," Star admonished.

"It's always about him," said Hendrick. "What a perfect excuse to bring over everyone I don't want to see." Hendrick took every opportunity to make everything about him, all the time.

"This is about John seeing the man he loves after he got the crap beat out of him by his father. You wanna go land a couple more punches so we can send your ass back to Rashad? Go upstairs, Scrap."

"There's nothin' to do upstairs."

"Fawn Bryan's diary is upstairs. Read it."

Star gave Hendrick a look that Scrap took as "go upstairs." It really meant *I'm over you.* Something clicked at a time it wasn't supposed to. Something that told Star that this damn dawg was responsible for most everything that went wrong in his life. He had to put it to the curb or put it down.

168

But not now. It was a horrible time to come to that realization, particularly with two legal teenagers in the next room. Just wrap the damn thing up, this isn't useful for anyone.

Darrock was laying down as some spirit from Ghana that had been consigned to the spare room watched over him. He felt best just laying with his eyes closed, feeling stitches settle in, feeling his body try to slowly repair itself, He heard his name coming out from John's throat and felt the smell and aura close by that was definitely John Taylor. Everything tensed up, almost as if he was ready for another beating.

"Darrock."

Darrock's eyes opened. He wasn't in the mood. He looked up at the face that once brought so much comfort but that at this point just regurgitated a recent horror. "Go 'way."

Star standing at the back, at the doorway, watching, feeling sorry for John. It seemed like a private moment, so he left the room. Not upstairs with Hendrick. To his own room, to think, to counsel whichever boy survived the meeting.

"Darrock! I love you. I'm sorry."

"Where were you?"

"I got scared, and I ran away. You're dad's a big boy."

"You're a big boy, John. You're tall and you got some muscles on you. I know cuz I've seen 'em all. You could'a fought back with me. Maybe saved me from this."

"You don't look so good."

"That doesn't matter. My father tried to kill me. All you could think about was your own skin."

"I didn't mean to run. I just did." He reached out, tried to touch Darrock's face. He was always more peaceful when he could touch Darrock.

Darrock knew, and denied. "Don't. It hurts."

"What can I make better?"

"Nothing. Go away. That'll make everything better."

John felt the words just like Darrock felt the fists.

"You let this happen to me. Now you come and say you love me. Now that it's easy."

John's voice cracked, and it got louder. "Man, I didn't know what to do!

169

Don't turn it into that I don't love you!"

"You turned it into that. If you can't stick through the hard stuff then don't come around for the romance afterwards."

"Where are you going to go?"

Darrock hadn't thought much past Star's guest bed. But there was too much tension here. Scrap was impossible, John was whiny, Star was saving the world at the cost of himself.

"Are those stupid kids gone yet?" Hendrick shouting from behind the pages of Fawn Bryan. That slavery thing was aggravating him. It was very hard for anyone to read Fawn Bryan without getting aggravated. Particularly anyone in the Bryan family, who had profited from her ever since.

"Shut up, Scrap!" Star had to calm down and think. Scrap wouldn't be easy to get rid of. Maybe he'd get over this feeling that Scrap had to go. But hopefully not. It'd been building, like high blood pressure before a stroke. When it struck it would be impossible to cure or control. And maybe impossible to survive, given Scrap's tendency towards violence.

Back to Darrock. Going through the same problem. He could soften his heart, but this was too important. A portent that if John would run now, he would run later.

People don't change just because they promise to. His father's response was expected.

This?

"Go home, John."

"Darrock, I came to take care of you."

"If I need you I'll call you."

"I need you!"

"Yeah, ya do. I need to sleep. I'll call you if I feel like it."

"What if you don't feel like it."

"Then I won't call you."

"You ain't breakin' up with me, are you?""

It didn't take a genius. "Yeah, I am. You broke up with me when you left me to face the mob. You left me to take all the blows. What for, bro? You were kissin' me as much as much as I was kissin' you." Anger made it hurt. "I can't talk any more now."

John reached to Darrock's hand, which Darrock jerked away. It hurt, in so many ways. John was the only one he'd ever touched like that. Now he had to walk away from it. Maybe it was okay. Life with John was all or nothing, and all was often too much.

"So you're gonna end it just like that?"

"Yeah." Darrock whispered, and closed his eyes.

"I love you. Dammit are you listening to me?" John whirred up and just about beat his head against the door; life without a man would be like living at the bottom of a well.

Darrock couldn't scream nearly as loud. He did his best. "Star! Make him go home! What'd you bring him for to begin with?"

John stormed out of the room, slammed the door. Forgot it wasn't his door to slam. It hurt Darrock all over. He hugged Star, the boy that was still so much a part of John was crying for help. He pulled Star so close as if the spirit of Darrock was locked inside. And Star, for his response, got hard.

John backed away horrified. "What did you bring me into your life for?" His head shook; all of him shook. "To fuck it up? You did good!" John flew down the steps like the athlete he was. Another door slammed. And from the third floor Star heard footsteps. He positioned himself in the doorway.

"I didn't say you could come down here."

Hendrick: "You got one fucked up family, you know that?"

"Get upstairs. I don't want to deal with you now."

"I fucking live here!"

"At my fucking discretion! And right now you fucking *live* on the third floor." He went up the few steps to meet Scrap and gave him a soft kiss on the lips. "Please."

Scrap's voice caught Star near the bottom of the steps. "Go ahead. Fuck the broken boy."

"I don't have to fuck *you*," Star looked straight ahead. "You're already fucked." Another door slammed. Darrock, over the edge already, cries in a strange room. Star opens the door slowly, goes in.

"I barely know you," Darrock says. "How come you're the only person in my life?"

Star took Darrock's hand. Held it tight. "We're gonna fix you up and figure out what to do. I'm a laywer. We'll take care of your father, and we'll take care of you."

"You gonna put him in jail?"

"Do you want to?"

"Fuck yes I want to! And John too."

"You can't put John in jail."

Darrock didn't like crying. He remembered back to the day of meeting at the Coffee Cartel. He was cool. The black guy who reads Faulkner. The dreds. The whole African thing. That boy was dead. Now his eyes were muddy pools of water. "Why did he leave me like that? Where we come from where he comes from in Lagos when you disagree with someone you pound them into the ground and kill them that's what he did to me that's what the rulers did to him do you know about that? What they did to him? He's carried that rage his whole life. He never had a chance to let it out. But now it came out all over me. John ran away and I don't know what to do. And if I stay here he's gonna kill me."

"Darrock. Your father won't find you here."

"Hendrick. He's gonna kill me. I see it. I can't stay here."

"Nothing's going to happen to you."

"I can't handle it anymore."

"You're a cool boy, Darrock. You'll get it back. You'll beat this."

Footsteps down the stairs, slowly, no one hears until a shadow comes to the door. Scrap is too big not to cast a shadow. He sees two hands holding each other. Sees Star's other hand lightly on Darrock's dreds, threading the hair through his fingers like he's twisting a rope. Hears Star chuckle just a bit. "I know what you are. And you're gonna be that man again. I'll make sure of it."

Star turned around and saw the fire Darrock was so afraid of. *The guy's a maniac. He's going to kill someone; either me or someone I love. Well, O'Ryan was safe, at least. The rest?*

It had to be a clean break.

And fast. This was getting ridiculous. Here Hendrick could support someone in dire need but chose instead to turn it into another round of "you don't love me." Or maybe he couldn't choose. Star couldn't either. His heart and mind collapsed around the truth like a popped balloon at the

Macy's Thanksgiving Day parade.

"Dawg does this look like the third floor?"

Scrap approached the two of them, Darrock tensed up so much he cried out in pain. Star blocked him more like a football player than basketball player. "This is one end zone you ain't crossing into." He said it before he even thought over the delivery. "Go away, Scrap. Just get out of my life."

There was a confused silence, as if Star didn't actually say what he said. As if it had come out of the mouth of a spirit. Maybe the one by the window. Everyone waited for the words to drop like so much confetti, flitting quietly to the ground in a ticker tape parade with the sound turned down.

"Huh?"

Star calmed down, now that he realized he'd finally done it. It felt so much better already. "Go away."

"I don't have anywhere to go. Star, I love you."

"Everybody loves me. Fat lot of good it's done me."

"You're just kicking me out so you can have at it with *boy* here."

"See? But you're out of my life. So suddenly who I have or don't have sex with isn't your concern. Get my sex life out of your head. You aren't part of it anymore. You can't kill every man I look at for the rest of my life."

"No, but I can kill a couple."

CHAPTER 20

It was a turning point for Star that he needed desperately since he left Brad: to be single. It felt good, like he'd passed his own 14th amendment.

"Where am I supposed to go?" Hendrick wasn't just going to up and leave without drama. "I'm gonna wind up out on the streets."

"It would serve you right. That's what you want for Darrock. I'm still bigger than you, if it comes to that. Six-five beats six-two."

"Maybe," Hendrick replied. "But you don't have the guts to use your size."

"Maybe not," Star admitted. "But you scare me. And you scare everyone I know." It became easier to tell the truth by the second. "I took you in and now I'm afraid to live in my own place."

"I just get that way. I can't always help it."

"Fine," Star said, seeing again the panic in Scrap's face that made him want to protect the guy, but that same panic that turned Scrap so vile. "But I don't have to stand by and let it destroy everyone. Man he's dying up there and all you can think about is it bugs you that I give a shit!"

"Fawn Bryan was a bitch. She was a motherfuckin' bitch."

"What does that matter? She's been dead for 150 years."

"You and your whole family are made of the same shit. You don't give a damn for your people as long as you get your own shit. You're just like George Jefferson up in his dee-luxe apartment in the sky spittin' on us stupid niggers."

Star thought for a bit. Took inventory of his life. "Nah," he rebutted. "It's just you I don't give a shit about. And my brother. But he ain't a walking death threat."

Hendrick started to tear up. He wasn't sure if it was losing Star or facing a life out on the streets, having to start all over again as he just had to start all over so recently, again with no one to care, going from being a semi-celeb as Star's boyfriend to a faceless ex con scraping off dishes.

And more.

"Man, I'm positive. Who's gonna take care of that?"

It was the sad beauty of gay relationships. Thanks to a legal system that didn't recognize them, no one owed anybody anything. Star could have possibly afforded to set up Hendrick. That would just give him a chance to plan revenge. On Brad, on John, on Darrock. On the entire Bryan family because of Fawn.

"How kind of her to release her slaves, upon her death, after so many years of keeping them in bondage."

Star thought hard. His rescue personality was kicking in. He could save someone. A good looking strong young guy that he loved. He could save – nope he'd tried that. "If I stay in your life we'll be right back to this. And I'll be scared again. I am too big a boy to be runnin' scared of some punk like you."

"I love you, Star. Don't that mean anything to you?"

"I love you too. That's the tragedy of the whole thing."

"Well you go up there and take good care of Darrock. That's what you want." A lot of looking, searching, Star felt his heart harden like Pharaoh ordering the Israelites to make their own bricks. He'd been pushed too far, too hard, and too much. He looked deep into Hendrick's eyes for the love he felt, looking to see if in any corner of his face anything still mattered.

"Sorry, I was wrong. I don't love you. You kicked it out of me."

Hendrick's eyes turned from hope to despair. The light in his face, in his life, flickered for the final time and went out. He turned away.

"I don't want to hear of you coming around anyone I know. Or you'll be paying your friend Rashad a very long visit."

Fawn Bryan was not a literary master, but she could spin a good tale. She had a chance to live with her husband without the constant fear of one of them being sold. She let her servants have the same peace of mind. She defended her decision on the grounds that she needed everyone to work on the farm. That she could make sure they didn't fall into worse hands. That she wasn't wealthy, at least at first. That it was closer to freedom than they could rightfully expect. And a better life than living in a hovel on the Master Bryan's plantation. No one ever tried to escape, or at least she never addressed it.

The manuscript was authenticated. It could have been written in Virginia in the 1830s and 40s. It wasn't something somebody penned in 1950 as fiction.

Lancer knew the family ancestry. Back to Fawn and Mack. More Fawn; Mack was a personality in their lives, but he didn't live and breathe like she did. Their marriage precarious until given their freedom, Fawn loved her husband deeply yet hesitantly. Who knew when someone younger, prettier, lighter, would take her place and they'd be separated forever? She cooked in the "house", he tended gardens around it. The Master's daughter griped that a black man had touched her, even though he did so to save her from drowning.

It was an enormous concession on the owner's part to grant Fawn freedom along with Mack, then to give him slaves off the plantation. Quietly a system of repayment was worked out, just as quietly Master Bryan went to market to restock his losses. They always called him Master Bryan, even now. "I believe it is the will of God that you have saved my daughter, and the will of God that I reward you thusly. You aren't like the rest."

Mack had to keep quiet; his freedom was at stake. Fawn took it upon herself to get educated; Mack took it upon himself to run a farm. She taught her slaves to read so they could better manage their freedom later on. Most of them stayed on the same land as free workers for her children. They became a family of pariahs, always looking over their shoulders, always feeling isolated because of a benefit no one felt they deserved. Now Hendrick was blaming Star for it 150 years later. *You're not one of us.* It made it so much easier to close the door.

Nobody in the family was comfortable with that diary in print. Perhaps people knew of it earlier, a hundred, eighty, fifty years ago, and left it in the box. "What it does," said Arielle, again on TV, "is humanize the African-American experience. It says over and over that black and white aren't any different. We all have the capacity of good and bad. And that the line between them is sometimes hard to draw. And I think – I know – that Fawn believed slavery was evil."

"But yet she held onto her slaves," ran the interview, several radio talk shows, blogs, and people who just didn't like the Bryan family.

"She probably thought it was better to protect them than let them go

176

free and have the whites mow them down as a bunch of uppity niggers. Don't you agree? You all were afraid to let is into your bathrooms for 100 years after the war, so maybe you don't need to question the motivations of a women to whom you denied education and then put out there to perpetuate a system you started."

"What would you like us to do?"

"I'm a teacher," said Arielle. "Read! Learn! Understand! I can't go back and change it. It's history. She didn't own a whip. I think we can learn something from her right there."

"Are you saying that slavery is ok under certain circumstances?"

"Do you *think* that's what I'm saying?"

"I'm asking you if that's what you're saying."

"And I'm asking you if that's what you think I'm saying. Or are you just trying to trip me up?" She'd learned her way around an interview by now yet she was often caught off guard.

"From reading this, it seems like Fawn Bryan justified keeping her slaves."

"She did," Honesty was the best answer. "Honesty with attitude. "She justified it. If she didn't think it was wrong she wouldn't have had to justify it."

"What would you have done?"

Hard question. She wanted to say, "I just *found* the damn thing, it doesn't have to be about me!" She thought for awhile. "I might have done the same thing. I think by treating her slaves well, she thought she was doing right as best as she could. At least more right than she saw done. What example did she have to follow, except that free people would own others? The thing to remember about slavery," she said in the city of St. Louis, "is that it happened right here. Here on our steps, here in our yards, here in these United States of America. Maybe what this book tells us is that any of us are capable of it."

Lancer watched in fear, Mary in fear of his reaction to their daughter's statements. Arielle's mouth could take them straight to hell, and he'd have to pay for it. She did reasonably well. There weren't talking about it at home. He'd forbidden her to – well he'd tried to. Now she was a small national celebrity in a family that had way too much notoriety and never for anything good. Came with the turf if you were a politician.

Once again it seemed like an entire people were being pilloried for the actions of a few. Folks who wanted to pillory found just the actions they were looking for. Arielle concluded her interview. "All in all, she sounds like a very generous woman. I'm glad I had a chance to get to know her."

And that's the difference between me and Scrap, Star thought to himself. I'm house and he's field. "We're still thinkin' that way, too," he said to Arielle later. "After all these years."

She'd always wanted to go to a basketball practice with Star and watch him work with the kids. She worked with kids, instilling pride through their minds as he did through their bodies. "You can't play ball without thinking," he said.

It was just a practice tonight; teaching folks some fundamentals so they wouldn't look stupid playing a couple days later. Too many 16-year-old boys thought they knew everything about hoops; Star's main goal was to remind them otherwise.

And tonight, to keep them away from his sister. "You're too pretty to hang around with a bunch of 16 year old boys," said Star, half serious. I'll have to spend the whole night teaching them to respect you."

"And my boobs."

"Oh, they'll respect your boobs. Trust me."

Basketball had been a team effort. Star and Scrap. Much of the "lesson" was learning to understand him and his gay lover. That if you want respect for who you are you have to dole it out as well as demand it. The guys liked Scrap. Put a ball in his hands and he was cool. He smiled. He ran. His face shone and for a short while he forgot who he was. But Star could forget no longer. He had to tell the troops and make as little of it as possible. Hard to do when you built it up as love between two men that was unshakable and inviolable.

"It's not the best example to set," said Arielle. Driving on the way down there, Star had everything but basketball on his mind. He felt more like he was in a TV series. *A very special episode; their lives will never be the same again. Yours will because you'll still be on this same couch eating popcorn watching them self destruct.*

"It's a better example than sticking by someone who's going to kill off your friends one by one." *Some guys accept things.* Star thought out loud, car winding its way through an old neighborhood to an old gymnasium. *You're here one day, you're not the next.* "I know a lot of kids. One day they'll love you forever and the next they accuse you of getting too serious." It might not be that big a deal.

He gathered them around; his personal life wasn't that important other than he made it so, more important was what Scrap meant to the group. That you could have a trashy background and recover from it. Or that he was just a good time. Either way – it was over.

Admir was harder hit than many, and he and Star were better friends than most. They spoke sitting on a bleacher, Star leaning back on his elbows with his feet spread apart a couple rows down, Admir trying to imitate that with his long thin frame. Black hair with a bowl cut, long nose, freckles, brown eyes, Slavic accent. "What are you going to do now?"

"I'll be happier," Star said, without thinking.

"I thought you loved him."

"I do."

"Then why can't you work it out?"

Admir was gay, most likely, and looking for a role model. "Scrap has too many problems. I thought we could fix them but we can't. It's not something I should talk about. But I didn't do it just because I felt like it."

"We know who you like," Admir said, innocently. "On the teams, I mean. We know who you look at, and we know who he looks at."

Star felt like someone was hammering him at the back of the neck. "What's that supposed to mean?"

"Nothing. It's just something we talk about. You've made it okay, so we watch you. We watch who you watch. Then we make fun of them when you're not looking." He smiled. He liked being friends with the boss.

"Who's been watching you?"

"He has. But you do too."

"You'll miss that?" Star asked. "We're just watching you as a coach."

"Maybe. It's cool having some important guys give a damn."

"Don't find him, Admir. He's dangerous. That's why I can't have him around."

"Sucks."

Sucks.

"Are you gay?"

"I like guys," said Admir. "That's where I got this scar." He pointed to his head.

"I thought you got it in the war."

"No, that's this one." He pulled his shirt away from his side, Star tried to imagine how that felt upon receipt. Yet now he smiled.

"You're too young to have all that happen to you."

Eyes big with humor. "That's why I live in America, dummy. You don't have it so bad here so quit your bitchin'."

Star ran his hand through Admir's hair, a quick rub of the head. Admir moved a bit closer. It turned into a hug, and later a disaster.

Most people were focused on another family member.

"That your sister?" Another guy asks in disbelief. Sixteen, his shoulders a mass of muscle bulging out of a uniform with Lancer Bryan's name on it.

"That's my sister."

"Dayam!"

"She's married."

"Dayum I wish I were him."

"If you were him you'd be babysitting," Arielle said.

The players least diverted by Arielle fared the best, there was a bit more showing off than usual. Star thought he'd use it as a teaching tool. "You got to learn to play with distractions," he said.

Arielle used her advantage to try to talk a few folks into an African studies class, after school hours.

"Man, I already got basketball."

"I'll give you a brain to go with it," she promised.

Maybe.

Star drove her back to his house to pick up her car. "We do so much good for this damn city," she told him. Pause. Took a long time to sink in for both of them. "You think dad will ever notice?"

"Not sure anyone ever will."

Star had an unsettling feeling of peace. Tonight at least, would be quiet. He could rest, uneasily. He didn't think it was over; he wasn't sure what his responsibility still was to Hendrick. He'd pulled him in this far only to cast

180

him back. But the guy was sick and didn't want help. The counseling idea never took off. Too much resistance. His jealousy was uglier every day, and he was creating havoc where there was no call for it. Star would have to spend a lot of time making things right.

"I feel so strange," he said to her, staring up at a red light, as usual waiting for change. "I can't believe it's over."

"What happened? Really?"

"I thought he was gonna beat up Darrock. Again. My head snapped. And my heart snapped. And I don't want it."

"What *do* you want?"

"To be a lot less important to a lot of people than I am."

He invited her in.

Be quiet. Listen. What do you hear?

Nothing.

Exactly. Nothing. I haven't felt this in so long. You should come see Darrock.

"What would you do without a problem?"

"Die, probably," Star laughed a bit. "Darrock's different. He's not drama. He's okay. I just don't know what to do with him."

"Keep him if he's cool."

"Everyone will hate me."

"Who, a few guys who want in your pants?"

"Does it feel quieter here?" He wasn't sure if what he felt was on the inside or the out.

"There's an energy that's missing." Star's African spirits felt relieved, Arielle pointed out, and they blessed the condo. "It hasn't been love for a long time. It's been fear."

"I think I kept his ass around to piss off my father."

That's a good reason.

Darrock was sitting up on the bed, leaning against the wall, legs out in front, reading a printout of the famous diary. "I heard y'all fighting about it," he said. "You know if there's a good book around I have to read it."

"How'd you get it?"

"I went upstairs."

"You feeling okay to do that?"

"Not really. But I did it. I'm 19 you know. I'll get better fast."

Star, drawn magnetically, sat down next to Darrock, took his hand. Arielle sat on the other side. She was still impressed with her success. Sometimes. She was getting used to interviews. People asking her how she felt about slavery. People discussing slavery in a different light. Not as white and black. When the white folks gloated over black slave-owners, they did it because they knew it was wrong. They took comfort in someone else doing it. Here, in America. "All I did was type it up," she'd say.

"Do you think Fawn Bryan's a good woman?" Arielle asked.

Darrock flipped through a couple pages. "I like her."

"I can't get it out of my head, if she did the right thing or not."

"Well, if she was white, would this be the right thing?"

"But she wasn't, and she lived in a world where that mattered."

Darrock pointed to a couple of his own bruises. "I'm not sure our own people have mastered the art of understanding. It still matters."

"Our father thinks I was wrong in publishing it. He says it makes us look bad. He says it gives white folks too much ammunition."

"Why are you asking me?"

"Because you're brilliant, Darrock. You read Faulkner for fun. So what you think matters more than what anyone else does." She took his hand, looked into his eyes, the cuts and scrapes that he so newly acquired, as he looked straight ahead. Thinking of other things. "You have friends here."

Star's hand tightened on Darrock's other set of fingers. He wasn't sure what he was doing, but it just seemed impossible not to have some kind of contact with anyone he was sitting next to. Maybe he was desperately lonely. Bad boyfriends will do that to a guy.

Darrock thumbed through it. His eyes came back to life because someone was speaking to his mind. He'd spent so much time with John he'd forgotten sometimes that he could discourse intelligently. "Everything that happens in the past affects how we live now. This book is the beginning of what makes you who you are. It all started right here. Well it started on a slave ship. But they could have worked their lives away and died, and you might still have been born from all this, but you still wouldn't be what you are now. Because of this, because this happened, and because the master's daughter fell into the river, that's why you are what you are. You can deny

182

it, you can say it's good or it's bad, but it's still part of you. You can be proud of it or not. That's up to you." Darrock was thinking hard. It was thought that made him beautiful. Thought that made his hand all the more worth holding. And thought that convinced Arielle that her family history wasn't evil.

He continued, only because he was comfortable. No one ever asked what he thought; his brain was locked in a vault very close to his sexuality. "Very few people have good fortune in this world. And that's why everyone tries to take it away from you." Darrock turned around; he and Star looked deeply into each other, past John, past Scrap, past anything other than what a different afternoon this could be *without* a past. Darrock picked up his hand, and Star's along with it. Smiled a little bit, but serious. "This has to be the worst idea in the whole world."

CHAPTER 21

There was a certain nostalgia in John's driveway. Star, Scrap, John, Roof, just a few guys throwing hoops and having a good time. Sitting out on the front porch talking with John, trying to make him see the good in himself. Turning him into a guy with confidence.

Maybe a lot of bigger things started out the same way, in someone's garage. And perhaps the person who started it lost control of it, or himself, somewhere along the line.

Maybe John never had the confidence. The mind didn't wrap around the new body. At this point John seemed like part of his past. John, Scrap, Brad; he used to beat himself up over stringing along three guys at once. Now none of them meant anything to him except aggravation. He wished they'd all go away. Yoyo in, yoyo out.

Morton Taylor greeted Star at the door. Star knew John had a mom around somewhere but she seemed to stay out of things most of the time. There was a warm handshake; Dad still remembered when Star was a star, then a shrug of the shoulders again. "I don't know what to do about him when he gets like this."

"I just need to tell you... um... if Scrap comes to your place, don't let him in. He's... sick... and he might hurt John."

"Does John know this?"

"That's why I'm here." Star mumbled through some random reasoning as to why without saying *he's jealous because we were making it while he was in jail and now that I've kicked him out he's snapped*. It was very hard to tell the truth without giving out any information.

"Is that why John's upset?"

"No."

"Well what is it? He's my son. Why do you know more about him than I do?"

Star tried to be dismissive. "Just be glad someone does." He looked at John's father, overweight and unattractive, wondering how John came from that. "It's a love thing. It'll be okay."

That got a small laugh out of Mr. Taylor. "That explains it."

"In my life it never stops explaining it."

"Why didn't you turn pro?"

Star didn't know what to say. *I wasn't good enough* was a truth he had to face every day. No one else had to share it. "It's a love thing."

The house wasn't so big. Living room and dining room in one combo, pass a bathroom, parents' room behind the living room wall, John's room at the back. Simply furnished; drab colors, someone bought the décor ten or fifteen years ago, put it up, and left it there. Newer TV, all-in-one remote, state of the art.

John's head was under a cloud so dark it was hard to see him behind the rain, harder to reach him without being struck by lightning. On the bed, jeans, no shirt, no socks, alternately laying, sitting, crying. Maybe none of this would have happened if Star hadn't tripped him at Bob Evans. Or maybe it would have, just with a different cast. This seemed so much like a whiteboy thing. Some little twink who thought love was the only thing to live for, and that it came from only one source. Some kid writing a howling poem of *what did I do to deserve this?*

John sat up on the bed, his limbs dangling over it. Star in a wooden chair nearby, again something that had probably been in there all John's life.

"What?"

"Hey... uh..."

"Don't matter." John looked to the floor.

"A lot more matters than you think."

"No. I can't undo it. I got scared and I can't undo it."

"John, um... I know. I..."

"Where is he?"

"At my place. He has nowhere to go."

"That's convenient. Darrock gets to stay with you."

"John-"

"Star, I know you. You take what you can. People love you and you take it."

"Is that what it looks like?"

"That's what it is!"

That was a misconception it would take way too long to undo, if ever. "John, I have to talk to you. You can't live like this, for one-"

"This is how I live! I'm never going to have anyone."

"How old are you? Seventeen? Eighteen? Whatever! You've already had two. You haven't even started your life."

"No, I finished it..."

By running like a scared nigger on a plantation. Star had slavery on his mind even when he didn't. "John, I threw Hendrick out of my house."

"What?" John finally looked up.

"He was threatening Darrock. It couldn't take it anymore. We broke up. Look, maybe you and D can get back together. When he feels better and he's thinking better. Maybe you can apologize one more time. But not if Scrap does you both in."

"Why would Scrap do me in?"

"Because you and me had something. Because he's a sick motherfucker and that's what he does. He goes around beating up people that like me. Maybe he's got some kinda mental thing goin' on. But you need to watch. If he comes here, if he finds you..."

"Run away? Man I'm just as big as he is. Look where runnin' got me. Hey, if we're both single then-"

"John!"

"Star! The only think keepin' us apart was Scrap being in the way. You got me Darrock so I'd get out of your hair. I'm old enough. You still love me, huh?"

This caught Star blindsided. And the answer didn't matter. There was a time when it mattered. Not now. "I need to be single. I need to get my shit together. You're in this position because my shit isn't together. And I don't want to make things worse for you."

"Scrap oughta be more afraid of me than I oughta be of him."

"I just came here to tell you."

"Is that all you came here for?"

"John, if you want Darrock back I'll put in a word for you."

John got jealous, quickly. "I know what you'll put in."

"Didn't I just tell you-"

"I don't care. What you just told me. I don't care. The two guys I've been with are living together and he can hardly get out of bed. Good for you."

"John, I just want you to know I'm here for you. I'm not going to let you flounder."

"What you just said? I don't care."

"Do you want me to get D back for you?"

"D don't care. He wants to read. I'm sitting there sexin' him up and he turns a page."

"Maybe it's time for *you* to turn a page."

John moved closer to Star, almost lip to lip, eye to eye. "If all this shit hadn't o' gone down, would you love me? Would I be your true love?"

"I don't know how to answer that."

"Yes or no!" It was so simple for John, but he didn't understand the ramifications of turning confused emotion into yes or no as much as did Star's legal mind did. John wasn't in any condition to hear either.

"Then I'll answer when I'm ready."

John moved the inch or so further, took his head just close enough to quietly touch his lips to Star's. Again, five, six times, his tongue reaching past Star's lips, past his teeth, beckoning Star to come hither, desperate to have someone back in his life. Finally Star gave in, let the kiss take its long wet ride. It felt more like a past than a future. "I never felt like this before I met you. I guess it's love. Next time I see you, you better have that yes or no."

What you just said. I don't care.

"Take care of yourself," Star said. "I'll still be here for you."

"And that's done what for me?"

"Fine. Never mind."

"No. Wait. We can hang out an' shit can't we?"

"Sure."

"Like we used to, before all this shit started."

"Think we can go back to that?" Star missed that. There was a good kid in here somewhere.

John shrugged. "I dunno. Love makes me feel like shit. Who needs it?"

"One day it'll make you feel good," Star replied. "This isn't love. It's hope. It's what you wish was love, but it ain't. It's a prison in which I lived for far too long."

"I can't stop thinkin' about Darrock."

"Well, John. You fucked it up. But his dad might have killed you. I'm a lawyer, so one thing I can say is there's no right or wrong answer. You gotta live with it. One day it won't matter. Freedom is good. Freedom is real good. But people hate you when you have it."

Star wasn't sure if he'd accomplished anything. He figured in the next couple weeks he'd grab John and take him out for a burger. Or something. See if it worked. Time was a good indicator of what mattered and what didn't.

Something was drawing him to his parents' home. So much had happened that he needed to talk about, so he arranged a visit in the hope that they might actually still serve the parenting purpose for which they were designed – to help a lost boy along the way rather than find fault with everything he was doing in his life.

And of course he had to ask for favors, without it appearing so.

Mom greeted him the way so many mothers do. "It's a sad day when I have to find out what my son is doing by reading the internet."

Arielle. Posted. Everything. Gotta keep my mouth shut.

"But I can't say I'm not glad to hear it."

The familiar sparring was back; Star looked around familiar surroundings, after his recent stint at John's house he was growing irritated with people who never redecorated. "You've had the same shit here for years," he said, not planning to say it out loud.

"It's home."

"Buy something new. Every traditional African-American household has JKF on one side and MLK on the other. You need to get a li'l Nelly in here, mama. We finally got a famous rapper from Saint Louis but you have locked him out of your home. Get with it."

Living ones life in constant fear of the ballot box imposed a bizarre conservatism from on high.

"Star," she said, and almost as if she were surveyeing her walls with an eye for self-improvement. "I will never 'get with it.' I'm your mother. You, however, still have a chance. Especially if you get all those annoying men out of your life. All of them."

Star brought them up to date, feeling good that for once he could tell his parents news they wanted to hear, feeling bad that his acceptance was contingent upon everything in his life going sour.

"Not necessarily," said Mary. "It's contingent upon you doing something about it. Like you were brought up."

Darrock's story was particularly compelling, and easy to tell because Star had nothing to do with it. He left out a few of the more lurid details, but that wasn't the point. The point was D's father was a raving lunatic and Darrock had to start his life over, or perhaps, simply, start his life.

"I know you have some influence," Star said to Lancer, not quite being able to read him. Dad was in a chair, wearing a small pair of glasses, reminding Star, disconcertingly, of O'Ryan. Like son, like father.

"If it ever comes to court, I'll see what I can do."

"This isn't fuckin' Nigeria," said Star. "It better come to court."

"You know better than that. We have to find him first."

"If you do, let me know. Darrock wants to press charges."

"I will do what I can."

Next order of business... Star wasn't sure. Hendrick? Hendrick hadn't done anything.

Yet.

"That's an alien baby *you* gave birth to," offered his mother. "When a tornado comes towards your house, you need to get out of the way. You saw that one coming. You fed it and housed it and let it grow into a monster."

"Mom, I know I know. Didn't you do the same with dad?"

"If it comes down to it," said Lancer, "I'll do what I can."

And one more. "What should I do about Brad? He's suing my ass."

"Settle."

"Settle?"

"Yep."

"Your father doesn't want-"

Star didn't want to hear his mother ever start another sentence with those words. He bit into a cookie she so sweetly provided him earlier.

"Can't he speak for himself?"

"No, Star," said Mary. "He's an elected official. He has peeps."

"Peeps."

"Yes, peeps. You wanted me to get with it, and now you don't like it. I'm yo' daddy's peep. And yo' daddy don't want his chillun' draggin' their personal bid'niss in some high falutin' on-the-down-low court-ass drama."

"You sound like-"

"Yes I do, because we both feel that strongly about it."

"I didn't have anything to do with it," Star said, his voice rising in pitch.

"Well, you did," said Lancer. "Besides, he's white and you're black. You and Scrap," he continued, putting as much vitriol into the word Scrap as possible, hitting the final p like a sledgehammer in a blacksmith's shop... it felt so good he repeated it. "You and Scrapppp are some big gentlemen to allow this to happen to an average sized well-off Caucasian man who just happened to be your lover for the five years previous. Do you think you have a chance?"

"Even with you as alderman?"

Mary's eyes lit up. "Lancer, I do believe he's just complimented you."

"And conveniently so. But I think the best compliment would be to take my advice. Star, you've become way too high profile."

"I'm doing good for the community. I didn't want it to-"

"We know how reluctant you are. Throwing a ball around with a group of teenage boys on the cusp of discovering their sexuality. We know how much it eats into your evening. And we know you've done a lot of good. So you probably don't want to put it in jeopardy through a high profile civil on-the-down-low court case." Lancer ended his sentence quickly, almost like a Wayans brother in an old TV comedy.

Star was waiting for the fateful words "your father's career" to come out of his mother's mouth. Peep indeed. Not a peep out of her. Something was amiss.

"He's going for a quarter million."

"Do you have a lawyer?"

"I *am* a lawyer?"

Louder. "Do you have a lawyer?"

"Venda Bratton."

"I'll give her a call."

"*You'll* give her a call?"

"I will. We'll work something out. You just sit tight and we'll work out a settlement."

"Why? I'm surprised you don't want me to sink on this."

"A couple reasons." Lancer was officious, yet cordial. "One is it's for the good of the family, two is I have influence, and three you don't need to drop a quarter million on that loser."

"But we still don't understand why you left him," Mary put in. "Especially for Scrap." Same ppppp inflection.

"Oh, and there's one more reason," Lancer added, deferring to his wife, because some words were never going to come out of his mouth.

"You're our son and we love you."

"Wow." It was like being wrapped in a warm blanket, like finding that blanket after so many lost years, still warm as ever. "Well... uh... I love you too."

"We are a family after all."

"Yep," said Star. "We certainly act like it." He was reading faces, and trying to plow his way through words of love delivered as if he were at a corporate board meeting. He'd had plenty practice trying to figure out if someone had something up his sleeve, whether it was sex, money, or swindling. A lot of loving families managed to twit a relative out of something substantial under the guise of being a loving family. But so far so good. They gave him everything he asked for.

"I know you're starting a lot of your life over," said Mary. "We just want to help you..."

"And relieve you of some unnecessary responsibility," Lander added.

"Well... uh... thank you." Nothing would come without a price. Damn good cookies, though.

CHAPTER 22

Brad Brad Brad. The list goes on; Brad was on every line. Probably best not to talk to Brad. That's what having a lawyer was for. Peeps. Representation. You talk to me, it's free. For $120 an hour or more, my peeps will talk to your peeps. If his dad was going to do something behind the scenes, so much the better. It was so "in the past." John was in the past. And Scrap? On the front steps.

"What? Git outa here. You're turning Soulard into a ghetto."

Scrap looked to Star with a Taco Bell Combo of emotions, none of them pleasant, all the same feelings stirred in a different formula. "I'm stuck stayin with my mama," he said. "In fuckin' north St. Louis."

Star put a foot up on one step, a big foot encased in a Nike, and looked down at him. Looked like someone blew out the light that glowed in his face. Gone. Wick, wax, nothing but an empty Scrap-smellin' glass for the recycle bin.

"That's where you belong. And you fuckin' better not touch my boys."

"She don't want me staying there. She gave me 30 days."

"Smart woman. It's more than I gave you."

"I don't know what I did to turn you so-"

"You *don't*? You know what? That's a bigger tragedy than *Antigone*."

"You threw me out with nothing. No shoes, no clothes. After all I did for you-"

"What did you do for me? You sucked my cock a few times so suddenly you get to destroy my life? What about what I did for *you*? Every breath, every tear, standing by you when everyone rejected me for it, paying your way while you made $7 an hour, and maybe you showed some concern about me, maybe some time, but not nearly enough, and not nearly recently. And you're still back here like the dawg you are begging for more scraps." Gee that felt good! Star pulled out his wallet and whipped out five twenty-dollar bills. "Here. Don't blow it on cigs and whores."

"You trying to buy me off?"

"I'm trying to do whatever it takes. You got a job. You might spend your 30 days looking for a place to live."

"My job don't pay for shit. I scrape dishes. Scrape scrape scrape. Scrape-dawg outghta be my name. I don't have any money for rent. Not in 30 days."

Star leaned on a rail. Weather was cooling down so he wore a leather jacket. Worth more than any rent Hendrick would pay in north city. Dark blue jeans. Cars slowed down for a rape fantasy. "I know it looks good but you ain't gettin' it," he said.

"You used to want me. You couldn't get enough. And I ain't no different now."

"Nah. Your face is pretty but your brain's fucked up. And you're not even *on* anything." Star thought it over. If he could keep Scrap out of trouble it might make life safe for John, Darrock, Brad, and himself. "If you find a place I'll give you two months rent and a deposit. Up to five hundred a month. You don't need a place that costs that much anyway."

"Man your family just talks with money. That's all they do."

"We do when the love doesn't work."

Scrap still didn't get up. He looked to the ground. He found a rock and threw it down. Looked at Star's shoe. Looking up at him was too humiliating, and too much a reminder of a recent loss. Nothing to lose, so he gave it a try. "Are you sure about all this?"

No thought for the answer. "Yeah."

"Just yeah. After all this."

"Well... yeah. If it wasn't for all this, I wouldn't be so sure. I never give up on anyone until I'm sure I can't put any more effort into him. So, yeah."

"So you're giving up on me," Hendrick accused.

"Yeah."

"You're the only one that didn't."

"You need to learn a little self control. A lot of self control. I'm tired of your jealous bullshit. I've spent so much time solving *your* problems I haven't been able to solve mine."

"Well I'm sure John and D-boy are so happy I'm out of your life."

"And mom too. And me! Look I gotta go in. I'll pack your shit up and

I'll call you."

"Star!" Scrap got up, finally, took a step up and looked Star in the eye. Two big men out on the porch with very set faces, very set agendas. A casual onlooker might not understand. "Star just one more chance."

Star's eyes grew hard. "I said no. Now you can leave civil-like or I'm just gonna have to close the door and call the cops. And I don't think you want that." Star took some steps towards the door. Turned around and leaned up against it, sliding in his jacket a couple inches down. Bent his knee. Head down, eyes up still at Hendrick. Staring him off the steps. *You have no idea how tired of you I am.*

It went on for a couple minutes. Scrap not used to this, thought no matter what, the love would be there. The understanding, the support. Now it all went to Broken Boy in the bedroom.

"So just send me out on the street, huh."

"Huh. You did it without me before. Look, we shouldn't have got involved. I was just coming out of someone, you were just coming out of jail. It was too soon. I did love you, Scrap. With all my heart. But the heart's turned it off, and there's nothing I can do about it. Wait here."

Star went inside and grabbed two armfuls of Scrap's clothes. Sweats, t-shirts, jeans, socks. He pulled out a trash bag from the kitchen. "Here. I'll get the rest later."

He shut the door. Shut Hendrick out. Hendrick on the porch looking lonely and lost, stuffing his clothes into a bag, dragging that bag down the steps like a lost dog. Got in his old car, rambling down the road into a wilderness of his own making. Dog out on the prowl will either die or turn mean. Star watching out the 2nd floor window with a tear in his eye, like a movie, end scene, fade to black.

Somewhere in a far corner of his imagination, a white bird flew away.

Darrock approached slowly. Darrock did everything slowly, but he was starting to pick up the pace.

"We gotta pack all his stuff up," said Star. "He doesn't have much. I only want to give him one excuse to come back."

"How you feeling?"

"About like you are. That was a lot of life I invested in him. A lot of love and..."

"Money."

"Money. And arguing. Could've thrown it down the trash."

"But the sex was good?"

"Man, I can get that without the hatin' attached. I don't hardly care anymore. I lost myself. I've been taking care of everybody else and I'm just for the first time noticing that I have a soul of my own."

"Maybe you should take care of that for awhile."

Star unloaded on Darrock, telling him everything about everything, bringing him up to date in Star-World. It was a mess, but maybe things would get better. His father was finally acting like a father, stepping in and neatly resolving several crises with the swish of an aldermanic wand. Maybe he could live like a normal person now and then. "You can stay here for awhile if you need to," Star said.

"I'll get a job and help out."

"That would be cool. Just whatever. You seem stable. I just want to watch you and see how you do it."

Darrock laughed a bit. "Sometimes I wonder how much life I missed out on."

"Shit. You ain't missed a damn thing. What are you gonna do about John?"

Darrock laughed again. "John was always *your* problem. Now he's your problem again. John was cool. I might see him again. John needs to educate himself. He needs to let me educate myself. He needs to realize that books aren't stupid. And he needs to realize that when the guy you say you love is getting the shit beat out of him, you don't run away."

"Can you ever forgive him?"

"I don't know if it's worth the trouble. It was sorta like 'The Rime of the Ancient Mariner'."

"The what?"

"Poem. It's the poem with the albatross hanging around your neck. It's gone now."

"Oh." Star looked at Darrock like he was a Swami on a hilltop in Nepal. "Huh. So that's where that came from."

The sound of boys and bouncing balls and macho coaches; cajoling, triumph, disappointment, selfishness, irritation, echoed up from the gym floor. Star was a little late, but enough people were in place to take care of it without him. Every team had a coach; enough adults to keep the guys in check, enough so all the city elders, involved or not, could pat themselves on the back that they had a program to keep the proverbial kids off the proverbial streets.

Star had Admir on the brain: the thin gangly limbs, the wounds, the accent, the chance to matter to someone without so much drama. It would personalize the whole league thing that he never wanted in the first place and make it more heartfelt. He looked over the proceedings, proud that his name was on top of it. For once he didn't mind seeing Lancer Bryan's name on all the shirts. *Seems like dad came through on a couple things.*

"Where's Admir?" Star looked out, noticed some Bosnian kid he'd never seen before.

"He don't play with us no more. He's too gay." Some other boy, giggling like Jack on *Will and Grace*.

"What?" Star was shocked; it was the last thing he ever expected to hear.

"Everyone knows he had a thing for your boyyyyfriend," said the guy, hitting the word boyfriend with another smarmy giggle. "Damir says we don't need that. And Admir's dad, he found out too."

"What, did you all tell?"

"We're a close group. We have family honor. *You* can do what you want, you Americans, but we do not."

It had never dawned on Star that there might be a culture clash over the gay issue. Never. Well, it did. But no one ever said anything. He came so strong out of the box that everyone was afraid to. He declared it a non issue, and it took a 16 year old Bosnian boy to make it otherwise. "You're not going to hurt him," he said. Thinking of Darrock.

"We need to turn him around while he's young enough. Or we'll just take turns fucking him in the ass." He laughed, as if they'd do it to teach him a lesson.

"Yeah, that's not gay." Star wasn't impressed and turned to walk away. Wow.

"Hey." The Bosnian called after him. "You live in your world, we live in ours. You be how you have to be. You have no honor doing it all out in the open."

It never occurred to him he could put the program in danger. He always figured being gay and out and proud and all that, no matter how much an act, was part of teaching the kids. Putting a bunch of Bosnians, Mexicans, Vietnamese, and city black kids together was an exercise enough. Perhaps homosexuality was icing on a cake no one wanted to eat. Perhaps people were getting nervous because the boys were teenagers. They were expected to know and care nothing about sex until they had an epiphany on their age-of-consent-in-Missouri 17th birthday.

It was the infamous "they" that finally pulled the plug. The "they" that your mother warns you about.

They won't like that.

They'll make fun of you.

They don't wear that anymore.

Finally you come to a point when you wonder just who "they" are.

Althea Howard had been talking to "them," and she related "their" message to Star. At about 5' 3", she had to carry herself with a lot of authority for him to even notice her, but at this court, everyone respected her, perhaps feared her. It was she more than Star who made it run; her temper that could make it stop. She took Star up a few steps into the bleachers where no one could hear them, where the balls and boys and emotions echoed a bit more faintly, warming up for games like an orchestra warming up for a symphony.

She was in pastels: yellow and blue. Pants; she'd learned the hard way about the incompatibility of bleachers and skirts. Over that was a floral print polyester shirt, white background with lots of purple and green. This was a woman who didn't know how to dress, or didn't think the basketball league demanded a matching wardrobe. Most likely she was used to shopping at Goodwill so she could afford to feed Roof's teenage appetite. She was special here, although very few knew why – it was because she, more than Star, was the reason it happened.

But she had that look. That "I'm breaking up with you look." The look of sympathy. The look of "they" made me do this.

"Star, we have a problem."

"We always have a problem." He felt way too big right now, talking to someone over a foot shorter than he was about a problem.

"People are starting to talk. The boys are starting to talk."

"When boys talk..." That song by Indeep. *When boys talk, they don't talk politics. When boys talk, they talk about their kicks.*

"They talk about you and Scrap."

"Scrap is on the scrap heap." He looked, she looked, to see people looking at them, wondering. No one went that far up into the bleachers if it wasn't serious.

"They think you're interested. You and Admir were messing around like you were on some kind of date."

"He hugged me. For a reason. The reason being I made a positive difference in his life, as is the point of the basketball program that everyone thinks is about everything but basketball."

"*Now* it's about basketball." There was a bit of disappointment in her voice.

Star's lawyer mind kicked in. "That's not good."

"Maybe, maybe not. These are high school kids. They're fifteen and sixteen. Maybe seventeen. That's it. It makes some of them uncomfortable. Parents are starting to hear about it. And now *I'm* starting to hear about it."

"Well what do you want me to do?"

"Well, it's sort of been decided..."

Star didn't like the way she put that. Passive voice. She got out of saying who made the decision.

"It's been decided that you shouldn't come around here for awhile."

This from one of his staunchest allies. "I thought part of this was to show them..."

"It's gone beyond that," she said, more and more upset. Perhaps she drew the short straw and had to deliver the news. "It's gone beyond five boys in a driveway. Now we have the city. The papers. The parents. We have to set an example."

"By kicking me out? It's *my* league! It's *my* fucking example!"

"It's *my* league!" she said, a proud reminder that he was just a pawn in his own game. "It's inappropriate when *you* see a 15 year old boy and your eyes bug out. Those aren't the values we want to present. We all know about John Taylor. We let it go. But it can't go any further than that."

Star couldn't stand up any longer. He sat down, eyes to the ceiling, fingers feeling the fuzz of his goatee. If he wasn't so dark he was sure his face would be flushed red by now. "Is that what they think of me? I would never... play in that sandbox."

"I know that. You know that. They don't know that..."

"They."

"They." Althea was sympathetic to Star, but she understood "them."

"It's the Bosnians, isn't it?"

"No, it's us folks," she said. "You've been living in this little island of toleration that our community doesn't have. We're churchgoing people. We have values. Most folks have values that say don't send your children to learn sports with a homosexual who looks like a ghetto thug."

"I do not look like a ghetto thug."

"Scrap did."

"Scrap was."

"You do. You dress like it, and you have a pierced eyebrow and a chandelier hanging off your ear, and Star, you're scary to some people. These boys need to focus on basketball and not gossip. And I can't risk their parents pulling them from the program. We already lost one."

"Well who's gonna..."

Althea dropped a hydrogen bomb on Star's very crowded Nagasaki. "You father's a major sponsor of this program. He's going to make sure it keeps going."

"I thought he just bought t-shirts."

Althea wasn't looking him in the eye any longer. They were both watching the court. A buzzer went off, a game was about to begin. Bosnia vs. Richmond Heights. "He's invested a little more money. For equipment, for administration... it doesn't take much to run it. But it has to come from somewhere."

"He never told me."

"I'm sorry, Star. I'm sorry I have to be the one to tell you."

"So he's basically taking it over."

"If I don't do this, I'll have a mutiny on my hands. And you know how much this means to me. But yes, the city is going to get involved. Maplewood and Richmond Heights might kick in too. This could be really big."

"Without me." Star looked at the door of the gym, on the other side of the bleachers. He'd have to walk and talk all the way to the other side, and out. All this would still happen. Without him. Funny, he thought he never wanted it. But now he'd lose Admir, he'd lose some friends, he'd lose the chance to finish making the difference he'd started. "Thank you for... uh... everything." Star wasn't going to hang that albatross around her neck. She was too short for one, and he had just gotten rid of it, for two. "You stood up for me when no one else would. I know you wouldn't do this if you didn't think it was for the best."

"I don't think it's for the best. It's the only choice I have. People aren't ready for you."

"I'm not that controversial."

Althea laughed. "It's your family's legacy to be controversial. Embrace it. Just not here."

Star walked across the court. He high fived, low fived, rubbed up on a couple of the boys he felt particularly close to. *Waddup, bro?*

I've been fired.

Man you can't be fired, it's your scene.

When a man loses what he has, he usually loses it all at once.

So you ain't comin' back, man?

No. But I better not hear that you quit. And I better not hear that yo' mama raised the stink.

You got my cell programmed, you call me.

Yeah. Huh. Yeah. I will. I promise.

CHAPTER 23

Star drove to Clementine's. He sat at the bar, knocked back a beer, stared straight ahead.

Man, I'd like to suck your big cock.

You ain't good enough to put it in your mouth. Still staring straight ahead.

Whoa, who made you so high and mighty?

Star curled up a hand, a big hand, knocked it on the bar. *Suck on this, first.*

The jukebox played old rock, the drunken men next to him were whooping it up, laughing at stale old sex jokes, guys that called themselves wild but spent every weekend sitting on the same bar stool. Wild, indeed. Everyone living in a different world, no one could possibly imagine his.

"You have beautiful eyes." The man changed tactics. "I like your goatee. And your eyebrow thing. But your eyes are beautiful."

Star uncurled his fist, held the hand next to him. It was white, older, drunk.

"I didn't mean to...," said the man. "Well I'm not what you think."

"Please don't talk to me about your life right now." Star couldn't bear one more set of problems he'd wind up trying to fix.

"If I can do anything to make you feel better. Sometimes a man like you just needs a little attention."

"Maybe sometime you can." What a lie. But he didn't want to hurt anyone else if it wasn't absolutely necessary. He couldn't stand it anymore. Couldn't stand being ignored, couldn't stand being paid attention to. Couldn't stand the Bud Light.

It was a short walk home, but he had to go to his car and move it to the garage, past groups of "people" having a Soulard good time. Loud women, raucous men, God he hated people tonight.

Darrock downstairs, reading.

"I've never seen anyone read as much as you."

He held up a book. "Best friend a man can have."

"You think my eyes are beautiful?" A bit of sarcasm, a bit that everyone seemed so interested in him but he hadn't heard a compliment in so long...

"There ain't *nothin'* wrong with you." Darrock laughed a bit. "Someone got a problem with the way you look?"

Star stared at Darrock for awhile. Not thinking of him. Thinking of Lancer. Not only had he stolen the league, he'd stolen Althea. That seemed like a bigger betrayal. Right now being gay really sucked. Being alive sucked more.

"Man I can put this down if you got issues," Darrock said. "I owe you whatever."

Star smiled a bit. *I want to hold you tonight. I don't want anything else to happen.* "I don't know if I can sleep." He couldn't very well tell anyone the truth. Not the whole truth. Not about the boys. His father was a politician, and he was a lawyer. It was something he learned to dance with.

It took almost an hour of looking into Darrock's eyes just to get started.

"I need to talk to Lucinda."

"You don't *git* to talk to Lucinda just because you ax to. You gotta be impawtant!"

"Tell her it's the Starman. And you tell that bitch to get her ass over to this phone or I'm gonna whoop it from here to north St. Louis."

"I can't believe you would botha the sista so early in the mawnin'. You know she be out late wit' her peeps."

"Yeah, her husband and her two kids."

Star had talked to Darrock until about four a.m. He wanted to share the bed, but he wasn't sure how to ask, or if. He didn't sleep well, and he had ugly dreams when he did. Waking up was a haze of wondering if yesterday really happened. Huh. Yeah. It did.

It morphed. Star didn't feel attracted to Admir. Kid looked like he needed a hug. They're still kids, after all. Sometimes they like to be treated like it. It morphed from a coach-student hug into "they were making out under the bleachers," into "Star Bryan is lip-locking the boys, pimping out the players for street cash, and worse, not giving the money to the league."

Colorful and creative versions of the story barreled through the organization like an old man running his car into a crowded bus stop. Parents were getting concerned and a number of them threatened to pull their kids out if Star wasn't replaced. "This is about basketball, not Sodom and Gomorrah," someone said on the evening news, under the impression she was expressing herself creatively.

Althea found herself fielding all sorts of lurid speculation, when actually what happened was one guy was drummed off his team by some homophobic teammates. But Star and Scrap had played the gay card too loud and too long. It might be okay in a driveway, but now there were too many people with too many values and too many interpretations of Christianity and Islam to allow one so high-profile to announce it so brazenly and continuously. One of the main tenets of the league, to teach adolescent boys how to get along with other kinds of people, became irrelevant.

As Admir's mother reported it, Star and Admir were kissing underneath the bleachers. Star growling and chowing, holding the boy in a death grip. Big black stud taking what he wants from a defenseless war victim. Sex as in a horror movie, sex as a prelude to murder.

Arielle and Lancer were strained. The diary had catapulted her into a national spotlight and, as feared, provided a shooting range for his local political opponents. It belied an entire generation of students who said history didn't matter. Here it was bashing them in the face – saving a drowning white girl in the 1830s came back to hinder someone's father's career in the early 2000s. It *did* matter what dead people did.

Star's prominence was more current. It was the basketball league, a lawsuit or two, and a harem of impossible boyfriends. O'Ryan never made any waves, but he wasn't about to do anything that would allow someone to take the sneer of arrogance off his face.

Lancer knew it was coming down to this. A final confrontation. Family Armageddon. He had to do something. If Star went down as part of the league, he'd go with it. Everyone in that league was wearing shirts with his name on it.

"There are times when your name is the only thing you have," he'd said on occasion.

Then why the fuck did you call me Star?

Arielle and Star approached the house they grew up in wondering if this might be the last time for a long while. "Have you noticed..." he said, still wondering why this was so bothersome, "that they've never redecorated?"

"They don't have to. They're comfortable with who they are."

Mom made cookies, Dad was sitting in that same damn yellow chair, O'Ryan on the couch – what was he doing there? Just to watch the walls of Jericho?

"Da sistah gave up her stories to come hear y'all, so y'all better have some better stories than the stories she gave up."

"Hey can we can her today?" O'Ryan was opening his big mouth.

"Can you go can some peaches or somethin'? Cuz' the only thing this sistah wants to *caaaan* is fruit. And not her opinions. Cuz she has plenty. Her cup of 'pinion runneth ovah this fine afternoon!"

"Arielle, shut it!"

She dropped back into herself. "You don't wanna hear what I think."

O'Ryan had a couch to himself because on one wanted to sit with him. Finally Mary took the honors. Star paced. His long legs took him quickly from one end of the room to the other. "Will you stop that?" Mary demanded. "I know you can walk."

"I can walk but I can't dribble."

Lancer had held back long enough and for once wasn't going to wait for his wife so start a sentence with "your father thinks."

"Star. You are lucky. That I did something. To save you." He was choosing words carefully, almost like his speechwriter had given him a blank sheet of paper on the most important night of his career. "The talk was getting pretty bad."

"By firing me. You told everybody. That I did it."

"No. By firing you, I saved my career until that damned diary brings it down. And I saved a lot of boys-"

"From what? My insatiable eight-inch black cock?" Star's voice louder than anyone had heard in a long time.

"No. Not from you. From themselves. From their parents taking this away from them."

"Do you know what they're going to do to Admir? Those boys? A lot more than I could dream up. Who's going to save him?"

"You're the one that kissed him under the bleachers."

"I did not – what the fuck kind of politician are you? You accept every opinion poll as truth!"

"That's how the story came down to me."

Star stopped pacing long enough to see O'Ryan smile. The smile of victory. He cuffed his brother across the face. "Don't you ever let me see that look on you again."

O'Ryan was in pain, but he didn't want anyone to notice. "Man. We got O.J. Simpson in the house."

"I fuckin' cared about those kids. Without me those kids wouldn't be there. None of 'em. They'd be sitting at home playing video games and sticking knives in white folks. Don't tell me I don't care about those kids. And don't tell me I've been fuckin' those kids. This isn't even about the kids. It's you getting the fuckin' league like you fuckin' wanted. Because you know what, you could have said *this is my son and I won't stand for any bullshit you say about my son!* You could have said that just once in your life."

Lancer's face set as hard as Star's. No one cared about O'Ryan. No one could figure out why they should. "I said it as long as I could stand to say it. Our African-American community does not want-"

"Some gay nigga upsetting the white folks by taking their boys to the woodshed. Is that it? I forget. You're a politician. The truth doesn't enter into it."

"Oh, it does. Badly."

"You took everything from me. You said you were gonna fix stuff."

"And I am."

"This is what you're charging me for it. You got it. Thanks."

Mary spoke quietly. "You still have a law practice. You have a nice home. You have a lot of people who respect you."

"How? When word gets out?"

"You just kept dipping lower and lower on the age thing..." That tone of voice she had, so conciliatory. So sweetly condescending. So much like a violin concerto gone on too long.

Star couldn't believe he was having this conversation. *This should be happening to someone else.* "No. You just said so. Everyone just said so. If something's going to ruin my life, can't it at least be something I've done?"

If anything good was coming out of this, it was that O'Ryan learned to shut up.

Arielle took up a mantle. "I don't understand. You people. At all."

"You people." Mary. Worse than nigger. *You people.*

"Yeah. You people." No more sistah.

"Do you know what publishing that book has done to our family?"

"Yes." She was still quiet. "That's why I did it."

Lancer. "I would have thought differently of you. I thought we taught you to respect how what you do affects other people."

"It's bigger than us. You only taught us in terms of you. How it affects you. All this affects everyone else. I don't know where I learned that from. Fawn spent the whole book-"

"I don't want to hear about fucking Fawn Bryan." O'Ryan wasn't finished yet. "Fuckin' bitch."

Arielle had lived the world of Fawn Bryan for a long time now. The defense almost left her short of breath. "She spent the whole book living a lie. Trying to justify something she knew was wrong. The same wrong put upon her, she put upon someone else. She didn't know how to get out of it. The world she lived in was set up to justify that wrong. But she wasn't supposed to live like that. She was supposed to be a slave. Not have slaves. She spent her whole life not understanding, and not fitting in. We do the same. I'm a teacher. Now I can show how what happened 200 years ago matters now. *How what you do now will matter 200 years from now.* You took him down, Lancer Bryan. You took down your own son. And that's how history will remember you, because you didn't stand up for what was right. And what was true."

"I had no choice. We had to sacrifice Star to save the league. Whether he did it or not. It's a mob mentality."

Arielle couldn't let go. Not just yet. "Then our whole city will go down for it. Today's white folks don't want to be held accountable for what their forefathers did. So we shouldn't be either."

"But that's not how it *is*!" Lancer screamed at her. Screaming because a whole life of establishing authority as a father and politician was crumbling because of his family's past and family's present. "And history has shown that time and time again. And you, as its teacher, should know it."

"And it will never change as long as you let it stay that way!" Arielle was smoking. "You know when I'll believe we've made it? When a black person can do something stupid, when one black person can make a big mistake and our entire race won't have to pay for it! You've used your position to keep our people down, and every time you say that you're just shoveling dirt on our graves."

Star was leaning up against a wall, but he slid down to sit on the floor. Elbows on his knees, hands over his face. Sometimes his size made him uncomfortable. He was never sure how he outgrew everyone else in the household by so many inches.

"Of course," said Mary, "we'll still help you with the legal issues as promised."

Star started to cry, silently. Arielle sat next to him; before long she joined in.

CHAPTER 24

Star was stunned. He never realized how much the league had meant to him until he had it snatched away, and in the most embarrassing manner possible. Time rambled by... ka-clunk, ka-clunk... like a refugee on a slow train trying to escape from under an atomic cloud. The next morning, the next days at work, picking up every minority-owned newspaper in town to see what was or wasn't being said, trolling the net, wondering what he'd been doing with Admir under the bleachers, what they saw, what they reported, why they embellished, why no one believed him.

He had to. Call.

Admir. Are you okay?

Not really, no.

Did anyone hurt you?

No.

You sure?

No.

You can tell me. Please don't. Please please please don't. Don't say they raped you to prove you were gay.

I know. I can. But I can't. It could be worse. There could be war.

I'll always be your friend. I just can't see you now.

I know. Same here. Maybe one day. Gotta go.

"Star." It was Brad's obnoxious way of starting a conversation.

"Shouldn't your lawyer be calling my lawyer?" Star's obnoxious way of continuing it.

"I want to see you."

"I'm tired of you."

"I want to drop it."

"Then drop it. I'm still tired of you."

"Please. I need to apologize."

That albatross was getting around. *Okay.*

Star wasn't about to believe that something good could happen to him without a corresponding something bad somewhere else. There was a Zoroastrian balance of good and evil fighting for control of his life. He met Brad at a St. Louis Bread Company in Creve Coeur. Coffee, sandwiches, the one-outlet shoppe that started in Kirkwood went nationawide under the name Panera's, apparently too embarrassed to use the name St. Louis.

A bunch of rich folks were eyeing Star hoping he wasn't as black as he looked. The dark skin, the bright eyes, the gold hoops, it wasn't a color combination most of these people used to decorate their homes. But the sandwich was nice. Brad eyed Star's big hands picking up a turkey-and-sprouts-and-avocado and chowing down on it; Star noticed, added as much sex as he could to turkey-and-sprouts-and-avocado. *I'm a fucking man! I should act like it just sometimes.*

"So why you being nice to me?" he asked Brad. "It's very white of you."

"Can you stop that?"

"Only when you do."

"I realized I was taking it out on you. There was nothing you could have done."

"Brad. You knew that all along."

"I was hurt."

"You dumped me," Star said.

"*You* left."

"I had to. You dumped me three years before. I stayed around hoping you would take me back. We were a couple but only officially. It's sad, because my mother liked you a lot more than Hendrick Pardee."

"I miss you."

"Funny way of showing it." Another big bite, another lost opportunity for the man across the table.

Brad was eating a salad; Star could see how his injuries impeded his daily life. A simple hand to mouth was at times hard work.

"I dumped him."

"I know."

"How the fuck do you know?"

"Family website. I know everything. I read it all the time. I feel..." Brad was almost angry. Too angry for the innocent lettuce he was jabbing, unsuccessfully. "I feel like I should still be there."

Star had never asked before. "Why did you treat me so badly? I loved you. Surely there should have been some kind of reward, sometime."

"It was too easy, I guess. I didn't have to work for it. It was just there when I wanted it."

"But you never wanted it." Star couldn't bear looking across his sandwich at what was now a broken wisp of a man and realize how much time and heart he'd wasted needing it. "If you want to take advantage of something, eventually you need to take."

"Well, expenses and all. You chucked in a bunch of money. I'm probably going to have to move. Somewhere cheaper. Somewhere that doesn't remind me of you."

"Scrap's looking for a place."

"Star, I don't know. I don't know why I did any of it. Power trip maybe. Big guy at my feet. I don't know. I just want to say I'm sorry because I've really been a dick. It's just an apology. Because I love you. If I can't have you the least I can do is be decent about it. The least I can do is not be like Scrap."

Star was dumbfounded. No one had done that in so long. Just apologized. He looked at Brad, let out that little "huh" that he found himself saying far too often.

"What? I mean it."

Star swallowed. He laughed a bit. Took a swig of coffee. Bread Company coffee was so hot he had to wait until the end of the sandwich for it not to singe his insides. "Why's it have to be the white guy?"

"What?" Brad was confused. "Getting a bunch of money out of you isn't gonna help. I can't get you out of my head and I can't get you out of my heart."

"You did a good job of it before. I was right there. I couldn't get into your heart. Couldn't get near it." Star let up a bit. Brad had been attacked enough. "Brad, thank you. It means a lot to me. I have so much going on in my life right now. I'm losing everything..."

"You don't have to lose me."

Star shook his head. "I... do. You've put me through hell. Before we split up..."

"Before you left me."

"You left me long before I left you. I just walked out the door. And after, you never let it go. If you're sorry I forgive you. I respect you. I wish you a good life. I never got my shit together after I left. That was thanks to Scrap. That's what I have to do now."

Brad's masticating slowed down. Everything slowed down.

"I should." Star said.

"Should what? Whatever." Brad finally recognized defeat.

"Move in with you. This African-American community I'm part of just kicked my ass. Kicked it to the curb. I'm a lost dawg with a bare cupboard. I'll be lucky," Star thought out loud, "if I have my law practice by the time my friends and family are done kicking me. Maybe I should be a white boy again." He looked at Brad. Brad looked at him. Star looked deep, trying to find the man he used to love, the man he used to need, the man it felt so comfortable to kiss, touch, flop down next to.

This wasn't the man.

"Have your lawyer send me a letter. And to my father."

Maybe it was time.

Another trip to TJ Maxx. A new identity for under $100.

Star drove home quietly. Thought everything through. Brad was over. No friendship, no love, no lawsuit. They could be civil if they ran into each other again. Like at a bar, that kind of thing. Just seemed useless. If Brad really loved him, always loved him, all he would have had to do that day was say so, say *please Star don't leave, we can make this work,* and it would have saved him everything that happened since.

Hendrick, John, basketball, all those goddamned teenagers, so much hope turned to so much pain. Well, life was like that.

Star half expected to find Scrap on his doorstep every time he drove home. Looking for rent money. Even if he didn't have a place to live, he might lie to get the cash. Whatever. If it took $1,500 to buy freedom, it wasn't that big a deal.

He'd have to keep a low profile now; word would probably fly around the community that he was a gay guy into illegal teenagers. He couldn't risk showing up places where it might be spoken aloud. Hopefully Arielle wouldn't post that little tidbit. She might. She might not. She was on his side. Who knew, anyway, how much she'd care about the family after the last meeting.

They still cared. That's why everyone cried.

Star stopped at TJ Maxx, bought more stuff. It seemed like a cure-all. Maybe it was time for some other kitch-culture. He could go Asian. Indonesian. Something that wasn't African so he wouldn't have an identity crisis every time he looked at his walls. He didn't want to be like the Taylors and the Bryans who didn't change their décor but once every two decades. He was gay, gol' durnit! He had to redecorate. It might just save his soul. Maybe D-boy could take some spirits with him. He'd need them.

Darrock was venturing out of his room more, the less he was afraid of Scrap or John showing up the more he took the run of the house; like a bruised cat from an alley fight he slowly acclimated to his new quarters.

Now, dressed only in a pair of baggy green shorts, he lay on the couch on his back, asleep, *The Scarlet Letter* open on his chest, one arm crooked up over his head, another bare arm resting towards the floor. Star noticed him and put his bags down quietly. He sat on a chair to watch Darrock sleep, soaking up his aura, his essence, his scent, his peace, feeling no need to say or think anything on his own. Eyes wandered up and down the contours of his body, artful, inviting, relaxing because he didn't have to look away. He wanted his lips, his tongue, his hands to make the same journey, to slowly lift D's other arm over his head, taste him, massage him with pools of spit, make him feel appreciated for providing, finally, some solidity. Wasn't sure if that would ever happen.

Finally the eyes opened, both men looked at each other telepathically.

"Man, how long you been here?"

"Awhile."

"You just watching me sleep?" D was flattered.

Star smiled. That felt unusual. "Yeah. You look better. You look less scared."

"My dad's in jail."

Wow.

"I didn't think. Being a gay black guy I didn't think they'd take anything seriously."

"It's a tradeoff."

"Not sure what to do. He's my dad. If he comes near me again though he'll..."

"Maybe you need to leave St. Louis."

Darrock put his book on the floor, sat up a bit. Head on the back of the couch, body curling downward. "I don't want to think about it."

"I do. I asked my dad to help find your dad. I guess he did. I guess he kept his promise." Backstabbing motherfucker kept his promise.

"Tell him thanks."

"Yeah if I ever talk to him again."

"Why wouldn't you?"

"He beat me up. Same way yours did. Just didn't use his hands. Ya know..." a light bulb went off in his head, incandescent wattage on a cloudy day. "Ya know I take risks for people I love. I don't know where I learned it from. Darrock." Star's voice almost a low whisper from far away, would have been sexy were it not filled with sorrow. "D-boy."

"What's with this D-boy?" He liked the nickname. Made him feel cool. Almost black.

"I dunno. It just sort of happened. It's who you are now. D-boy. You're all I have. And I'm all you have. But I gotta set you free. I don't want you to get caught in this downward vortex known as my life."

Star moved to the floor by the couch, Darrock laid back down. Star did move D's arm slowly up over his head, exposing more tender skin beneath. Darrock gave himself over to it, slowly rising, slowly falling, a very subtle but loving domination. It felt like the best sex ever, just that. *Maybe this is love, maybe love is peace.* Star put his arm around Darrock's chest, looking at his dark skin resting over the slightly lighter body. He rested his head on Darrock's chest. Darrock took his own thick ropy hand, ran it over Star's head, his ear, his face, through his goatee, let it rest over his lips. Draped the other over his shoulder. A fallen celebrity, fallen at his feet. Too much history for them to admit liking each other; too much danger.

"What's in the bag, bro?"

"Buncha shit from India."

"Buncha shit from India."

"Ya. I gotta take down these African spirits. They've cursed me."

Both thinking the same thing; both thinking of the other. *This isn't the man I met. It's just what's left of him.*

Star made the call. Time for Scrap to get his stuff, time for Star and D to move a few things around, put up the new decorations, put the old in a closet somewhere, maybe in a box under some other box where the spirits couldn't communicate and cast spells on the Bryan family.

"Is this Krishna?" Darrock looked at some seated Indian figure.

"I dunno. Does he look pissed?"

"No, he looks pretty happy."

"Good."

"What do you want to do with this?" Darrock curled his hand around the giraffe's neck.

"I'd like to throw the fuckin' thing out the window. I'd like to throw fuckin' everything out the window. Let's put it in the basement."

Doorbell rang.

"Nothing worse than someone's past lover coming upon two gay men happily redecorating," Darrock whispered. "This should be good."

Star thought telling Scrap he could even come over, even for a hand-over-the-bags-in-the-doorway transaction, was a bad idea, but that it might end things once and for all. He was even prepared to write out a check for $1,500 whether Scrap needed it or not. Just get him out of the way.

Darrock was awkwardly walking down the steps with the giraffe and hoping to get it out of sight but the pounding on the door was incessant so he changed course to open it up. He and giraffe greeted a very disturbed John Taylor.

"What are you doing with that?"

"We're moving it. What are you here for?"

"I need to talk to you."

"Yeah, fine."

"Are you and Star-"

"No. Get that out of your head. No."

John looked around. "Wow you're redecorating. You must be. If you're takin' that to the trash I'm gonna..."

"John, chill bro."

Star came down the steps. "What you doin' here? You need to go!"

"I need to talk to Darrock."

"You need to do it later. Scrap's on the way and I don't need him seeing you."

"I need to talk to D."

"Now?"

"Yeah," John had a determined gait to his voice and his face. "Now."

"I know what you wanna talk about," said Darrock. "I know exactly. It's not like you ever have anything else on your mind. I don't know if I want to." But that "I don't know if" left open the possibility that he did, just a smidge, and John took that opportunity to push the door open.

"Darrock, put that down!"

D stuffed the outgoing giraffe in a corner of the room next to the incoming Krishna. They both looked uncomfortable.

"Darrock I can't stop thinking about you. I can't stop needing you. I can't stop saying I'm sorry over and over and I just had to come. I couldn't wait any longer. I miss you. Forgive me. Please. You're better. I'm glad you're better."

John talked like a pot of macaroni boiling over while Darrock tried to stay steadfast in refusal. The water falls out of the pot to sizzle on the burner below. Everyone else runs to the kitchen to turn it town. Yet, it still boils over.

Star was out of water and his pot was starting to burn.

"John you have to go *now*."

"I ain't afraid of no Scrap!" Again hitting that P.

"You should be. He's dangerous. I just..."

"Then what you go bringin' his black ass over here for? You all got a death wish? I'm the one that needs to die. Thanks to both of you kicking me out of the house so you can fuck while you put my present on the wood heap."

"John, please."

"John." Darrock relented. "Call me and we'll talk."

"Why don't you come with me? We'll talk now. Please!" So much rode on a yes.

"I gotta help here. And I gotta make sure Scrap doesn't pull any shit."

"And who's gonna protect *you*?" John asked before he could pull that train back into the station.

"Certainly not you."

John went down the front steps as Scrap walked up.

"What you doin' here motherfucker?"

"Just comin' back to get what's mine."

"Yeah right." Hendrick was already on the verge. "Just waiting for me to get the heave ho."

"Star ain't what I'm here to get."

"Liar." Scrap's insanity kicked into high gear. "Look motherfucker. I'm gonna find your motherfuckin' ass. I know where you live and I know where you work. I know where you are all day long. And now I know you're here. It's only a matter of time."

"Leave him alone." Star at the door. "John, git."

"I'm not gittin'." John grew a backbone at a bad time. "Last I *got* I got fucked up for gittin'. So I'm stayin'. Maybe it'll prove something useful to someone."

"Yeah maybe some other time," Star said.

Hendrick said *motherfucker* enough times, full volume and outdoors, that he that was inciting and confirming the worst fears of every bigot west of the Mississippi. John was scared, even standing his ground. He knew what Scrap could do. Star was getting worried. Family teaching crept in to point up future ramifications rather than to help solve an immediate menace. *What will the white folks think?* Always about someone else. Still, it was time for Hendrick and his belongings to go back to north city.

Four bags of crap. Scrap crap. Scrap didn't have anything so he'd need it.

"I'm down to just a few days with my mama," he said, accusingly.

"You got yourself a place?"

"Yah. You're throwing me out of it. Looks like you're taking *in* the garbage instead of throwing it out."

"Well you find yourself a place. This is no dearth of abandoned buildings up in crack-ho-ville. You find it; I'll give you your fuckin' money and you get out of my fuckin' life. And them too. Keep your hands off the boys."

"Yeah, that's a great piece of advice comin' from your horny ass. You're the one usin' the high school as a recycle depot."

"Curb it, boy." Star barked. He looked mean. Meaner that Scrap had ever seen him. He obeyed, temporarily.

Star put the bags on the sidewalk like they were clothes for the Goodwill. So much misunderstood tension among four misunderstood men. Almost looked like there was a "do not cross" tape strung up around the yard. Only an idiot would walk though it. "Get the fuck in your car and get the fuck out of here!" Star was screaming. The neighbors were looking. *Great. Four black guys fighting on the front steps. And we moved here why? For a jazz bar?* More words, more threats, more accusations. Finally a back seat full of black plastic and a car rumbling away up the street. Anger subsides, neighborhood heaves. One more nail in the coffin of Star's reputation.

"Yeah, see I stayed," said John. "Now maybe you'll talk to me."

It wasn't that easy.

Cop car coming up the way, everyone knows to let them park, take their time, close the door. Everyone's taught young.

Everything okay here? We heard there was a disturbance.

Yeah, there was. He's gone. Sorry about that. It won't happen again.

Hey, are you...?

Yeah, I am.

I read the book.

The book.

Your sister's book. Your relative's book. I read it. On the website. Interesting.

Yep. You never know who's got a slave in their back pocket.

Keep your ass outa trouble. Everyone's watching it. Don't make me have to come back here again.

Cop pulls away. Everyone sits on the steps, dumbfounded. Scared. Realizing what just happened, and how it looked. Always how it looks.

We're not like that.

"I can't go home if he's gonna follow me." John was truly frightened, plus it was a good excuse to stay behind.

Darrock went inside first. Life was so quiet back when he was lonely.

Maybe that was better.

Words fly between them, allegro and staccato.

John I don't want to talk about it now.

When?

I don't know.

When?

I told you I don't know.

Why not? I'm here. I'm sorry. I love you. Dammit I love you. Why doesn't that mean anything to you? God Darrock.

I want to think. So when I say something I say the right thing. So if it's yes or if it's no it's the right thing. For me, and for you.

You're fuckin' Star, aren't you?

No! And you were cheatin' with him when you were so get off that horse.

The symphony over, John went to Darrock and hugged him tight, D relented finally, put his arms around John. John wants a kiss. Darrock says ok.

"You miss that?"

"Yeah I do."

"You want more?"

Darrock hurts but he's digging in. *It was more than sex, more than dad. It was who you are and who I am. It was so much more.* His silence was too long for John's patience.

"Fine. I'll go jump off a bridge and when you're ready to talk you fish me out." Turned to go.

"Careful of Scrap." Star warned.

"Who gives a fuck? Let him kill me. I'm sick of this."

CHAPTER 25

The pressure cooker that was Hendrick Pardee had simmered quietly on a low burn for the entire month. His mother stoked the flame, turning it up ever so slowly by reminding him daily how long before he had to get out. She loved her son, but he was a jailbird and he was trouble. She was only trying to have some peace, and the undercurrent of looniness he tracked into her house robbed her of what peace she could find living in poverty in a drug zone.

Scrap parked his car a few blocks away from the Taylor's place, on a route he knew John would take to get home. Damn them! Kicked out the life he knew, the life he loved, the man he loved, not to mention his financial support; anything that mattered to him taken away so some stupid kid could come in and claim all that he worked for. Maybe Darrock didn't know better but he should have. And Darrock had a protector. Darrock had Star. John would have to come home eventually.

Sooner than he thought, John's car ambled down the street; John had his usual look of self-demolition on his face. Scrap recognized it, even in its brief automotive passing, from all their time together at Bob Evans. Sure he'd grown up, sure he'd turned from geek-a-zoid into sexy young man, sure he'd done all that. Deep down he was still sullen and scared, but not so deep down, Star couldn't get enough of him. And Star could wipe that sorrowful look off John's face all too easily.

John went to his room, again Morton Taylor wonders what he can do about this kid who always comes through the door as if he'd lost a large portion of his territory to conquering Mongol hordes.

"John, what is *wrong* with you boy?"

"Nothing."

"Is this how you are all the time?" Morton stands in the door of John's room, blocking him from escape. John is on the bed, wants to cry in peace. The two guys he's given everything to ditched him out of his life, and at this very moment they're howling out in pleasure. He knows what they both look like when they're hot and sexual. He knows what they both do. He knows what they both like and he can see it plain as a picture on the wall *dammit dad get the fuck out of here!*

"Can't you ever leave me alone?"

"I'm afraid to," says dad. Morton was easy going, tried to live and let live. "We're going to have to talk about this. This isn't you. It hasn't been for a long time."

No one had bothered locking the front door; there was no call to from the time John came stumbling in. People weren't often robbed and raped and brutalized in this part of Dogtown. Morton turned around to see Hendrick looming in the doorway.

"Where is that motherfuckin' kid?"

"Scrap!" It had been a long time. Far different Scrap than he remembered. Scarier. Meaner. Mad dawg, drooling, snarling, with wild eyes.

"Where is he?" No reason left in Scrap's mind but one. If John were dead, life would be ok. Everything wrong was now the fault of John Taylor. With him gone, Star would take him back. Darrock has to go too. Fuckin' *D-Boy*. But one at a time.

"Get out! And stay away from my son!" John had never been in a fight in his life.

"What the fuck do you know about it, motherfucker!" Something about Scrap using *motherfucker* repeatedly was ominous. "I'll find him. The place isn't that big."

John, huddled in his room. This time it was Dad in danger. Again he was frightened. Out on Star's porch nothing would happen. He knew it. He played bravado. Why was everyone important getting the crap beat out of them? Why was it up to him to stop it?

Hendrick pushed Morton into the dining room table. He was stronger, bigger, angrier, more adrenaline. John's father crumpled to the floor, Scrap kicked him, threw a chair over him, knelt down, picked up his head and punched him across the face. Father and son both screamed, father in pain, son in fear, John in the living room screaming *go away*, John screaming *help*, John lost as Hendrick picks him up and carries him back to his room.

"You know what I should fucking do is see what's so delicious about that ass of yours that everyone wants so damn badly." Hendrick, rabid, salivating, that light in his face glowing again, but a red, ill-omened theater of the absurd; John could smell the sweat and the paranoia falling from Scrap's face and his chest; the hard muscles in his arms ready to deliver a painful message. "But I don't have time to waste." Breath coming hard, Hendrick had a hand under John's chin, ready to strangle at any moment. "So you and me are gonna play a little game, where I beat the shit out of you, and you try to stop me. It's a lot more fun than basketball. It'll teach you" WHAM! "to fuck" WHAM! "my man!" WHAM.

Wham.

John tried in vain to fight back. He didn't know how, his arms landed squarely in Scrap's open palms and were twisted backwards until he screamed. Father on the floor hearing his boy in pain, helpless, trying to get up, dazed.

Sirens up the street, police rushing to the door, Scrap lays a few harder blows, like the Germans killing as many Jews as possible before their inevitable defeat. He wasn't going down alone. They burst in the door. Four, maybe five. Nearly trip over dad, run to the back room where the screaming stopped and Hendrick fell against the wall, panting, sweating, moaning, resting up for one last lethal blow.

It takes four guys to subdue him, cuff him, take him out while he's cursing at life and at John. Morton in shock, his body trying to process what just happened, his head hearing things, hearing things from Hendrick; John and Star did what? A lover's quarrel. Jealousy. John and Star. *Oh, God. It's come to this.*

Ambulances swoop down the street. One for Mort. One for John. Paramedics, wires, older man will be okay, *John is salvageable but we have to hurry.*

Across the street the old guy watched. The white guy with the radio show. The white guy that's stuck in the neighborhood but won't leave because it feeds his truth about the black community. He saved John's life by calling the cops. He heard the screaming, the fighting. Maybe it would or wouldn't make the papers. He could crow. Jim Crow, perhaps, about how he'd saved some black kid so he could spend more time flunking out of school and selling drugs. And debate if a life like John Taylor's was really worth saving. Wait until he found out, as everybody would, that this was the result of a gay love triangle with old-news Saint Louis University basketball stars, one now a druggie and the other an alderman's kid. And a barely legal teenager. John languished in the hospital while so many in the city called in to mock his pain.

Star found out through an anguished phone call from Scrap; the scuffle, the handcuffs, the booking all served to bring his tortured mind back to reality, particularly the reality of more jail time and a much less sympathetic justice system. The same clearing of the mind, the same Greek woman staring into the clouds and recoiling in horror at finding her son's ripped head hanging from her fingers. He remembered vaguely that last time, Star understood. It wasn't his fault. It had been weeks since his mind was this clear. It was all a blur until now.

Star, for all his caring about other peoples' fate, turned the microscope farther and farther inward. "Yeah, that's too bad." *Do you know what this is going to do to me?* "Where's John?"

"I don't know."

"What the fuck for did you have to go beatin' up on John?"

"Star, I'm sorry. All I could think about was-"

"I don't think you could think about anything."

"Are you going to help me? I didn't mean it. I just... it just happened. God Star you have to believe me."

"Well, you found a place to live, and just in time for your mother's deadline."

"Call your father. He'll do something."

"Huh. Yeah." He clicked the button on his cell. Quietly. Just like closing the door on Brad. Maybe that was the end of an era. "D! We need to see John."

Star made a couple calls to area hospitals, found a John and a Morton Taylor admitted to a place nearby. Morton was beat up but more or less okay but for some scrapes and bruises. And a busted dining room table. He'd miss some work.

John more serious. "He'll come through," said an ER nurse. "But he can't have visitors now."

Darrock sat in a waiting room while Star went in to see Morton. Just to apologize, just to say I care; just to see if everything was going to be all right. Morton respected him; he respected what Star had done with John. Until now, when he found out more specifically what Star had done with John.

He lay in his bed, an IV tube pouring into him, the ubiquitous blue pitcher of water full of crushed ice, a blue cup with a bendy straw on the table next to him. Infomercial on the TV. There was little room for anger in his battered body, but just enough to share, to refract through Star's eyes so that the sheer force of his quiet tirade magnified and sanctified into a divine wrath attacking Star's broken heart.

"I heard what you did."

"What do you mean?" Star assumed his visit would be welcome.

"With my son. I thought you were taking care of him. I thought you were helping him grow up and turn into a man. And play ball."

"I was. And I did. And I'm glad to have had that opportunity to-"

"You were fucking him."

"What?" Anger and spittle came out of Morton's mouth with the "fucking."

So many months of not understanding John finally came to fruition. "That's what this was all about. I thought you were like... like some big brother or something. Some celebrity that took a special interest in my boy. Man I was proud! Basketball star taking care of my boy. You took him home and you fucked him."

Star went through all sorts of defenses. *He was of legal age. He asked for it. He wanted it. He begged for it. He wouldn't leave me alone until I did it. Morton I did love him... sort of!* None of that would calm an outraged father.

"I have watched him, all my life, grow up lonely and unhappy. And you came into his life from somewhere..."

"Bob Evans." Star tried to lighten the moment.

"You came in and promised to make it better. But it never was. I watched him sulk and withdraw, and as he turned more and more into a man, he turned less and less into a human being. He sat there in his room staring out the window. Now it all makes sense. He's just a kid. Just a lonely mixed up kid. If he gets out of this alive, I'm going to have to clean it up. Me and his mother."

"If you need anything…"

"What I need is for you to stay out of his life. Of all the people in the world, I trusted you with the most precious thing I have. You'll never know what it's like, having a son, a son you love and will never understand." Morton was losing strength and vitriol. His overwhelming need for sleep turned his anger to sorrow, rage to tears. "God why did you all have to break him in two?"

"I'm sorry." Star realized in some way, he was responsible for what happened to the man on the bed. And more so, what happened to the younger man now in intensive care. The broken bones, the internal bleeding, that damned white bird had landed on the windowsill of John's bedroom. He would live there for a long time.

Recently turned 18, John's name didn't have to be kept under wraps. It was too good a story not to print all the lurid details, most of which were confessed by a very delirious Hendrick "Scrapdawg" Pardee. The *Argus* couldn't wait to get its hands on it, the scandal-loving *Whirl* had a blast, the *Post-Dispatch* ran it under a pretense of treating it seriously: it was crime, it was love, it was the alderman's son. Lancer and Mary fell victim to the fear of every parent, to have everyone find out their kids are a failure, and to have the press put the blame on the procreators. "Star Bryan is the son of long-time St. Louis City alderman Lancer Bryan." That said it all.

From there the myth took wing, flew across the water like Daedalus escaping from King Minos' tower. More happened with Admir under the bleachers. Under the covers. Lots more. Whether it happened or not, now it did. Setbacks for tolerance, understanding, race relations, just about anything possible. The gay community, accused constantly of pedophilia, over-reacts. They decry the deed, if it happened. Guys hitting up 15-year-old boys on MySpace are outraged. The black community trots out the "down low." The basketball league gets on the news, every sport in the city is scrutinized for coaches who want the boys in the bedroom rather than on the court. Althea Howard is sorry. The radio guy is a hero. John is a victim, a poster boy of potential for what can happen to anyone involved with a coach. The soccer team, the baseball team. *How safe are your children? Story at ten. In the mean time, throw them under the bus.*

Hendrick gets a state appointed lawyer who's going to try to plead insanity so they can lock him up in a different institution. He sits in a cell and cries. If he wasn't insane then, he will be now.

Star isn't quite sure what this will do to his law practice. Maybe this will blow over. Maybe his jewelry and his unorthodox approach to the mundanely legal will keep his peeps around. Or maybe the phone will stop ringing, except for other professionals asking to transfer documents to someone less in the public eye.

He's afraid to leave the house. His city, his family, his community have tattooed him with a scarlet alphabet.

Arielle comes over, wears tight jeans and a tight white t-shirt. She's stunning. *Wow. That's my sister!* She walks past a for sale sign. It jars her, brings up a lump in her throat. It means so much more than a Century 21 real estate transaction. Star was her only ally, and her good friend. But she doesn't have to fight the family anymore. They just don't talk. Nobody was sure who won, and the next conversation would have to either produce a winner or an apology. No one had the stomach for either.

"Where are you going?"

"I dunno. Just away."

She hadn't been over for awhile; she looked around at the new decorations as yet to be packed. "Are we Indian now?"

"I am," Star said. "I can't be African anymore. Too fucked up."

"Yeah you can. It's everyone else. It's not us."

"Arielle I'm gonna miss you."

"You too." He hugged her, tight. She was so slight. But she was the rock he could never be. "What about Darrock?"

"He's coming with me."

"Oh. Are we two..."

"I'm not saying." Star had learned his lesson. "From now on it's no one's business who I'm with, and who I'm not with. I might not ever have

225

sex again," he tried to laugh. "D has nowhere to go. So he's coming with me."

Arielle sat on the couch, watching her strong older brother wilted in defeat. She could still help him pack, help him close up, but eventually the inevitable parting would come. "Well, we still have e-mail."

"Still have a cell phone. And that silly website."

"Yep. That silly website." She reached into her purse and pulled out a hardback book. One hundred eighty four pages.

The Negro Slaveowner's Diary. By Fawn Bryan. Arielle's picture on the inside back cover, as editor. A stern picture of Fawn, more like a sketch on the front. One of the old pictures from the trunk. Everyone assumed it was her. Now the assumption was the truth.

You should have this.

Aw...thanks. I already read it.

Read it again. Read it and... weep.

Yeah. Huh. Yeah.

June 23, 1855

This will probably be my last entry. I believe I have said all I have to say. I have lost my husband, my rock, my everything. I have directed our children, upon my death, to free our slaves. They deserve no less. And perhaps, for their sake, I will be with Mack very soon. Perhaps they will all work together, my children and their charges, to build a better life. I do not know where else they can go, except to work our land.

We have done well. Our family is rich. We have been forced to sell our goods cheaper than the whites. But this means more people buy from us. Their reviling us has in fact caused and increased our good fortune.

I can not help but wonder if we have committed a grave sin, keeping other human beings in the bondage we so despised. We believed by being better masters we could earn the Lord's forgiveness. Or at least His understanding. But it is forgiveness I ask most, because I have always known we were committing wrong. I fear we have proven no different than our former masters. This is the world in which we live. My hope is that our children and grandchildren will live to see a world without slavery, without human beings being bought and sold like cattle. Without white and black making every difference in every detail of every person's life.

I pray that our transgressions will die with us, and not live on to haunt our children in generations to come.